EVERY LAST MINUTE

BOOK 1 OF THE TIME WRECKER TRILOGY

....

ELLEN SMITH

ESW BOOKS
WASHINGTON, DC

ESW Books
Washington, DC

Editing: Shayla Eaton, ShaylaRaquel.com
Cover Design: Monica Haynes, TheThatchery.com
Book Layout ©2017 BookDesignTemplates.com

Every Last Minute/ Ellen Smith. -- 1st ed.
ISBN 978-0-9961999-2-6

For my husband,
A.B.S.
and our children,
G.B.S., R.N.S., and V.M.S.

ACKNOWLEDGMENTS

True story: there was actual time travel involved in writing this book.

Okay, maybe not fancy time travel with a time machine or timeline rectification or anything snazzy like that. Every Last Minute was the first novel I ever wrote. Poorly, I might add—but I loved the characters of Mara and Will and I desperately wanted to tell their story. After revising that first version many times, I finally put it down, stepped away, and got to work on my next novel: Reluctant Cassandra, which became my first published book.

After Reluctant Cassandra was released, a good friend asked me about that first book I had written; so I found myself looking back at the original draft. Revisiting a fictional world I had abandoned years ago was very much like traveling back in time. The world had changed since I last worked on this story, and so had I. Going back and trying to write the book again was exciting, scary, and incredibly challenging.

Thankfully, I had a lot of help along the way.

First, I want to thank my friend Sarah, who read my first

draft years ago and encouraged me to try again. I'm grateful to her for bringing me back to a story I loved and helping me believe that I could write it.

During the long process of rewriting and revising, I received incredible feedback from fellow writers and readers. Many thanks to the Waterfront Writers critique group, to the Curiouser Author Network, and to the beta readers who read over the final draft: Sarah, Jocelyn, and Peter. I'm indebted to each of you for your help in drawing out the story that needed to be told.

In the publishing world, I've been extremely fortunate to work with Monica Haynes of The Thatchery and Shayla Raquel of Curiouser Editing. Monica always brings her passion for great books and beautiful images to her cover designs. I'm grateful to her for bringing the setting of Every Last Minute to life on the cover. Shayla went above and beyond as an editor, patiently working with me to correct everything from punctuation and grammar to fine-tuning the characterization and plot. I'm so thankful to both of them for getting Every Last Minute ready to send out into the world.

And finally, the greatest thanks are due to my husband, Andy, who lights up my life simply by sharing it with me. Out of all the love stories I've seen and read and even written, ours will always be my favorite.

EVERY LAST MINUTE

Chapter One

....

MARA

ONE LIFE, ONE TIME
Join Conrad Gibbons, new president of ONE LIFE, ONE TIME
at the National Mall
Wednesday, March 30, 2011
for a community rally against the sin of timeline rectification
REMEMBER, NO MATTER WHAT . . .
TIME MARCHES ON!

Mara Sterling rolled her eyes at the postcard and threw it into the recycling bin. She stuffed the rest of the mail inside her heavy laptop bag, which bumped against her thigh as she crossed the lobby and climbed the staircase. Days like this made Mara wish she and Will had rented a garden apartment, or at least picked a building with an elevator. Walking all the way up to the third floor was easier some days than others.

Today was one of the "others."

The stairwell was empty, so Mara took her time. She

shifted her bag and tucked her right arm closer to her side, like an injured wing. In public, Mara usually kept her right hand tucked discreetly in her coat pocket or laid it casually across her lap. But there was no one around, so if she wanted to move slowly and cradle her arm, she might as well. Trying to keep up the appearance of an ordinary, perfectly healthy twentysomething was exhausting in its own right. Especially on days like today, when chronic pain made her feel more like eighty.

Then again, the workday was over now and she was almost home to Will. Seeing her husband made Mara feel more like eighteen. So there was that.

Predictably, Mara's right shoulder was already seizing by the time she reached her apartment door. It had been a long commute home on the Metro and now it was past time for her next dose of painkillers. Then her key got stuck in the lock. Mara shifted her weight and jiggled the key again, leaning into the door as hard as she could. Every time she moved, a lightning bolt of pain zinged from her injured shoulder, radiating down her arm and up the side of her neck.

At last, the key turned. Mara lost her balance as the door swung into the apartment. She barely caught herself on the doorframe before she landed face-first in the living room. The flap of her laptop bag flew open, scattering the mail across the floor. Thankfully, the laptop stayed securely in place.

"You sure know how to make an entrance, don't you?" her husband said, crossing the room in three long strides. Will Sterling stood just over six-foot-three, so by comparison, Mara always felt as tiny and delicate as Thumbelina. Even after Will took her workbag and helped her upright, he had to lean down to give her a kiss.

It was a good kiss—the kind that overpowered the pulsating pain in her shoulder and made her feel light and breathless. When Will straightened up again, his fine blond chin hairs barely grazed the top of her head.

"But seriously, are you okay?" Will asked. His green eyes were narrowed with concern. From Mara's angle, they looked even smaller through the thick lenses of his glasses. "Are you dizzy or anything?"

"From you or from the painkillers?"

Will grinned. "I meant the meds, but feel free to feed my ego."

Mara wrapped her good arm around him and rested her cheek against his crisp blue work shirt. "I'm fine, really. I just lost my balance. How was your day?"

"Unreal. A bunch of kids forgot their instruments, I broke up a fight in third period, and I don't think a single class played through a piece without having to stop and start over. You'd think the kids were excited for the long weekend or something."

"Too bad you don't get a long weekend too." It would have been nice to have Will home for an extra day, even if she still had to go to work.

"At least I get a teacher workday tomorrow. I should have plenty of time to catch up on emails and put in grades for the quarter too."

Mara had heard that before. She waited a beat before saying, "So you're going to be bringing some work home with you tomorrow night, huh?"

"Pretty much."

Her shoulder seized again, so badly that she couldn't help but wince. Will's fingers found the stiff, knotted-up muscles and gently began to work them loose. Mara both ached and relaxed. He worked closer into her shoulder blade, making tiny circles around the long, curved scar. When she couldn't stand it anymore, Mara motioned for him to stop.

"I'm going to go take a shower," she said. "Try to calm this shoulder down a little." Heat did wonders on her damaged nerve. Since she'd started her new job, she'd begun taking hot showers almost every day after work. Good thing water was included in the apartment's utilities. That was one perk to living in this building, at least.

"Want me to order something for dinner?" Will asked.

"Sure. I think the new Greek place has a delivery special on Wednesdays."

"Gyro and fries?"

"Perfect."

"Nope, *perfect* would be eating our gyros and watching Netflix," Will said. "You want to pick the show?"

"You can." He would probably pick a stupid comedy show or some kind of overzealous courtroom drama. That was okay. Will had been teaching rowdy middle schoolers all day and he'd probably be up to his ears in paperwork tomorrow. The least she could do was let him rule the remote for the evening.

Mara gave him a one-armed squeeze before she headed down the hall to the bathroom. She could take her next round of pain meds and then relax under the hot water. Maybe she still had some of that passion-fruit-scented shower gel. That would be a nice way to scrub off the grit and grime of the city.

"You better hurry," Will called after her. "If the food gets here before you do, I'm eating all the tzatziki sauce."

"You wouldn't dare."

♦♦♦♦♦

Mara gritted her teeth as the hot water pulsed over her aching shoulder. She rotated her arm again, leaning and stretching as gently as she could.

Don't overdo it. That's what the physical therapist had cautioned her, over and over again. *Overworking a damaged nerve is as bad as underworking it.*

Mara gave one more stretch under the running water before turning and letting the shower stream run over her face. She tried to imagine the shower washing away her worries, like it said in the positive thinking self-help book her friend Robyn had recommended. *Breathe in. Breathe out. Breathe in . . .*

The water stung her eyes and Mara backed away from the stream.

No luck. Her worries were all still present and accounted for. The only thing going down the drain was a knot of her long, dark-brown hair. *Gross.* Mara fished it out with her big toe and reached down to pick it up, sending a sharp *pang* all the way down her right arm. She jerked it back, knocking over the shampoo bottle as she did.

Mara massaged the angry shoulder with her left hand, chewing the insides of her cheeks as the pain worsened and then eased. *I need to be more careful. Can't let something like that happen at work.*

In her first six weeks as one of Dr. Olivier's research assistants, Mara felt that she was the one being studied more often than not. Elliott, who ranked one step above her as Dr. Olivier's head researcher, double-checked every word she said and every move she made.

At first, Mara thought it was because she'd checked "Asian" on her job application. People were always questioning her mixed-bag ethnicity. Mara could never just check "white," even though her dark-brown hair and eyes weren't all that different from her father's. Her face shape and features were distinctly Japanese, just like her mother's. Enough so that her ignorant prep school classmates used to call her "Dragon Lady" and "Geisha Girl," or ask where she learned to speak English.

Mara turned and angled her right side under the shower spray. Maybe race did have something to do with Elliott's initial reaction to her, but as the weeks went on, Mara realized that Elliott was probably suspicious about something else. It was in the way his eyes lingered over her when she used the mouse with her right hand—painful, but doable in small doses—but typed with only her left. Or when he handed her a stack of papers and then watched carefully to see which hand she used to pick them up. Mara had run into his type plenty of times before. Self-appointed watchdogs, out to make sure she was really as disabled as she claimed to be.

Thank goodness the other two people in the office were easier to be around. Colleen, who sat at the desk next to hers, had been nothing but friendly. Dr. Olivier seemed overly eager to make sure Mara was comfortable. Mara supposed there might have been some truth to Elliott's mutterings around the office. Dr. Olivier had probably wanted to hire her because it looked good. A trauma survivor working on a research study about trauma. How poetic.

Elliott can think whatever he wants. At this point, Mara was just grateful to have a job. After two and a half years of unemployment, it felt good to have a paycheck and a retirement fund and something to put on her résumé, just in case she ever wanted to put herself through another job search. That probably wouldn't be happening any time soon. It was hard to squeeze in much besides work anymore.

The steam from the shower fogged up the bathroom. Mara tested her arm's range of motion again. Good. As good as it was going to get, anyway. She shut the water off and wrapped up in a towel. Dinner had probably already been delivered. Better get moving.

Mara took two pumps of lotion and rubbed it up and down her arm, working closer to her shoulder and even, bravely, down through the shoulder blade itself. No twinges. The hot water had helped so much that she felt almost normal.

Almost.

With the edge of her towel, Mara wiped the steam off the mirror. Her reflection was cloudy, but she could still see the angry pink scar that underlined her collarbone. That was from the first surgery. She turned her head as far as she could and looked at the long scar that curved along her shoulder blade. It framed the pucker marks where the bullets had hit. Two of them.

Mara was glad she couldn't remember that. Unfortunately, Will could.

She reached around and traced both marks with her finger. After eight years, they looked more white than pink, pockmarks rather than wounds. *I'm still here,* she told herself. *Jason Mann didn't win. Will and I did.*

Mara said the same thing every day. And it was true. Every day.

◆◆◆◆◆

Will had already set out dinner on the coffee table when Mara emerged from the bathroom. Even though she was 98 percent sure Will had been kidding earlier, Mara was still a little relieved to see a cup of tzatziki sauce on each of their plates.

"We're not just eating out of the containers tonight?" she asked. "Fancy."

"Only the best for my girl," Will said, offering her a paper napkin. "Now get ready—there's something playing on TV I think you'll like." He pressed the power button on the remote.

Mara squealed when the familiar Spanish-style mansion appeared on the screen. "They brought it back for another season?" She curled up on the couch beside Will, tucking her legs underneath her.

"I cannot believe you got me to start watching this," Will said as the words *Engaged or Enraged* appeared on screen. He popped open her can of ginger ale for her. Mara took one fizzy sip as the voice-over began:

"While most engaged couples are shopping for wedding gowns and picking out favors, these ten couples are taking the ultimate challenge. They're putting their marriage to the test before they take their vows. Will extreme sports, team challenges, and unbelievable drama bring them closer together? Or will their relationship shatter under pressure? It's an all-new season of *Engaged or Enraged!*"

The theme song began and Mara hummed along. Each of the ten couples appeared in turn, dancing a little and pretending to shoot each other with fake bows and arrows when their names flashed up on the screen.

"Every time I watch this crap, I die a little inside," Will said.

"We don't have to watch this," Mara said, shooting him a mischievous grin. "I did say you could pick anything you wanted."

"No, I know you really like it. I don't mind," Will said.

"Uh-huh. Plus, you're the one who looked up spoilers for the finale last season because you couldn't wait to find out who won."

Will pretended to be too busy eating his dripping gyro to respond.

Mara nestled back in the deep sofa cushion. On screen, the couples had been issued their first challenge. They were going to play some type of capture-the-flag game on an obstacle course complete with fences, rope courses, and rock walls.

"There's one more twist," the host said, pausing over each word for dramatic effect. "One partner in each couple will be blindfolded." The couples groaned as the host passed out bandanas emblazoned with the show's logo.

"We're going to win this, no question," said one man as his fiancée nodded happily beside him. "Our communication is on point. We're just like . . . I'll be talking and she'll just know . . ."

"Exactly what he was going to say!" the fiancée finished sweetly.

Mara nudged Will's leg. "Hey. How come we never finish each other's—"

"Fries? Don't mind if I do," Will said, hovering a hand over her plate. Mara swatted him away, and he smirked.

The show switched to a commercial. As a businessman deplored the effects of his chronic dry eyes—just in time to discover a drug that could help—Mara took the first bite of her gyro. Good, but not nearly as good as the ones she and Will used to get from the food trucks when they were in college. Food truck gyros were the best.

The dry-eyes commercial ended and the next began. As

the camera panned over a dimly lit room, Mara watched Will from the corner of her eye. The foreboding music rose to a crescendo and there it was: a sudden flash of light, a bloodcurdling scream, and a half-hidden ghostly figure. The voice-over intoned the title of the horror movie due out in theaters next month.

Will nonchalantly ate his fries. If he were triggered by anything onscreen, he didn't show it. Hopefully that meant he really was okay. Even after eight years, it could be hard to tell with Will. He barely admitted to having post-traumatic stress disorder, never mind admitting that he needed some help.

Mara reached over and squeezed her husband's hand. He squeezed back.

"What are you thinking about?" she asked.

"How much money people have to get paid to be on reality shows."

"Probably not much," Mara said. "Some people like the spotlight."

"Fair enough." Will munched on another fry. "I'd need at least a million to consider it."

"Only a million? There's not enough money in the world to convince me."

For a moment, it looked like *Engaged or Enraged* was back on, until Mara realized it was an ad for another reality show. The image of a wide-eyed woman with puffy blonde hair filled the TV screen.

"What if you found out that your life was a lie?" the woman asked dramatically.

Mara thought her eyes were going to pop out of her skull. "Is that . . . ?"

The wide-eyed woman onscreen sniffed and dabbed at her eyes. "For years, I've felt as if my life was blown off course," she said. "I was haunted by thoughts that this wasn't who I was meant to be—that there was another life, my authentic life, just out of reach."

The camera panned to her sitting at a kitchen table, sorting through boxes of photographs and newspaper clippings. "Even if the government can't confirm it, I think the evidence is clear: I've had a timeline rectification, and my life isn't what it seems. I'm on a mission to uncover the truth about my other life." The woman turned and faced the camera straight on. If she were bothered by anything she'd uncovered, she certainly didn't look it. "I'm Deirdre Collins: entrepreneur, TV show host, part-time actress, and full-time personality. Who knows what else I could have been?" She gave the camera an exaggerated wink. "Tune in next Wednesday at eight central for the season premiere of *Déjà Deirdre!*"

"You have to be kidding me," Will said. "What is she famous for, anyway?"

"At this point, I think she'd just be famous for being

famous," Mara said. Why was her heart suddenly beating faster? "This is ridiculous. I thought the whole point of a timeline rectification was that people wouldn't remember having one."

"Plus, even if there was a way you could find out—why would you want to? If someone goes to the trouble of time wrecking, they probably want to forget," Will said.

"Seriously." Mara thought back to the postcard she'd found in their mailbox. Another day, another protest. Timeline rectifications had been legal for over a decade—since 1999, 2000, somewhere in there—but most people called them *time wrecks*. Anti-time wreck organizations like One Life, One Time were getting more popular every year. "Still—it's kind of creepy to think about, isn't it? That people can actually time travel."

Will seemed unconcerned. "Meh, not really. Science was bound to get there eventually. And of course, the government had to get their hands on it."

"It's not a bad idea," Mara said. "On the surface. Criminals actually going back and undoing their crimes instead of sitting in jail forever."

"Only if they can be rehabilitated. And unfortunately, a lot of people can't."

And that's why we'll never get a time wreck. Jason Mann would have to be sorry for what he did. Jason had to be one of the most unrepentant and incompetent school shooters in history. His attempt to shoot up the Adams Morgan University Student Union—during a school break, no less, when almost no one was around—had only been witnessed by Mara and Will, and only Mara had been shot.

Granted, she wouldn't have wanted Jason to be a more competent shooter. God, no. But it would be nice if he were at least a little sorry.

Mara leaned back into the couch cushions again. Well, whether Jason was sorry or not, he was rotting in jail now. Besides, they didn't need a time wreck, anyway. It wasn't like she and Will couldn't handle the life they'd been given. They'd made it this far. Mara swallowed and tried to will her thumping heart to slow down.

Engaged or Enraged was back on. As the camera panned in on the couples lining the obstacle course, Will nudged her. "Your turn. What are you thinking about?"

Mara forced herself to make her voice light and cheerful. "That if we were on this show, you'd be wearing the blindfold," Mara said. "I give better directions."

"Not a chance," Will said. "I'm not banging my head on every dang obstacle because you can't see around me. Tallest guy plays navigator. Always."

Mara laughed. She leaned against her husband and inhaled his clean-boy scent of soap and shaving cream. They fit together so neatly, his arm around her, her head on his chest.

All in all, it had been a good day.

Scratch that.

It was a good life.

Hey, Deirdre Collins, Your Show Is Nothing New . . . Literally

By Sarah Kapelli

Guest poster for the One Life, One Time blog

By now, I'm sure we've all seen the latest in the movement to normalize time wrecking: Deirdre Collins's new show, *Déjà Deirdre.* The premise is simple: Deirdre Collins, in yet another attempt to stay relevant and regain her stardom, believes she has had a timeline rectification because she has many déjà vu moments. She moves to New York City (a place she claims to have never lived but for which she feels a strong affinity) and attempts to discover who she might have been in her first life map, before her supposed time wreck.

There are only two problems with this premise: 1) There is no evidence whatsoever that people with completed timeline rectifications will feel any sort of "déjà vu" when they encounter the people or places from their original life map; and 2) the show glamorizes time wrecking. It suggests that the worst possible outcome would be a wistful sort of melancholy, wherein the time wrecker occasionally wonders about who they might have been.

Let's be clear: time wrecking affects a lot more than one person's experience. Yes, it (supposedly) gives the criminal the opportunity to go back and choose not to commit his or her crime. Yes, it (again, supposedly) gives the victim or victims the opportunity to live without the effects of that crime. Both of these things are understandable or even admirable in principle.

However, changing a life map (as the Department of Timeline

Rectification so eloquently puts it) doesn't just affect the criminals and victims. The proverbial ripples from a single event have the power to touch us all. I don't live a singular life, powered only by my own actions and limited only by my own shortcomings. Neither do you. We all touch and shape each other's lives in thousands of different ways.

Here's the thing, Deirdre: *this isn't all about you.* If it is true that you're a time wrecker (which we can't prove, either way), that's not just an entertaining little part of your human experience. That's evidence that you are so selfish, so conceited, so absorbed in your own experience, that you chose to change time—which affects everyone—to benefit yourself.

That, sadly, is nothing new. Not just for Deirdre Collins, but for all of us. We frequently put our own selfish wants above our concern for the greater good. That's not entertaining. That's sad.

And we normalize this self-centered behavior in so much of our daily lives. Our culture has become obsessed with supporting everyone's individual dreams and ambitions, catering to every little whim, assuring ourselves that we're each special and unique. We need to bring back our concern for each other and focus on building our community.

The concept of time wrecks may be relatively new, but the sin behind it is a tale as old as time. *Déjà Deirdre* is nothing new . . . literally.

Chapter Two

....

WILL

Today was not a good day to be late. A teacher workday was a rare gift in their school calendar, and Will was determined to make the most of it. Mara always teased him about bringing work home—but truthfully, he did spend most of their evenings answering emails and lesson planning after dinner. Tonight, he wanted to come home with nothing on his mind except the weekend.

Will knew that wasn't going to happen as soon as he saw the traffic jam on the Beltway. As soon as he could, he jumped off on an earlier exit and took a roundabout way to work. He wouldn't be early, but at least he made it to the school on time. If he hadn't forgotten his workbag in the trunk, he would have made it to his desk on time too. Will was already halfway to his classroom before he realized what he'd done.

By the time he'd retrieved the bag and reentered the building, huffing and puffing down the hall like he was out of shape—which, to be fair, he was—Will had already resigned himself to the fact that he'd be bringing some work home that night, exactly as Mara had predicted.

"How's it going, Sterling?"

Will's heart dropped when he heard the principal's voice. Cliff was a retired army officer who'd improbably chosen public education as his second career. He'd been running the school for the past two years, after Ms. O'Reilly had retired to Florida to spend time with her grandchildren. With a short, silver buzz cut, perpetually tanned skin, and his collared shirt unbuttoned a bit too low, Cliff often appeared to have wandered off the set of a *Miami Vice* re-run.

"Running late this morning," Will panted, hoping that Cliff would nod and move along. No such luck. Cliff stopped in front of him and gripped him in a knuckle-popping handshake. With his other hand, Cliff delivered three solid whacks to Will's back.

"You ready for today? Going to bring the fire?" Cliff asked. "Bring the fire" was the staff motto Cliff had chosen for the 2010–2011 school year. It was supposed to remind the teachers to ignite their students' passion for learning. Something like that. Since this had been a record year for everything from online bullying to an actual bomb threat, the teachers had privately started telling each other to "extinguish the fire."

"It's a busy day," Will agreed. "Lots of work to do."

"Good on you! Make it happen, captain!" Cliff boomed, finally stepping aside so that Will could pass. "But first—I'm planning an assembly for our anti-bullying program the week before spring break. I want us to finish the year strong. I was wondering if you'd be willing to speak out about your personal experience. Maybe seeing how bullying has affected someone they know—a teacher they look up to—well, maybe it would scare some of these kids straight."

"Um." Will wanted to say no and saw, at the same moment, that Cliff was fully expecting a yes. "I don't really think a school shooting falls under bullying, per se."

"Neither do bomb threats, but here we are. Gotta put a nicer label on it." Cliff waited a beat longer before saying, "Give it some thought, okay? Make it a good day, Sterling. Bring the fire!"

Will was starting to hate that motto.

◆◆◆◆◆

Will watched the first two hours of the workday tick by on the orchestra room's clock. He was losing precious time to put the rest of his students' quarterly grades into the online grading system. The school fairly hummed with tension. All around the school, teachers frantically typed in progress reports. Will realized he probably should be too.

But Will was not a deadline kind of guy. If anything, his

late start this morning had made him move even slower when he finally got to his classroom. A more motivated person—someone like Mara—would simply sit down at the desk and push through until the job was done. She'd probably have gotten it done yesterday. There was no reason he couldn't enter all of his grades in the system before lunch.

Instead, Will found himself using a bent paperclip to clean lint out of his computer keyboard.

The school bell rang, even though there were no students in the building today. Will looked at the time on his computer monitor and groaned. He had to find a way to focus.

Music. That was always the answer for him, wasn't it? Will opened a new tab in his web browser and typed in a familiar website. Listening to the online stream of Then Sings My Soul—the official hometown radio station of Deer Hill, North Carolina—was an odd habit he'd developed back in his college days. It wasn't that he had a particular hankering for gospel music and bluegrass. It was just nice to take a break from DC sometimes. Growing up in Deer Hill hadn't been perfect. There was a reason Will had pieced together a music scholarship, a Pell Grant, and a Stafford Loan to fund his way through college at Adams Morgan University. But life back home had been simpler.

Will turned up the volume and hummed along to an arrangement of "Swing Low, Sweet Chariot" and "Down by the River." He was lucky to have his own office. Most teachers were confined to a standard teacher desk jammed in the back corner of a classroom. He had the luxury of a five-by-ten-foot room, separated from the orchestra room by a frosted glass door. In here, he could play music as loudly as he wanted without worrying that anyone would overhear.

On the computer, Will clicked over to his inbox. Listening to the music made it easier to think about what he was supposed to be doing. That was good, because his email count had already jumped from twenty unread messages to sixty-two. Will scanned over the subject lines.

Subject: Just a quick question re: Matthew's progress

Subject: Concerns on Janelle's performance

Subject: Staff, a few brief reminders for our teacher workday

Subject: Do we have to practice over break?

Will tapped out a little percussion part on his desk in time to the music and sighed. He would answer ten emails and then get back to doing grades, he promised himself.

Bang.

Will jerked back from the computer so fast he hit both knees on the desk. He whirled around just in time to see the outline of someone on the other side of the frosted glass door.

"You okay there?" It was a familiar voice. Hector. Will realized he had been holding his breath and refilled his lungs in one greedy gasp. He barely heard Hector continue: "You know I like to announce myself when I come into a room. Didn't mean to drop the mop, but you know how it is. Slippery little sucker."

"It's fine. Just caught me off guard," Will said, fully aware that his voice was far too high. He inched toward the door, rubbing first one aching knee, then the other, and twisted the knob open.

Hector gave him a strange look. "I could hear you jump from all the way out here. What are you reading on that computer? Someone email you dirty pictures or something? You know the folks down at the board can read your emails, dontcha?" Hector smirked. "I'm just messing with you. I know you and your lady. Classy girl. Don't know what she's doing with a guy like you."

Will smirked back. "Wouldn't you like to know." His voice had returned to a normal register. Good. "What are you still doing here? You're usually gone by now."

"Eh, you teachers aren't the only ones who got a workday today. Cliff wants me to go over all the floors again while the students are out of the building." Hector warily eyed the tiered floor of the orchestra room. Stacking the chairs and mopping each level of the room was a daunting task, especially when he'd already done it once this week. Will followed his gaze and imagined how long it would take Hector to go over the already-clean floors.

Will shook his head. "If anyone asks, you were here. I saw you go over the floor with a toothbrush and a can of Pledge. I got your back."

"Thanks, man," Hector said, turning around and starting to wheel the mop bucket out. He held onto the mop handle with an exaggerated grip. "Sorry I scared the bejesus out of you earlier. You should lay off the caffeine."

Just then, the radio station changed to an upbeat revival version of "My Savior's Love." Hector turned back and shot Will another questioning look. Will grinned and belted out a few verses, arms outstretched, eyes rolled back like he was singing in the choir of his childhood church. Hector laughed and walked out, shaking his head.

Will sat back down at the desk. Grades. He was going to sit in this chair and work until every last one was in. Starting right now. He adjusted his desk chair a little lower, clicked to the online gradebook, and cracked his knuckles.

He'd left the door to the office open. The song on the radio didn't quite drown out the sound of the air conditioner going full-blast from the orchestra room, or the sounds of people walking down the hall outside. Will got up and scanned the orchestra room twice before shutting the office door.

It wasn't cool that Hector had seen him jump like that,

but at least it could be explained away. Too much caffeine or whatever. That was fine. What Will didn't like was the stuff only Mara seemed to notice. The way he'd scan a restaurant or a movie theater before they went in, noticing how close they were to the exits, just in case. The dreams that still woke him up at night—each so real it took him hours to settle back to sleep. If he ever did.

Mara always wanted to comfort him when that happened. She used to offer to get him a drink or rub his back when really all he wanted was to stare at her. He wanted to admire every perfect, healthy inch of her body until he could convince his brain that this moment, right now, was real. In his dreams, he could still smell the blood soaking through her shirt and feel the weight of her when she lost consciousness.

It wasn't just in his dreams, though. That image came to him when he was driving and saw a banged-up car on the side of the road, or when the news showed the skeleton of a burned-down house in the city. This school year, after the bomb threat, he'd seen the image whenever he looked at his students.

You never knew when something could happen. Or who you could lose.

♦♦♦♦♦

Will finished submitting all of his grades just before the

deadline at the end of the workday. Then he stayed an hour later, sorting sheet music for next week's classes and scribbling notes into each square of his planner. He still had emails to answer, but finally, Will decided to pack up and go home.

It was to Mara's credit that she didn't say "I told you so" when he got to the apartment and immediately pulled out his laptop. She made peanut butter and jelly sandwiches for dinner and brought him one while he worked. Will rolled his head back and luxuriated in the little neck massage Mara gave him. This was definitely better than staying later and trying to do everything at school.

On the other hand, it was more distracting. Much more distracting. The soft scent of Mara's sweet, citrusy lotion made him think of all the things he'd like to be doing instead of work.

"Can I get you something?" Mara asked.

"Stay here and keep me company?" Will gestured to the other chair at the little dining table. It was just the right size for the eat-in nook of their kitchen, framed on one side by the closet with the washer and dryer and on the other side by a large window that overlooked the parking lot. They almost never ate there, unless Mara got it into her head to make a romantic meal for Valentine's Day or their anniversary. Instead, the table functioned as a computer desk for two. Their laptops sat side by side, with stacks and stacks of unopened mail littering the rest of the table.

Mara sat next to him and started up her laptop. "We really should do something about all this," she said, picking up a fistful of catalogs. "Do we need anything from here? They're having a thirty percent off sale."

"They *were* having a sale," Will said, pointing to the date. "That was for Presidents' Day. In February."

"Oh, good grief," Mara said. She tossed the catalog into the recycling bin. "Same with these coupon inserts . . . and this housewares store . . ."

"Rats. I was dying to go housewares shopping."

"I bet. What about this catalog? Need any new suits?"

"Do I ever wear my current one? Why do these companies keep sending me catalogs? Like I need to wear eighty-dollar shirts to teach kids how to play their scales."

Thump. The last catalog briefly hit the edge of the recycling bin before falling in.

"Rim shot," Will said.

"Still counts."

Will turned back to his laptop. His inbox had seemed to double in size every hour. That was Cliff's fault. Since starting up the anti-bullying program this school year, the principal had urged concerned parents and staff to "keep the lines of communication open." Since at least a hundred students in each grade level were taking orchestra this year, Will had to keep communication open with a lot of students and parents.

Will cracked his knuckles and clicked on the first email. He'd answer at least twenty emails tonight. And he'd make it quick too. No need to spend hours on this. Will tried to answer each email in one or two lines.

Matthew does seem to have improved in his class participation and in working together with the other saxophone players. Thanks for your note. I'll see you at the IEP meeting next week!

No, I haven't noticed any signs, but I'll keep an eye out. I'd like to bring the guidance counselor into this conversation—she has several good resources for parents dealing with this issue.

Yes, participation in both the fall and spring concerts is mandatory for a passing grade.

Beside him, Mara was still sorting through the mail that cluttered the table. Every so often, he heard the soft sound of more papers hitting the bin, or he smelled her shampoo when she brushed her hair out of her eyes.

"Am I distracting you?" Mara asked.

"Yes," Will said. "You're my favorite distraction."

Mara smiled. "I hope you're getting enough done, anyway. I want to go to bed before too much longer."

That was motivation enough. Will clicked on the next

email in his inbox. It was from Cliff.

RE: Continuing our conversation today—are you interested in speaking at the assembly?

Will wasn't in the mood to discuss that again—at least, not with Cliff. He turned to Mara. "Cliff asked me something interesting this morning."

"Interesting good or interesting bad?"

"I'm not sure," Will said. "He wanted me to talk about the shooting at an anti-bullying assembly after the break."

"Talk about . . . *our* shooting?"

Well, it was clear what Mara thought about that. "I don't think I'm going to do it," Will said.

"Do whatever you think is right," Mara said, eyebrows raised. "I'm a little surprised he'd ask you."

"I think he's scraping the bottom of the barrel. Things are looking bad at the school and he needs to show we're working on addressing school violence. A lot of the parents have been pretty unhappy."

"I'd be unhappy too if my kids had to evacuate the school for a bomb threat."

Hearing Mara say *my kids* like that made his head swim for a minute. Someday. When they had enough saved. And if Mara's pain was under control—she couldn't get pregnant with the types of painkillers she was on.

Will was realistic enough to know that someday might not come. They were only twenty-six, though. Things could change. Miracles happened all the time.

Mara slowly shook her head. "I don't know how you stand working there. How do you do it every day?"

She meant handling the school violence—at least, Will thought she did. Maybe she was thinking about their if-when-maybe-never future children too. How hard it was to see classrooms full of kids every day and know that he and Mara might never get their turn at parenthood. Will shrugged and turned back to his laptop.

Mara dropped a kiss on his cheek before she started sorting again. Some of the tabletop was almost visible as more and more of their piled-up mail sailed into the recycling bin. Will imagined that this was what she might be like at her new job. There was something about Mara that made even efficiency look elegant.

Back in college, they used to study together—in the same room, anyway. Will spent more time studying her than his notes. No regrets. He could learn music theory anywhere, anytime. There was only one Mara.

Will skipped over Cliff's email and answered five more messages from parents. Then ten. Then another six.

There. He'd responded to more than twenty emails, and he was going to call it a night. He hit the red X on his browser with an extra flourish. He turned to see if Mara had noticed—and, more importantly, if she was ready to expand on that going-to-bed idea.

Mara was still and quiet. She didn't even look up at him. She was holding a letter, her eyes tracking each line.

"Hello?" Will asked. "Mara? Whatcha reading?" No answer. He waved his hand in front of her eyes, half-joking. "Earth to Mara. Come in, please."

She didn't smile. When she looked at him, it was impossible to read her expression—she seemed blank, almost, as if someone had zapped her out of her body for a moment. She put down the letter and handed him a sealed envelope.

"You got one too," Mara said, so softly he could barely hear.

Will inwardly groaned when he saw the seal—Department of Justice. *Not them again.* Even after they finally got a conviction against Jason Mann, he and Mara had still been treated to countless notifications of petitions and requests for appeal. It had been almost a year since they'd gotten anything. Naively, Will had hoped that meant Jason had finally decided to stop making excuses for himself and had accepted his sentence.

Guess not.

But then, why was Mara staring at her letter like that? It wasn't like anything ever came of Jason's appeals. Will slit open the envelope and started to read.

Notice of Request for Timeline Rectification

March 16, 2011

Dear William B. Sterling,

This letter is to notify you that a Timeline Rectification Case has been opened regarding the incident at Adams Morgan University Student Union on October 18, 2002. The offender(s) has/have requested a timeline rectification under Code 67b.

A timeline rectification may be requested to a) lessen the impact on victim(s) of the crime and b) reduce or dismiss the sentence against the offender.

Your participation is vital to the resentencing process. Please report to an intake appointment with Nayana Patel, Corrections Specialist on

March 31, 2011, 10:30 a.m.
Suite #200
Bennington Building
940 Pennsylvania Avenue
Washington, DC, 20530

If you have any questions regarding this case, please visit the Applicants for Timeline Rectification portal on the Department of Justice website. You may use this portal even if you did not personally apply for the timeline rectification. Please have the Case Number on this letter and your Social Security number ready for login. For your convenience, you may use the portal to submit any questions or concerns electronically before the meeting.

Sincerely,

Nayana Patel

Corrections Specialist

Department of Timeline Rectification

Chapter Three

....

MARA

"A time wreck," Mara said. The words tasted as bitter on her tongue as any of the painkillers she had to swallow. "They want us to be time wreckers."

"Timeline rectifiers," Will corrected. "Wow. Never thought that would happen."

"It probably won't," Mara said. "Jason's applied for continuances and appeals before. This guy has tried to beat the system with every trick in the book."

"Let him!" Will said. "If he's willing and the corrections officer or whatever says he's clear, why not? I mean, I'm not going to stand in his way."

"Well, I guess. If Jason's actually ready to change."

"That's . . . what a time wreck is," Will said. He frowned slightly, as if he were trying to understand her. "That's the point. He's rehabilitated enough to take back what he did. You know. 'Go back in time. Undo the crime.'" He made air quotes with his fingers as he repeated the slogan.

"People started saying that at a protest rally. Against time wrecks. Remember that? I just saw a postcard about another rally yesterday. People come to DC from all over the place to protest this stuff."

"To be fair, people come to DC to protest a lot of things."

Will's eyes were begging her to laugh. He wanted her to relax, to be happy, to not take everything so seriously for once.

Sorry. Seriousness is in my DNA. Mara groaned when she thought of something else. "Oh my gosh, and my parents. Your mom. What would they say if they knew we'd been offered something like this?"

"Nothing."

"Really? Your devoutly religious mother won't have a thing to say about us turning back time? I'm sure she'd think it's going against God's will or something. And Dad's always worried about another scandal, especially since last year's election was so close. He almost lost his seat in Congress. And my mom—I don't even want to think about what she'd have to say." Mara's mother, Mrs. Augusta Gaines, was one of the top-tier attorneys in northern Virginia. Even though her office didn't represent criminal justice cases, Mrs. Gaines had used her connections to hire—and fire—each of the lawyers who had represented Mara and Will against Jason Mann.

"My mom won't say anything because she won't know," Will said. "Neither will your parents. We don't have to tell anybody beforehand. And if the time wreck goes through and Jason fixes everything, nobody will ever know. Even we won't know. It'll just be like it never happened at all."

"But think about why that is," Mara said. "A time wreck wouldn't just change time for us. If we go back and change this crime, it's going to change time for the whole world too. What if we erase something important?"

"Yeah, change one flap of a butterfly's wings and the whole world goes to hell," Will said, sarcasm dripping off his words. "I'm sure the people who say that are exaggerating. Time wrecks have been legal for years and the apocalypse hasn't happened yet."

But we met because of the shooting. Mara stared at him, trying to force the words out of her mouth. *If Jason hadn't shot me . . . if you hadn't seen it happen, if you hadn't saved my life . . . would we have met?*

Will reached out and grabbed her good hand. "Don't worry," he said. "Jason did wrong. Now he's finally trying to make it right. This is a good thing."

Could he really not realize? Finally, Mara found the words. "But we have a good thing. We have a good life. And as awful as it is, what Jason did—that's how you and I met. If it hadn't been for him—"

"Stop," Will said. On the rare occasions Will was angry—like now—his pale skin turned blotchy and red. "Stop. We do not owe one damn thing to Jason Mann."

"I'm not saying we owe him anything," Mara said. "We don't. I'm just saying that when we change one thing, we change all the things that happened after that too. I want to change what he did, but I don't want to miss meeting you."

Just as suddenly as Will had gotten angry, he calmed down again. "Of course we'll meet each other," he said. "We were in the same building on the same night, for God's sake. We both went to Adams Morgan for the same four years. We were bound to bump into each other at some point."

"But we don't know that," Mara said. "I don't know every single person who went to college with us. Neither do you. We could have missed each other."

"We won't miss each other," Will said. He smiled at her, as if a simple assurance could be enough.

"You don't know that." She threw her hands up in exasperation. "We have to be practical. We can't just trust that everything is going to work out. What if Jason isn't even sorry? What if he's just saying that he's rehabilitated, but he hasn't done the work? We could go back in time and have him decide to shoot us all over again."

With a sigh, Will pushed back his chair and stood up. He leaned back, stretching until even Mara could hear his spine pop in three places. "I'm going to get myself a soda," he said. "Want anything?"

"It's ten-thirty. We should be going to bed."

Will grabbed a can of Mountain Dew from the

refrigerator and popped it open. He took two long, thirsty swigs before coming back to the table.

Mara watched as he opened a new window on the browser of his laptop. *Are we still arguing? Is he changing the subject?* It would be just like Will to bring up some stupid video on YouTube to make her laugh right now. Anything to break the tension.

Will looked at the letter before typing a web address into the search bar. Mara realized with a sinking heart what he was looking up. There was the Department of Justice seal in the corner, and the words "Applicants for Timeline Rectification Portal" emblazoned across the top of the screen.

With a few more taps, Will had entered the case number from his letter and his Social Security number. There was a pause before a new window popped up: "Thank you for registering, William B. Sterling!"

"Here we go," Will said. "Look. They already have a bunch of stuff uploaded. Here's the PDF of the police report after the shooting . . . and here's the summary of the trial . . . copies of Jason's appeals." He clicked each file as he spoke.

"That's a lot of information to have on the Internet," Mara said.

In response, Will pointed at the secured icon in the corner of the webpage. "Besides, most of this was probably online before, anyway." That didn't make Mara feel better.

"Okay, here it is. Jason wrote a statement declaring his intent to seek a timeline rectification—"

"It just says that he believes he is capable of making a different choice now, if he were faced with the same circumstances." Mara rolled her eyes. "Excuse me if I doubt his sincerity on that one."

"He probably signed a form letter. I doubt they make each criminal write their own essay. And here's one from a corrections officer who oversaw his rehabilitation." Will squinted through his glasses at the PDF. "It looks like a questionnaire. Says he believes Jason is highly qualified for a rectification."

"Looks like he circled fives for every question. Do you think he really oversaw Jason's rehabilitation or just rubber-stamped it?"

Will sighed. "What do you want, Mara?"

"What?"

Will took off his glasses and rubbed his hand over his face, hard. He put his glasses back on and stared at her. "What do you want? Do you think we should call this lady"—he glanced at the letter—"Nayana Patel, and say, 'No thanks, we're not interested'?"

"Well, I'm not crazy about the idea."

"Obviously. But it seems like you've already decided it isn't going to work. How do you know? Maybe Jason is rehabilitated. Maybe this can happen."

"Maybe," Mara said.

Will sighed again. He logged off from the website and closed the browser. "I'm going to bed."

It was strange to go through their nightly routine in silence. Mara swallowed her pain pills and brushed her teeth, leaving the bathroom door open for Will when she was done. He changed into his pajama pants in the bedroom, leaving his clothes in the hamper instead of on the floor, like usual. They trimmed down their dialogue to the bare minimum:

"Do we need another blanket?"

"Have you seen my cell phone charger?"

"Ready for me to turn out the lights?"

They lay in the same bed, but not together. Mara fiddled with the bank of pillows under her shoulder, adjusting them until she found the perfect position. On his side of the bed, Will was perfectly still and straight. Mara watched the minutes go by on the digital, glow-in-the dark alarm clock. Closer to morning. Longer since they'd sat side by side at the kitchen table, before they had opened those stupid letters.

Finally, Mara couldn't stand it anymore. She could tell by the sound of Will's breathing that he was still awake. She rolled to her left and faced him, his profile barely visible in the dark.

"I love you," Mara said.

Will's response was immediate. "I love you too."

"I'm sorry I was a grump. It's just so sudden. The appointment is next week—if we'd opened the mail sooner, we'd have had more time to think about it." That sounded like an accusation, even though they were equally guilty of letting the mail pile up. Mara hurried to change her tone. "I just don't want to get our hopes up and have it all be for nothing."

"I know." Will was quiet. "And we'll be okay, no matter what. With a time wreck or without it."

Mara slid closer. She wanted to wrap herself around him. She wanted to fall asleep with her head on his chest like she did so many other nights, listening to his strong, steady heartbeat, sure that nothing and no one could change what they had.

Will held her for a few seconds, then patted her hand and rolled over. His back was facing her now. Within minutes, Mara heard his long, slow breaths. Will was asleep.

Mara readjusted her pillows and lay back down again. When things weren't so hectic, they'd talk again. Will was right. They would be okay whether Jason was granted a time wreck or not.

Mara thought back to the brightness in Will's eyes when he'd first read the letter, the way he'd talked, as if it were a golden ticket to a better life. Their should-have-been life.

If Jason Mann hadn't fired those shots, that night would

have been boring. Predictable. She would have walked out of the Student Union with the soda and mozzarella sticks she'd ordered. Back to her dorm room, probably, to read a book or catch up on sleep since midterms were over. The dormitory would have been so quiet, with most of the students having gone home for fall break. Of course, Mara hadn't gone home—when she'd mentioned it to her parents, they'd replied that they were sure she'd rather rest and study for the remainder of the semester. Point taken.

Will hadn't gone home that weekend, either. A Greyhound bus trip all the way down to Deer Hill, North Carolina, and all the way back would have taken up most of the long weekend, and it would have been too expensive for him, anyway.

If it weren't for the shooting, Will probably wouldn't remember going to the Student Union that night, either. He would have checked his mail, probably looking for another prepaid phone card so he could call his family long-distance. His life, like hers, would have taken a very different path.

For one thing, Will wouldn't have nightmares anymore, because he never would have seen Mara running away as the shots sounded closer. He wouldn't have seen her fall right in front of him. He wouldn't have had to press down against her bleeding shoulder or seen her lose consciousness.

Maybe he wouldn't have seen her at all.

Ridiculous, Mara thought, but her rational mind was

already going over the facts. She and Will had been in one of the biggest freshman classes to attend Adams Morgan University—almost two thousand students, to say nothing of all the other undergrads and graduate students.

Will and Mara hadn't had any classes together that first semester. They did afterward—they'd made it a point to take whatever elective classes they could together, once Mara had been discharged from the hospital. Everything had been so much easier with Will there. The two of them against the world.

Of course, we'd find each other anyway, she thought. She tried to hang on to Will's easy assurance. They didn't owe their romance to Jason Mann, for crying out loud. It didn't take a tragedy to bring them together.

Mara reached over to Will and grasped his hand. *If only we could be sure.*

Chapter Four

....

WILL

When Will woke up on Saturday morning, the day ahead felt deliciously lazy. Yesterday had been a long one—and to top it off, it had ended with an argument. He and Mara would work it out, though. Now that they'd slept, they would talk things through again. They had plenty of time. It was the weekend, and he couldn't think of anything they had to do until Monday morning. Will stretched and rolled over in bed.

The Mara-shaped dent on her side of the bed was still warm, Will noticed. Within seconds, he realized why he'd woken up: it was the unmistakable sound of Mara throwing up.

Will jumped out of bed and sprinted across the hallway to the bathroom. "Mara? Can I come in?"

She got sick again, and Will winced in sympathy. "I'm a little busy," she yelled back.

Will hovered his hand over the doorknob. He wanted to

help. But—as Mara pointed out whenever this happened—throwing up was really a one-person job.

After a few minutes, Will heard running water and let himself in.

Mara stood at the sink, rinsing her mouth. She offered a weak smile when she saw Will. "Didn't wake you up, did I?"

"No," Will lied. "How are you feeling?"

"Great."

Okay, so that was a stupid question. Will tried again. "Did you skip breakfast this morning?"

"No, I ate when I got up to take my pills, but then I lay back down to try to get some more sleep." Mara made a face. "I guess I can't lie down after I take this medicine, either."

"So, you have to take it with a meal, you can't have any alcohol, and now you have to stay upright for a few hours too? I sure hope this painkiller actually kills pain."

"Meh." Mara drank another paper cup full of water. "It's bearable."

"For all the trouble this stuff gives you, you should feel a lot better than bearable."

Mara shrugged her left shoulder. "I think the side effects are worse because the doctor upped my dose last time. I'll talk to him about it."

"When's your next appointment again?"

"The thirty-first. Thursday."

"Oh," Will couldn't believe he hadn't made the connection

earlier. "The same day as our meetings for the time wreck thing."

"Different times," Mara said, in between swigs of water. "The neurologist appointment is in the afternoon and our other meetings are in the morning."

Our meetings. Will wondered if that meant that Mara was on board with the time wreck. This probably wasn't a good time to ask.

"How about you just take it easy today?" he said instead. "Let your stomach settle and everything. Or if you're feeling better, maybe we could do something tonight? Catch a movie?"

"Can't." Mara rinsed again, spat, and threw away the paper cup. "My parents' anniversary dinner is tonight."

He'd forgotten. Will watched his face in the mirror to make sure he kept his expression neutral. "Ah. Sure you're going to be up to that?"

"I have to be," Mara said. "I'll push through."

For her sake, Will hoped she could.

•••••

If it were possible to make time physically move slower, Will would have sworn it was happening on their Metro ride that evening. Mara's jaw tightened every time the train started or stopped. Will reached over and covered her left hand with his. Her engagement and wedding rings dug into his flesh, but Will didn't mind.

"How are you doing?" Will asked. His blazer was hitched up around his shoulders, as if the coat were wearing him instead of the other way around. "You ready for this?"

"Me? I've been preparing for this my whole life. I could write a book. Always order a cocktail. Don't talk about politics unless Dad does, and if he brings it up, agree with him."

"You can't have a cocktail," Will reminded her. "It'll mix with your painkillers and turn you into Superwoman. Or Sybil."

"I know. Have one for me," Mara said. "Pretty please? And make it strong. Not one of those girly ones that look like fruit punch. I want to imagine myself getting a little loopy."

"I'll do my best."

It was their stop. Will braced his feet and grabbed a handlebar as the Metro came to a halt. Mara tucked a hand under his elbow, making him feel tall in a good way—protective, kind of. They navigated through the platform and up the escalator together.

"Where's the restaurant again?" Will asked, when they had to let go of each other to walk through the turnstiles.

"It's just a few blocks," Mara said. Through the station's entrance, they could see a steady drizzle of rain.

"We didn't bring an umbrella."

Mara squeezed his arm. "Come on. Let's hurry."

The sidewalks were slick and little dots of rain splashed onto his glasses, blurring his vision. They had to stop twice at the crosswalks, going from damp to drenched as they waited for the signal to cross.

Finally, Will made out the green awning ahead. The twinkle lights reflected against the water droplets on his glasses. Once they had ducked under cover, Will used the edge of his blazer sleeve to dry his lenses.

Mara pulled off the hood of her coat and ran a hand over her hair. She caught him looking at her and asked, "What? Did I do something?"

"You look beautiful."

She was already standing one step above him, so she didn't have to lean far to kiss him lightly on the cheek. Will opened the door for her, and they ducked inside.

Congressman and Mrs. Gaines were waiting just inside the door. Posed, like they'd just stepped out from a catalog. Congressman Gaines wore his usual navy-blue suit, and Mrs. Gaines wore the red dress she'd donned to that fancy Christmas party last year. Will was immediately aware of two things. One, he was underdressed. Two, he probably looked like he was having too much fun with their daughter.

"Happy anniversary," Will said, reaching out to shake the congressman's hand. At the same time, Mrs. Gaines pulled Mara into a long, perfumed hug.

"You look wonderful, dear," Mrs. Gaines said, throwing an arm around Mara's shoulders. Mara flinched, but Mrs. Gaines didn't appear to notice. "Are you wet? Where's your umbrella?"

"We didn't have far to walk," Mara said. Will avoided looking at his father-in-law. One mark against him so far: he hadn't been prepared.

"Well, you'll dry off," boomed the congressman. Will helped Mara out of her wet trench coat and hung it on the rack outside the door. That should be one point in his favor: a little chivalry always impressed the in-laws. Mara's coat—coral, she'd called it, although it looked orange to Will—stood out brightly against the dark-brown and black wool coats hanging beside it.

When he returned, Mrs. Gaines looked Mara up and down. "I like your blouse," she said. "Although it would have been nice to see you in a dress for once instead of pants."

"I thought you'd like it," Mara said, smiling in a way that was all manners and no warmth. She called it her "prep school smile," although it looked like she'd learned it directly from her mother.

This evening's off to a great start. Will tugged at the cuffs of his blazer.

The maître d' appeared then, ushering them to the far side of the restaurant. Their table was lit with candles and a bottle of wine was on standby in the ice bucket. Will hoped there wouldn't be too many forks and knives. He knew the salad fork from the dinner fork, but the others always left him confused. He pulled out Mara's chair for her—that should be another point for him—and sat down opposite.

The prices on the menu were even higher than he'd feared. Will tried to smile and make small talk while he scanned for something they could afford. One of the chicken dishes could work. Fish would be all right. The salads were a safe choice, but he couldn't tell if it was the kind of salad you could eat for a meal or the kind of salad that had to go on the side of something more expensive.

When the waiter came by to open the wine and take their orders, both the Gaines ordered steaks. Mara was next.

"I'll have the steakhouse salad, please," Mara said. So, he could order just a salad. Will scanned the choices to see if there was one without anything French drizzled over the top. No luck.

Across the table, Mrs. Gaines nudged her daughter. "It's our treat. Go ahead and get the steak if you want one," he heard Mrs. Gaines whisper.

"I'll have the steakhouse salad, please," Mara repeated to the waiter. There was that plastic smile again.

The waiter turned to Will next. Was it his imagination, or did he look like he didn't believe Will knew what to order? "I'd like the mahi-mahi," said Will.

"Are you sure?" asked Mrs. Gaines. "The steak here is

divine."

"Mahi-mahi," said Will. "It sounds wonderful wonderful."

Nobody laughed at his joke. The waiter took their menus and sauntered away. Will wished he could leave with him. The table was so silent Will could hear the classical music playing lightly in the background. Something he recognized—Will tried to figure out what it was. Sounded like Mozart.

"So, Will, how's work?" asked Congressman Gaines.

"Great, thanks. We're getting a new coffeemaker in the teacher's lounge. The old one kept shorting when someone would use the microwave, so the principal brought in a new one." He meant for that to lead in to a funny story about Cliff, striding into the teachers' lounge carrying the coffeemaker like it was God's gift to educators, but he stopped short when he saw Mrs. Gaines frown.

Will looked across the table at Mara and widened his eyes. *What'd I do?*

Mara raised her eyebrows. *Who knows?*

"I think it's just dreadful how underfunded the schools are," Mrs. Gaines said.

"We increased funding this past year," Congressman Gaines said. "Surely there should be enough in that extra quarter of a million to buy basic appliances."

"I meant in general, Joel," Mrs. Gaines said. "Teachers are priceless—it's impossible to pay them enough."

"I would think it's possible to buy them a coffeemaker," Congressman Gaines said. "Is there anything else the school needs, Will?"

"Oh no! No, we're good. Thanks. I was just . . . that was all that sprang to mind. I wouldn't call it a problem or anything."

Mara blinked twice at him. *Stop talking.*

"And how is your new job going, Mara?" asked Mrs. Gaines. Emphasis on *new*.

"About the same," Mara said. "Nothing special. I mostly arrange for the participants to come in and put in the data from the interviews." She gave a wave of her hand, as if to brush away the topic.

"It may be nothing special now, but you've got your foot in the door," Congressman Gaines said. "That's all you need. Everybody's got to start somewhere. I'd be surprised if you weren't running the experiments yourself before long."

"It doesn't work like that, Dad," Mara explained. "Dr. Olivier has a doctorate in psychology and fifteen years' experience. She's not so much doing experiments. It's more like questionnaires and interviews. We're tracking long-term data on the effects of traumatic events."

"Well, you certainly have some experience there," Congressman Gaines said. "And look at you now. It goes to show that people can overcome just about anything if they put their minds to it."

Mara flashed that smile again, and Will saw the congressman smile back at her, as if they were sharing a normal father-daughter moment. It reminded Will of one of the first times he had met Mara's parents—at an awards ceremony, of all things, not any of Mara's physical therapy sessions or post-surgery appointments.

"That's Mom and Dad for you," Mara had said. "They only show up for the applause."

Under the table, Mara's foot touched his. It had been a long eight years. They had done almost all of it together, from Will's first visit to her in the hospital to the last long years of Mara's unemployment.

"Well, that's all in the past now," Mrs. Gaines said. Her tone was a little sharp, even though she was smiling too. "No need to dwell. This is a celebration."

That seemed to jolt the congressman to attention. He raised a glass to toast his wife of thirty-nine years, who glowed in the light of the attention she'd asked for.

Under the table, Will nudged Mara back with his foot. *Hey, it's going to be okay,* he wanted to tell her. *If we told them about the time wreck, they'd understand. They'd be on your side.*

Even Will knew that was a lie.

◆◆◆◆◆

Sitting next to Mara on the Metro ride home was like

approaching an active volcano. Will had seen a documentary of that once—Mara had made him watch it, actually—and he had held his breath the entire time the scientists circled closer and closer to the mountain, measuring the activity underground with instruments and predicting how fast and how far it would erupt.

That was Mara right now. She looked normal enough. Certainly the other passengers on the train weren't edging away from her. She'd been body-slammed three times since they got on the train.

But underneath the surface, something was simmering. Something big.

Mara erupted the second the door to their apartment closed behind them. "I swear, after that I'm actually looking forward to Thursday," she said.

Will tried to follow. "Because of the neurologist appointment?"

"Because of the time wreck appointment. The meeting with the time counselor or rehabilitation specialist or whatever. Let's hear what she has to say."

For a long, terrible moment, Will wasn't sure if she was serious or joking. "I didn't think you were sold on the idea."

"I don't love it, but I don't love the way things are, either. Seriously, why are they like that? To hear people talk, you'd think getting shot was the best thing that could have ever happened to us."

"People like your parents," Will said, connecting the dots.

"It's not just them. Whenever someone hears about what happened, they have to give their fifty cents worth of philosophy. You know? 'At least he didn't kill anyone. Most school shootings end so much worse.' Or 'At least you can still use your arm. What if they'd had to amputate it? Think about that.' Or—oh. What about when people say, 'You're so strong. Such an inspiration.' I hate that one."

"You don't want to be an inspiration?"

"Not for this. What are we inspiring people to do? Keep existing if they ever get shot? Act like nothing hurts? Take the most crap with the biggest smile?"

"I'm sure that's not what they mean," Will said.

"At least the time wreck people are being honest that this sucks. Because it does suck. And they're actually willing to do something to make it not suck instead of just trying to convince me that this was all a big character-building exercise."

"I know," Will said. Mara was willing to go to the meeting on Thursday. He'd wanted her to be open to the idea, hadn't he?

But he hadn't wanted her to feel like this. He never wanted her to feel like this.

"Hey," Will said, catching her up in a hug. He tried to be extra careful of her right side, but he still felt her wince a little. "So, we'll go to the meeting and we'll see what they say. But we're going to be okay with the time wreck or without it."

Mara pulled back enough to look up into his face. "I thought you wanted the time wreck. I thought you were excited about it."

"I thought it was a lot better than getting a letter saying Jason had filed another appeal. There's only so many times I can stand to hear him say it wasn't his fault and he shouldn't be blamed and blah blah blah."

"No. Uh-uh. You were all gung ho about it, like a time wreck was going to solve all our problems."

"I wasn't trying to be. You were acting like he was going to shoot us all over again. I just wanted to see what he had to say."

Mara sighed so deeply Will thought he could see her shoulder hitch. "It sure sounded like you were ready to throw in the towel."

"I don't think a time wreck is throwing in the towel," Will said. They were edging closer to an argument he didn't want to have, but he wasn't sure how to pull back, either. "Jason's admitting he did the wrong thing. He's offering to fix it. What more can we ask for?"

"I don't know." Some of the fire had gone out of Mara's voice. "It just feels like another hoop to jump through. I'm so tired of going back and forth with the legal system over a guy who never seems like he's even sorry. That's all. I wish I could just say I'm tired without people jumping all over me for not being more positive."

"You can always tell me you're tired," Will said. "You can always talk to me."

He was relieved when Mara leaned on him again. He held her even more gently, barely touching her when he felt for the tender muscles that knotted themselves up around her shoulder blade. They felt like a kind of self-made armor, tightening up around the scars and the flaring nerve underneath. If only those knotted muscles really did protect her instead of hurting her more.

At least there was something that could protect her now. Something that could even keep her from getting hurt in the first place. Will tried to feel hopeful but realized he had a sinking feeling in the pit of his stomach instead.

Chapter Five

....

MARA

Mara's phone vibrated with a new text message just as Elliott walked by her desk. He came to a full stop and shot her an accusing look.

Mara didn't even glance at her phone. She held Elliott's gaze and smiled with what she hoped was icy politeness.

"Can I help you?" she asked.

"I just thought I heard something," Elliott said. His eyes lingered on her desk for a beat before he asked, "Still typing those reports?"

"Yes," Mara said. "They'll be done well before the deadline to submit."

Elliott harrumphed and walked away. His lab coat flapped behind him like a superhero's cape. He probably *did* think he was some kind of superhero. Wonder Elliott, saving the office from frivolous distractions while Dr. Olivier was away at a conference. The knee-length lab coat did little to disguise the fact that he was just a regular lab tech, whose beige hair and beige skin matched his beige voice and beige personality.

When Elliott was a safe distance away, Mara sneaked a peek at her cell phone. The text was from Will.

Hope your Monday is off to a good start. Love you.

Mara smiled and slid the phone into the drawer of her desk. With her left hand deep in the desk drawer, Mara texted back quickly.

Love you too!

The phone buzzed a little when the text sent, clattering against the metal drawer. From the desk beside hers, Colleen grinned. She looked meaningfully at Elliott's retreating back and shook her head at Mara. Keeping her voice low, she asked, "What are you doing for lunch? Want to walk to the food trucks and grab something?"

Mara smiled back. Colleen was probably old enough to be her mother—she'd mentioned approaching her fifties once before, and her short, dyed-orange curls revealed some gray at the roots. Despite the age gap, in the six weeks they'd worked side by side, Colleen had proved herself to be something like a friend.

"Wish I could," Mara whispered back. "I've got to work

over my lunch break to get this data in, though."

At once, Colleen's expression switched from friendly to motherly. "Elliott is harder on you than anyone else. You should really say something to HR. You can, you know. It's harassment."

"It's fine," Mara said, looking straight ahead at her computer screen.

Colleen didn't seem interested in getting back to work. She leaned back in her desk chair and examined her long, fake nails. "It's not fine. You should say something."

"It's not that bad," Mara said.

Colleen made a noise in her throat and smoothed the edge of one pink nail with a file. *She* would say something, if it were her. The expression on her face said as much.

Well, I'm not making waves after two years of unemployment. Mara looked back at her computer monitor, scrolled until she found her place in the spreadsheet, and continued typing.

"Honestly, HR guaranteed you extra time to type because of, you know," Colleen said. "He's got no right to hound you. You should let them know." She examined her nails again. This time, she seemed satisfied.

"Yeah," said Mara. "If it goes on longer, I guess I will. Don't want to be a nuisance right after I was hired."

"I'm telling you, nip it in the bud," Colleen said. "But I can pick something up for you when I get lunch. Just let me know."

"Thanks," Mara said. "I really should get to work now. I've got twenty minutes until my next appointment."

"Right, right," said Colleen. "Of course."

Mara sighed as quietly as possible. In a perfect world, she would take it up with HR. Unfortunately, she didn't live in a perfect world.

But if the time wreck was approved, maybe I could live in a better one.

Mara tried to push that thought out of her head. She didn't want a time wreck. She was going to the appointment on Thursday with an open mind, but that was it. Jason was the one who had applied for the time wreck. Jason was the one who needed to go back and fix his life. She wasn't asking anyone to fix her life.

But if Jason's offering to take back what he did . . . maybe that's good for Will and me too.

◆◆◆◆◆

Five minutes before her appointment, Mara admitted to herself that she wasn't going to finish typing the data before lunch. She'd have to add it to her ever-growing to-do list for the afternoon. Mara saved her work and tried to put it out of her mind. There would be time. She would catch up.

For now, she needed to prepare for the interview. Mara

glanced down at her notes. Female, early thirties. Single-vehicle accident, rainy weather, no alcohol involved. Spinal injury. Mara grimaced in sympathy. It was the woman's third interview, so she was at least two years out from the accident. Dr. Olivier liked to do an intake interview as soon as possible after the trauma, and then a follow-up interview each year afterward.

Even after glancing at her notes, a quick jolt of surprise coursed through Mara's body when the woman rolled in. "I'm your eleven o'clock," the woman announced, thrusting the wheels of her wheelchair forward with quick, forceful bursts. She was wearing black sweatpants and an oversized T-shirt. The gaping collar revealed intricate tattoos down her collarbone.

"Welcome. I'm Mara Sterling. I'll show you in."

It happened. The woman held out her right hand for a handshake.

Mara clasped it with her left hand and gave an extra-wide smile. *Please don't say anything.*

No such luck. The woman eyed Mara's limp right arm. "What happened to you?"

"Just an old injury," Mara lied.

The woman offered a harsh laugh. "Uh huh. That's how everyone ends up dealing with people like me. No one wants to work with trauma unless they've been messed up themselves."

Mara stiffened her back and chose not to look at Colleen as she walked past. *Not everyone.* She showed the woman to the interview room instead, matching her steps to the woman's pace down the long hallway. As she opened the door to the interview room, Mara began her rehearsed speech. "Thank you for participating in our study today. The interviews help us track long-term data on the effects of trauma. Your time and honesty are appreciated. There are no right or wrong answers." She couldn't help adding, "Dr. Olivier hired me because of my background in the field of psychology, not because of my injury."

"Of course she did." The woman wheeled past Mara into the room.

Mara took a deep breath. *She's hurting. She's angry. Be kind.* Mara followed the woman in and closed the door behind her.

The woman had already parked her wheelchair, so Mara chose a chair close by—but not too close. The side table held a clipboard filled with paperwork and a cup full of pens. Mara took one pen and passed another to the woman, along with the clipboard.

"We have just a few consent forms for you to sign. This one explains our privacy policy. The data is encrypted when it is stored, and it is never matched with any of your identifying data. This form gives your consent to be part of the study and for us to use the data gathered today in our research. This form explains your reimbursement. You'll receive twenty-five dollars for your participation today."

"That's why I'm here," the woman said. She signed each form with a quick scrawl and passed the clipboard and pen back to Mara.

"Thank you." Mara took a deep breath and flipped to the next pages. The interview questionnaire had thirty questions. Mara already wished it was over.

Apparently, the woman did too. She gave short, clipped answers to the first ten questions. Whenever Mara asked her to rate an experience on a scale of one to ten, the woman quickly responded "one"—the most negative answer she could give.

"Please describe any ways your traumatic experience has led to positive changes in your life." Mara usually looked forward to this part.

"I found out my so-called family and friends aren't worth anything. What's that they say? You don't know who you can count on until you need them? I've got nobody. Guess it's better to find that out sooner than later."

Mara kept her hand hovering over the paper.

"What, you can't write sarcasm? Fine. No positive changes."

Mara hesitated before writing that down. "Final question: What support do you wish you had received immediately after the trauma?"

"What kind of support?" asked the woman. "I got counseling."

Mara read the pre-scripted response on her page. "Support can mean anything from professional services (such as counseling) to personal support (such as strong friendships or relationships)."

The woman shrugged. "Even if I had all the support in the world, I still can't live the way I used to. The only thing I wish for is that it never happened."

There was a long, horrible silence as Mara painstakingly wrote out each word. The woman couldn't possibly know that Mara had been contacted about a timeline rectification. Still, the words felt like a personal accusation. Mara's cheeks burned.

Finally, the woman spoke again. "They have that talk-to-text software, you know. Maybe that could help someone like you."

"No software is as accurate as I am," Mara said. Her prep school smile was good in professional situations too. "Thank you for taking the time to participate in our study. You should receive your check in four to six weeks."

"Four to six weeks? Good God. Last year it took two." The woman rolled herself out, barely acknowledging Mara as she held the door open.

"Have a nice day," said Mara, with all the sincerity she could muster.

"Oh, you too," said the woman, biting off each word.

Mara closed the door again, leaving her alone in the interview room. She sat down again heavily, balancing the clipboard in her lap and tapping the pen against the top. She flipped to the last pages. "Interviewer Questionnaire," it said across the top. Mara looked at the lines left for her to fill out and sighed.

Mara was glad Elliott and Colleen hadn't heard her last exchange with the woman. Elliott would have smiled to himself, silently confirming what he already believed: that Mara wasn't good enough to do this job. She could guess what Colleen would have said. *I'm so glad you're not like that. Some of these people we meet—they just never move on, you know? So angry all the time.*

That was the thing that Mara kept buried in the deepest part of her, in the dark corner of her mind where she hid all the thoughts she couldn't share.

It had been years since the shooting. She had built a whole life since then, a life she was proud of. And she was still angry at Jason Mann for what he'd done to her.

♦♦♦♦♦

All afternoon, Mara couldn't stop thinking about the woman she had interviewed. It wasn't like it was her first time dealing with a negative participant. She was just so brazen about it. The woman had made no apologetic reference to "being bitter," "needing therapy," or "having a tough day." The accident had made her life worse, and she said so.

Was that allowed? Mara chided herself for the thought. Of course the woman could say whatever she wanted about her own life. She was living it, after all.

That dark space in Mara's mind wished that she could get away with being so honest. Mara hadn't even been discharged from the hospital yet when she'd started to learn the new rules. What happened to her wasn't a tragedy—it was a setback. Having survived a shooting should make her count her blessings. This would build her character. She was an inspiration.

Mara had been exhausted just thinking about it. She still was.

If that woman had gotten the kind of letter she and Will had, she would have had no hesitation. But, Mara realized, the woman wouldn't ever get a letter for a time wreck. It was a single-vehicle accident. There was no crime to rectify. Just very, very bad luck.

Mara typed up the last of her data into the spreadsheet minutes before the end of the workday. She glanced over it quickly before uploading it to the group folder. Perfect. Slow or not, she was a good worker. Mara hung on to that feeling of pride as she gathered her raincoat and purse.

Elliott was already headed past their desks toward the door. "I see you finally got your spreadsheet in," he said to Mara. "Thanks."

"Yes, right on time," Mara replied sweetly. "Have a good night."

Colleen interrupted. "Mara, where'd you get that coat? It's so cute!"

"Thanks!" Mara said, easing the sleeve of her trench coat over her right arm. Her shoulder was starting to seize. She set her jaw to keep her expression normal. "I got it at a little shop in Georgetown. Sorry, I don't remember the name. I'll have to look it up for you."

The coat was a bright coral, dotted with little white flowers, so light and happy. She'd bought it on a particularly gray and rainy day to celebrate her first paycheck. It was a splurge, but Will had encouraged her. "Get something fun, for once," he'd said. "Get something that makes you happy." Mara smiled at the memory and cinched the belt around her waist.

"A little shop in Georgetown, huh?" Elliott said. "Must be nice."

Heat flushed her cheeks. She knew that tone. It was the same tone she'd heard since she was a child, whenever she came to school with new shoes or a monogrammed backpack or her own cell phone. She'd gone to a private preparatory school, after all. Most of the other kids were just as well off.

But most of the other kids' fathers hadn't been congressmen. And most of their fathers hadn't been accused of embezzling public funds, either.

"I think it's adorable," Colleen said firmly, glaring at Elliott. "Come on, Mara. Let's get to the Metro station before the next train."

It was nice to have a friend, but Elliott's words still followed her all the way home.

Demonstrators Converge on Mall to Protest Timeline Rectification

Wednesday, March 30

WASHINGTON, DC—An estimated three hundred protestors gathered at the National Mall Wednesday to protest timeline rectification, a criminal justice program that some claim does more harm than good. The protest was formed after the abrupt dismissal of Alicia Barnes, founder and former president of the anti-timeline rectification organization One Life, One Time. Barnes was dismissed from her position after it was revealed that she had been privately conversing with pro-timeline rectification rights lobbyists. In a leaked statement to the press, Barnes revealed that she thought the anti-timeline rectification sentiment had become too strong and had accepted money from lobbyists to discourage her organization from protesting the criminal justice program.

Newly minted One Life, One Time president Conrad Gibbons organized today's protest to "show Washington that we do not support altering the lives of hard-working, law-abiding Americans to give criminals a free pass." Timeline rectification, which has been legal in the United States since 1999, has been bitterly opposed by the group since its inception. Specifically, One Life, One Time claims that allowing rehabilitated criminals to make adjustments to the past, however small, could be producing potentially disastrous ripple effects. Despite numerous attempts to challenge the legality of timeline rectification, the 1999 Supreme Court decision has held.

Across the street from the mall, a small but determined group of counter-protestors held their own signs. They chanted, "Go back in time, undo the crime," in unison, competing with—but not drowning out—the chants of "One life, one time," coming from the National Mall.

One counter-protestor, who asked not to be identified, had traveled all the way from Florida to speak out in defense of timeline rectification. "All through history, whenever there's a new idea or new technology introduced, we see a bunch of people saying it's going to be the end of civilization and a bunch of people saying it's the wave of the future. Timeline rectification is progress. I'm here to say I was on the right side of history."

Staff writers A. Milner and C. Lindsey contributed to this report.

Chapter Six

....

WILL

On Thursday morning, Will and Mara stood on the sidewalk of Pennsylvania Avenue, looking up at the Bennington Building. It was sandwiched in between the FBI building and the Department of Justice, so the sidewalk was teeming with business people, police officers, and tourists. As usual in Washington, DC, everyone was on the move. No one was wondering why Will and Mara were stopped there on the sidewalk—or why they were looking up at this particular building. More likely, the other pedestrians were just wishing they would move out of the way.

After perusing the Timeline Rectification website over the last week, Will knew several things about the Bennington Building: it was named after Dr. Charles E. Bennington, inventor of timeline rectification technology; there had been a competition among architects to create a design that balanced the traditional architecture of DC with new, sleek, modern elements; and the only natural light came from three long, narrow windows across the front. The website had droned on about how the architect had to reconfigure the rooms to ensure they would have enough escape routes in case of a fire. Looking at the building now, Will wished the website had talked more about the real reason behind the mostly windowless design. However time wrecks were performed—and he still wasn't sure exactly how it worked—they didn't want to risk a security breach.

Finally, Mara tugged at his arm. "We should go in," she said. "We don't want to be late."

Will wasn't sure whether Mara was actually interested in the appointment. She'd promised to keep an open mind, nothing more. But Mara definitely didn't like to be late.

Will held Mara's hand for as long as he could in the first security line, until they had to empty their pockets and walk through a metal detector. When the terse security guard nodded him through, Will gathered his wallet and belt and rejoined Mara.

"Good thing I didn't wear any jewelry today," Mara said as she re-zipped her boots. Will stooped down to help, but she waved him aside.

"So, do we know where we're headed next?" Will asked.

"Let me help you," said a uniformed guard. "Suite two hundred? You'll get on this elevator and go straight up to the second floor. I'll escort you." She walked Will and Mara the ten feet to the elevator and pressed the button for them.

"That was . . . helpful," said Mara, when the elevator doors closed and they started up.

"They don't want anyone wandering around," Will said. "Here we are."

The elevator opened onto a second-floor lobby. It had marble floors and smooth, white walls that held framed black-and-white pictures. Mara pulled Will a little closer to the side so that they could read the plaques underneath.

Dedication of the Bennington Building for Timeline Rectification, November 1, 2000

Dr. Charles E. Bennington Receives the 1999 Medal for African-American Leaders in Science in Recognition of His Contributions to the Field

Congressional Medal of Honor Awarded to Dr. Bennington and colleagues Dr. Nguyen and Dr. Wczerski

In the middle of the lobby was a large bronze statue of Dr. Bennington, standing with one foot propped up on a pedestal and staring off into some imagined future. The plaque underneath read,

DR. CHARLES E. BENNINGTON
LEADER—INVENTOR—VISIONARY

Will looked over at Mara to see her reaction, but she didn't seem to be looking at the pictures or the statue anymore. She was turning slowly on her heel, scanning up and down the hallway.

"Over here," Mara said, leading him through a gray door marked with a brass plaque. Suite 200. "It's almost ten o'clock. Come on."

Suite 200 reminded Will of his dentist's office. The walls were upholstered in the same mottled gray fabric. The maroon chairs in the waiting area were pointed toward a television playing the news. If there had been posters of cartoon teeth happily holding floss and toothpaste, Will would have sworn he *was* at the dentist's. Instead, the walls were decorated with gilt-framed posters of vague landscapes and shore birds.

"Hello," said a voice to his right. A woman's voice, melodic almost, in contrast to the crisp, stern tones of the security guard. The woman was tall with dark skin and darker hair, dressed in a navy-blue suit. "You must be the Sterlings. The ten and ten-thirty appointments." She thrust out a smooth brown hand with flawlessly painted nails. "I'm Nayana Patel, the specialist for your case."

Their case. Will bristled a little at the words. Talking

about *their case* made it sound almost as if they had wanted this. As if he and Mara were the ones who had instigated the whole mess.

Will shook Nayana's offered hand. He noticed that Mara was keeping both of hers tightly curled around her purse. Mara didn't like shaking hands, since most people tended to pump arms furiously with no regard for her damaged right side. Will was relieved to see that Nayana warmly smiled at Mara instead.

"It's nice to meet you both, although of course I wish we were meeting under different circumstances. Please, follow me."

Didn't we get letters for separate appointments? Will looked at Mara, who looked equally confused. Well, if they got to go in together, he wasn't going to argue.

Nayana Patel's heels made soft indentations in the carpet as she led them out of the waiting room and down a narrow hallway. Her black hair looked like it was probably the same length as Mara's—just past her shoulders—but it was tied up in a bun.

Her office was on the left side of the hallway. It looked dark, even though three sets of fluorescent lights hummed from the ceiling. There were no personal touches. No framed photos of family or pets or anything. Just a wooden desk and beige filing cabinets. Two maroon chairs that looked just like the ones in the waiting room had been arranged to face the desk. Nayana herself sat back in a rolling desk chair.

"Please, sit," Nayana said. She poured the remnants of her water bottle onto the tiny bamboo plant in the corner of her desk. "This poor thing gets so thirsty in here," she remarked. "No sunlight to keep it going."

She's trying to keep things upbeat, Will thought. He smiled back. Beside him, Mara stayed tense. He put out a hand and realized that her right side was closest to him. He dropped a hand on her knee instead.

Nayana tapped the topmost file with a shiny polished fingernail. "All of your paperwork is in order. I was just double-checking everything before you came. So. During this initial intake, I like to start by letting you take the lead. So much of this process will involve us tossing information at you. What questions do you have for me?"

Will felt like a young child who had been suddenly called to give an answer in class. All the thoughts he'd ever had seemed to evaporate at once.

Mara cleared her throat. *Thank God,* Will thought. Mara always knew what to say.

"My primary question would be—why now? We've had several interactions with the offender, from the trial to numerous appeals, and timeline rectification was never presented as an option before."

Mara was using her professional voice. The one that sounded nice but demanded answers. Will moved his hand up a little higher on her knee.

"Great question," Nayana said. "I did see in your file that the applicant—Jason Mann—had gone through the appeals process several times, which certainly could be a cause for concern. However, the paperwork from the corrections officer is in order—he's completed a rehabilitation program, which is very intense for a timeline rectification."

Mara waited a beat before asking, "And what does that involve, exactly?"

"Oh. Well, I'm not personally involved in that end of things, but I do know that the program runs for six months. Offenders meet with licensed counselors and psychiatrists to determine their ability to understand the program, articulate what they would change, and show that they understand the effect their crime has had on others. Many people begin the program and drop out. Only sixty percent of the offenders who apply for the rehabilitation program actually complete it."

That sounded rigorous to Will. Sounded like Jason had done some work, at least.

Mara's dark hair had swung over her face, blocking her expression. "And if a timeline rectification was approved, how quickly would things move from this point on? I read online that the process can take around six weeks before final approval," Mara said. "Is that accurate?"

"Six weeks is a fair estimate. Sometimes it takes a bit

longer, and sometimes things move along more quickly. In your case, for example, there's a minimal number of participants, a strong recommendation from the corrections officer, and a straightforward argument that a time wreck would reverse a physical injury. I would anticipate that the process would be six weeks or possibly even less."

Mara frowned. "Why is the physical injury most relevant to the case? Shouldn't the emotional and psychological effects be just as relevant?"

"Or justice for the offender," Will added quickly. *Please take the focus off me.* "I would think that giving the shooter a chance to take back what he did is a pretty good argument on its own."

Nayana nodded a few times after they'd finished speaking. "Exactly. What I meant was, in the context of the resentencing trial, we need to prepare our arguments carefully. Timeline rectification has only been around since 1999, remember. The morality of resentencing is still under debate for some people. Some judges tend to press harder about whether, for example, a rectification would take away a hardship or growth opportunity that ultimately benefited the victims."

Beside him, Mara drew herself up, tall and stiff. They knew about that perspective, all right.

Nayana continued. "Now, in this office, obviously we understand how psychological and emotional effects of trauma—such as PTSD—are just as harmful as a physical injury. However, it can be harder for those cases to gain traction. Having an obvious physical injury—such as a gunshot wound—is a more clear-cut case."

"But the time wreck would benefit everyone," Mara stressed.

"Correct. We absolutely want to change the event and the negative effects for all involved." Nayana finished her statement with another smile.

"So does this mean . . ." Will started. Nayana nodded encouragingly. "Does this mean the time wreck would be a sure thing? The letter and the website made it sound like we could still get denied."

"Great question. At this point, there are only a few things that can derail a timeline rectification. For example, as I'm sure you know, a rectification cannot move forward if a minor is involved—and yes, that does include embryos." Nayana laughed, as if she'd said something funny. "So, Mara, if you were to get pregnant, that would take the possibility of rectification off the table. Similarly, if you two had had any children since the crime, Jason's case would automatically have been dismissed. Fortunately, that's not the case for us."

Mara swallowed and tucked her hair behind her ear. Will could see the hurt etched onto her face.

Nayana continued. "Obviously, a case also couldn't go forward if either of you or Jason were to pass away—but all three of you are young and healthy. That's more of a concern when one of the participants has more critical health issues or advanced age. For your case, the most likely obstruction would come from the judge at the resentencing trial. That's always a consideration, but it's fairly unusual for a judge to dismiss a timeline rectification application. Generally, judges tend to rule in favor unless there's compelling evidence that the offender or victims aren't ready to redress the crime."

"What does that mean? What kind of evidence?" Mara asked.

"Before the trial, you'll each meet with a psychiatrist to determine whether you understand the ramifications and that you're capable of making this decision. That's more of a concern in other situations, where the crime might have actually harmed a victim's cognitive ability."

"So assuming everyone's sane, the judge approves everything, and the rectification goes forward—then what happens?" Will asked. Both Nayana and Mara turned to him at once, and he realized how blunt he'd sounded. "I mean . . . I don't understand how a time wreck actually works. I get that the offender proves to you that he's rehabilitated and that we prove we're okay with living without this crime, but what happens that makes us go back in time? What do we actually have to do?"

"Right. That moves us into the second phase of what we're here to talk about today," Nayana said.

Oh, no. This sounded like the beginning of a lecture. Will shifted in his chair and tried not to sigh.

"I'm going to start with the phrase you used—I'm not trying to embarrass you, Will, but this is a common misconception. Timeline rectifications don't send you 'back in time.' We think of time in a linear way: first one thing, then the next, and the next, and so on." Nayana used her hands to demonstrate making points on a line. "But truly, time is much more complex. Rather than a point on a straight line, each moment of your life is like a set of coordinates on a map. Each point affects multiple moments in your life in many ways." Nayana fumbled a bit with the folders on her desk before reaching into a drawer. "I like to use this to explain. Here." She smoothed a rectangle of graph paper on the desktop. "So, we might see this edge of the paper as the beginning of your life and the other as the end. However, the chronological order of events is only one factor. There is also your comprehension of time—you don't remember being in the womb or being born, for example, but those events occurred and obviously profoundly impacted the rest of your life. Your first memory might be at age three or even two years old, but the event you remember might not be significant to anyone but yourself."

Will nodded. Made sense so far, but Nayana looked like she was just getting warmed up.

"The first event you considered life-changing might not

have happened until you were ten or twelve years old, or even twenty. Meanwhile, the way the events in your life affect other people is important as well. If you were in a car accident, for example, that likely affected not only yourself but other passengers, the driver and the passengers of the other car, the police, the medical personnel, et cetera. We also have the ways in which each moment affects our life—perhaps an event in your life changed your relationship with another person, changed your future career path, and changed your spiritual beliefs all at once."

This was sounding more complicated, and she still hadn't answered what they would have to do for a time wreck. Will shifted his weight, and one of the chair legs squeaked.

"So," Nayana said, glancing at him. "All of these elements create the fabric of your life. We don't see time travel as moving backward on a chronological line. We see it as returning to a set of coordinates that mark a specific event."

"Interesting," Mara said, without a trace of sarcasm. This was exactly the kind of thing Mara loved. Once, she and her friend Robyn had bored Will half to sleep debating whether the *Back to the Future* movies were science fiction or science fantasy.

"A timeline rectification is simply returning a person's consciousness to the precise coordinates of the event. Our brains process time as through we are moving along from one minute to the next in a straight line, but truthfully, our consciousness is elastic enough to hop around a bit. For example, you can probably remember some long-ago events as if they just occurred. You might even dream that you are reliving a different time in your life."

Had she even read the file? Obviously, I would know about that.

"The rectification itself is quite easy. You'll be sedated and we'll induce all of you to return to the time coordinates of the crime in a dreamlike state. The only difference will be that, in fact, your consciousness really will return to this point in time and the offender will be able to change what happens by behaving differently."

"So you're going to hypnotize us," Will said.

"No, I wouldn't call it hypnosis," Nayana said. He'd obviously hit a sore spot, based on how quickly she corrected him. "The procedure is very scientific in nature. Very well regulated."

"It sounds like you're going to put us in a coma," Mara said. "Is that safe?"

"It's not a coma either, no," Nayana said. "A coma would put you into a deeply unconscious state. Sedation will keep you semiconscious, but allow us to use your brain's plasticity to change the exact point in time when your consciousness will reemerge."

"So as far as we know," Will said, "the judge rubber-stamps this, we get sedated, and boom, we're back to being eighteen years old in the Adams Morgan University Student

Union."

Nayana laughed. "There will be a bit more to it than that. To ensure that the rectification will go smoothly, we'll practice the desired outcome until it feels habitual. The idea is for you all to feel so comfortable reenacting the event in the new way that it will feel perfectly natural to behave that way during the actual rectification."

"We'd have to act it out? Together?" Mara cried. Her voice was high and tight like a violin string.

"A number of times, yes. Again, we'll practice the desired outcomes until they feel perfectly natural."

They were going to be in the same room as Jason Mann. They wouldn't be separated by an aisle or protected by lawyers.

Never. Not in a million years.

"How long would that go on?" Mara asked.

"The reenactments are very intense, but you'll be able to devote your full focus to the process. After the resentencing trial, you'll be moved to a secure location. Once a judge agrees to a timeline rectification, they prefer for it to happen as soon as possible. It lowers the risk of possible complicating factors."

"Such as?" Will asked.

"It's really just a precaution," Nayana said. "Think of a time when a jury is sequestered, for example, to limit outside influences that might affect their verdict. It would be difficult for you to focus on the rectification process if you had a friend or family member actively discouraging you. As I'm sure you know, timeline rectification can be a bit . . . controversial."

"Sounds like the Witness Protection Program too," Mara said. "If someone were trying to stop us from participating in a rectification, moving us to another location could give us some security."

"Yes," Nayana said, hesitating. "But we don't anticipate that kind of issue in this case."

Mara reached for his hand, and Will squeezed it.

They weren't going to do this. Will knew it, and he was sure Mara knew it too. They would end the appointment, make their pleasantries with Nayana, walk out, and never return to this creepy-quiet building. Jason Mann would just have to rot in prison. Too bad, so sad.

Nayana made an obvious glance toward the clock. "Well, I'm afraid I've talked for quite a while. Now, if you're interested in moving forward with this process, we do need to complete some paperwork."

"Oh. I don't think we're ready to agree to anything today," Mara said. She was using her polite voice. The professional voice that sidestepped arguments and backed away slowly.

Nayana didn't seem to register the brush-off. "This is the first step in the process—let me explain. The papers I have for you today simply say you're interested in moving forward with the timeline rectification process. It's not a guarantee that one will be granted. If you do sign today, we'll line up interviews with a psychiatrist for each of you and for the offender. If each of you passes that interview, we'll go from there."

Will squeezed Mara's hand again. "And if we aren't interested?" He kept his eyes trained on Nayana, who had suddenly dropped her smile.

"You and Mara each have the right to stop the process at any time," she said, choosing each word carefully. "Right up until the moment of the rectification, either of you could say you're no longer willing to participate, and it would be canceled immediately. However, if you do decline to participate at any point, you won't be able to pick up the process where you left off. The offender would have to go through the rehabilitation program and apply again; both of you would have to agree to participate; we would need new psychiatrist interviews and a new trial. And"—Nayana pursed her lips here—"if you do decline to participate at this point, the offender may choose not to apply again. If you're sure you would never want to do this, you don't have to sign today. But if you think there's a possibility you might be interested, I strongly advise that you do."

Will's stomach flipped.

Nayana reached into a folder and passed each of them a set of neatly paperclipped forms. "Why don't you look these over first," she said. "You'll see that this is just expressing a willingness to continue the process."

"Can Will and I take a moment to talk this through first, please?" Mara asked.

"Certainly. I'll step out to give you some privacy. Take all the time you need," Nayana said. She exited the office and clicked the door closed behind her.

"I didn't mean to kick her out of her own office," Mara said.

"I don't want to sign anything. I thought we were just going to find out more about it. I didn't think we had to do anything about it today." Will wanted to pace. He hated pacing. Only people in movies paced back and forth when they were upset. He jiggled his foot instead.

"Do you want to walk away now?" Mara asked. "Because we can. If you don't want to do this, we don't have to."

"But you do."

Mara didn't confirm it, but she didn't deny it, either. She pressed her lips together and seemed to be thinking for a few minutes before she answered. "I said I would keep an open mind, and I am. I'm willing to meet with the psychiatrist. That doesn't sound so bad. And that gives us a chance to think more about it."

"I hate psychiatrists," Will said.

That made Mara smile. "Seriously? Meeting with a psychiatrist is the part that freaks you out? Not altering time?"

"I'm a complicated guy." Will took a deep breath. Mara hadn't said no. She hadn't said that this was too much, too drastic, too risky. She was considering it.

If Mara thought a time wreck might be the right thing to do, he couldn't take it off the table for her. Will looked back at the papers. This wasn't a decision. This was just keeping the possibility open.

"Okay," Will said. "I'm willing to sign if you are."

Chapter Seven

....

MARA

After they left the Bennington Building, Will and Mara had just enough time to grab lunch at McDonald's before taking the Metro back to their apartment building. They'd have to drive Will's car into northern Virginia to get to the neurologist. Mara leaned back in the passenger seat as Will drove, watching the clock and crossing her fingers that they would make it in time. A missed appointment meant a fee, and rescheduling, and another day off work.

Mara closed her eyes and took a deep breath.

They arrived just in time, but it didn't matter anyway. The neurologist was running forty-five minutes behind. Mara rubbed her left hand up and down her forearm, squeezing gently as if she could wring the pain down and out her fingertips. She didn't usually do that in public. Here in the neurologist's waiting room, though, nearly everyone was in the same boat.

Beside her, Will stretched.

"Thank you for coming with me," Mara said. "Not the most fun way to spend a day off, going to this and the other appointment." She stopped and looked around the waiting room, even though she'd whispered the words "other appointment." Nobody was listening to them. Or at least, no one was looking at them.

Will stretched again and shrugged. "I don't mind. Besides, we only have one quarter left in the school year. I doubt I'll use up all my vacation days by the end of the year."

Unless the time wreck gets approved, Mara added silently. Who knew how many appointments they'd have to get through. They'd have the psychiatrist appointments for sure. That was another vacation day. Would they have more meetings with Nayana? Would there eventually be a trial date?

That is, if they moved forward with it at all. Secretly, Mara was already hoping that the psychiatrist would rule them out of a time wreck after meeting with them. She didn't want to be the one to make this choice, one way or the other. It had been one thing to move on with their lives after the shooting. What else could she and Will have done? But now, they had to choose between continuing this life map and doing a time wreck. Turning down the rectification felt like saying that she was happy the shooting happened, that she literally wouldn't change a thing. Going through with the time wreck felt like saying that she hated what Jason did more than she loved everything that happened after.

For one minute—just one—Mara wished Jason hadn't applied for the time wreck at all.

"Mara?" asked the nurse. Mara cut her musings short. She and Will followed the nurse back to the same room they usually had. It was a monthly appointment to refill her pain meds. Mara answered all the nurse's questions by rote. Height, weight, current prescription, current symptoms.

"And on a pain scale of one to ten, with one being no pain and ten being the worst pain you can imagine, where are you at today?" The nurse hovered her pen over the clipboard.

"Seven," Mara said. Both Will and the nurse looked surprised. On a good day, she usually hovered between two and four. On a bad day, five or six. The last month had been especially bad.

"Right," the nurse said, handing her a sealed cup. "You know the drill. Come back to this room when you're done. Dr. Ricci will be in soon."

The monthly urine sample was something Mara hated most. They were testing for pregnancy before refilling her prescription. The medicine had warnings all over it about potential birth defects and cautions for expecting or breastfeeding mothers. It was a terrible idea to get pregnant while she was taking this medicine—Mara knew that—but a part of her selfishly wished that one month, she would test positive for pregnancy. It would be a surprise, to be sure, and totally unplanned, and they'd have to take her off the pain meds and watch the baby to be sure it developed normally, and of course there were no guarantees . . .

It was totally impractical. But then, wishes usually were.

When she got back to the exam room, Will greeted her with a smile. Sometimes she felt like he could read her thoughts, even though they didn't talk about pregnancy—or non-pregnancy—very often. Then his expression changed to concern.

"I didn't know your pain level had gotten that much worse," Will said. "When did that start?"

Another wave of pain rolled through her right arm. She closed her eyes. "I don't know." She could feel him watching her. Mara couldn't say anymore, not now, or Will might think she was the one who needed a time wreck. Which she didn't. She needed her meds adjusted a little, but that was all.

Mara didn't open her eyes again until she heard the door swing open. This time, Dr. Ricci sauntered through, carrying a sizable medical file. For someone who was running so far behind schedule, Dr. Ricci certainly didn't seem stressed. He took his seat on the rolling stool and ran a hand over his gray-and-white-striped goatee, as casually as if he were just sitting down for a leisurely lunch. Mara wondered, as she often did, what the hair on his head would look like if he weren't bald. Would it be evenly salted and peppered, like his beard, or would the grays have grown in patches, like her father's had?

"So I hear things aren't going so well," Dr. Ricci said. "Why don't you tell me what's going on?"

Mara recited it all again, ending with her pain levels over the last month. She was never exactly sure whether he was checking her answers against what she'd told the nurse, or if he just hadn't stopped to read the file before meeting with her. Either way, Dr. Ricci nodded as Mara spoke, underlining and circling the top page of the file. Finally, he tapped the end of the pen on the page.

"We have three options going forward," he said. "Further surgery is useless at this point, because it would create more scar tissue and press on the nerve rather than removing the pressure completely. That leaves us with medication and lifestyle changes. I can increase the dose on your painkillers, but that's going to increase your side effects as well. If you're already having trouble with nausea, you're not going to want to do that. If you start experiencing more drowsiness and dizziness, we'll have to revisit whether you should have a driver's license or whether you'll be able to continue working at your current schedule."

Mara balked. "I hardly drive at all as it is. Even if it's limited? I couldn't keep my license even for a few trips now and then?"

"If we increase the dose the way we would need to in order to address the pain, then driving at all would be inadvisable," Dr. Ricci said.

Mara bit her lip.

"The other option is lifestyle changes. If we choose not to up the medication right now, you could still benefit from more rest and less exertion. You may want to start with taking a break from everything for a while, and slowly adding things back in as you feel able to tolerate."

"How can I possibly rest more?" Mara asked. "I barely do anything besides work."

Dr. Ricci raised both eyebrows.

Mara closed her eyes again.

"Certainly, we can continue exploring pain management options," Dr. Ricci said, his tone gentler. "However, I'm going to be up front with you. There is not a medical solution that will significantly improve your quality of life. Maybe ten, twenty years down the line, there might be new medications and new treatment options. But for now, this is what we have to work with."

Mara opened her eyes. It wouldn't hurt anything to ask the doctor, would it? She looked at Will, who shrugged. Her choice.

Dr. Ricci looked back and forth at her and Will, clearly waiting for someone to clue him in. Mara cleared her throat. "There's a possibility we might be able to have a timeline rectification."

"Really?" Dr. Ricci asked.

"This morning, we actually met with the coordinator— what is she, Will? The specialist?" Mara asked.

"She's called a timeline rectification specialist, I think," Will answered. "It was our first meeting with her," he said to Dr. Ricci.

"So to be clear, this is a timeline rectification for the shooting itself?"

"Yes." Mara felt strangely exposed, talking about the time wreck with someone she knew. Someone besides Will. It seemed to make it more real.

Dr. Ricci didn't look horrified by the idea. He didn't even look that surprised.

"Well, that would certainly take care of your medical issues," Dr. Ricci said. "If I understand correctly, your consciousness will be returning to your eighteen-year-old self. If you don't get shot in the rectified life map"—he spread his hands apart—"then there won't be any injury to deal with at all."

Mara didn't say anything. Neither did Will.

Dr. Ricci continued. "Timeline rectification isn't my area of expertise, but my colleagues and I have certainly been interested in how it can change things for our patients. Medicine has always had limitations. There are some things we can't fix."

Mara struggled to keep her voice steady. "And my shoulder is one of them."

Nobody said anything to that.

"If this were you," Will said finally, looking at Dr. Ricci. "If you were in Mara's shoes, I mean. Would you do it?"

Dr. Ricci didn't even hesitate. "Absolutely."

◆◆◆◆◆

It rained on their drive home. Mara looked straight ahead, stealing glances to her left. Will squinted a little through his glasses and turned up the windshield wipers. He hated driving in the rain. Mara stayed quiet, letting him concentrate.

It had rained the day her mother drove her home from the hospital too. Mara had been there for weeks after the shooting, shuttling from one surgery to the next until the doctor declared her fit to continue her recuperation at home. Whatever relief Mara had felt at leaving the hospital evaporated when her mother closed the car door.

"Our first stop is the mall," Mrs. Gaines had announced. "You'll need some new tops that you can take on and off yourself. Some new flats and boots too. You don't need to be asking people to tie your shoes for you."

"What I'm wearing works fine," Mara had said, glancing down at her loose pullover sweater. "I've got some more stuff like this. Let's just go home."

Mrs. Gaines's lips were pinched tight. Her dark hair was pulled back severely into a low ponytail and secured with a plain brown clip. She looked austere. Impenetrable. "And sit around feeling sorry for yourself? Nice try. We're going to get you out and active."

"That's not why I wanted to go home first," Mara said, stung. "I wanted to see Dad."

"Dad's not home now, Mara. Home's the same as it always was. Errands first. I would think you'd have had enough sitting around by now."

It was pointless to argue. Mara stayed silent while her mother pulled in to the mall parking lot. Her shoulder throbbed before they made it up the escalator to the Junior Miss section of the department store.

Just push through it.

After an hour, Mara had three new pairs of flats, four blouses she could button herself, and skirts she could pull off and on one-handed. Mara could still remember the way pain had radiated down to her fingertips and how hard she had worked to make sure her mother didn't see her flinch.

On their way out of the store, her mother had insisted on stopping in front of a hair salon. The sharp smell of hair dye and bleach wafted out into the mall, mixing with the scent of pretzel dogs and cinnamon rolls that emanated from the take-out place three doors down.

"What do you think, Mara?" Mrs. Gaines asked. "As long as we're here."

It wasn't a question.

"Mom," Mara said. "Do you think we can do this tomorrow? I really want to go home."

Mrs. Gaines had already started walking toward the store. She turned and leveled Mara with a look. "Mara, you need to be practical. Who's going to help you take care of your hair? You don't want to depend on someone to fix your ponytail and wash your hair for you every day. You need to be self-sufficient."

Mara bit her lip. *Be calm. No tears.* "Mom, can we talk about this later? I really need to rest."

"This is exactly what I mean. If you're this tired after a few errands, imagine what life will be like when you're back at school. You need something easy to care for. Something that will let you be independent."

The fireball beneath Mara's shoulder blade burned. The lump in her stomach rose and burst. "Mom, please. I'm tired. I hurt. I want to go home and lie down. Please." Defeated, she let a few tears leak out.

Now the other passing shoppers were staring.

"Everything okay? Do you need help out to your car?" an older lady had asked.

"Oh, no thank you. We're fine," Mrs. Gaines had said, waving a hand airily. Mara pressed her lips together and willed herself to stop crying. The older lady shot Mara another concerned look but moved on.

When Mrs. Gaines spoke again, her voice was dangerously low. "Don't ever let me hear you do that again," she said. She leaned in close to Mara's ear. "Carrying on like that. What happened to you is awful, and I'm sorry, and I know you don't feel well. You can choose to let this motivate you to be stronger and work harder, or you can let this tear you down. I am not going to let you turn one bad decision from one bad person into a tragedy. It is not going to define your life. You can hate me for now if you want to, but someday you're going to thank me."

Mara swallowed the lump in her throat. She focused on keeping her voice quiet, reasonable. It shook a bit anyway. "I'm not saying no, Mom. I'm saying not right now. Please, take me home."

"*Now*, Mara. I promised myself I would be firm with you, and I am. No excuses. If you take it easy today, you'll always be looking for the easy way out. You're not going to be like that. Go in there and give your name to the receptionist."

There was no line, which didn't give Mara much time to compose herself. She walked into the salon with her mother and waited for the spiky-haired receptionist to look up. Her nametag read JILL.

"Do you have an appointment?" Jill the receptionist asked Mara.

Mara couldn't bring herself to speak.

"Are you a walk-in? Either way, we do have some availability right now. You're in luck." Jill looked back and forth, from Mara to Mrs. Gaines. Her mother stared at her, waiting for her to say something.

"Do. You. Speak. English?" the receptionist said slowly, enunciating each word.

Mrs. Gaines rounded on her. "Of course we speak English. My daughter grew up in this country and so did I." Mara was waiting for Mrs. Gaines to keep going: *and so were my parents, who were placed in the Japanese-American internment camps during World War II even though they were born in America too. Don't ask me if I can speak English, or if I'm an American.*

But Jill had already started apologizing. "I'm so sorry. I didn't mean to assume. I'm terribly sorry. I'll just get your name and take you on back."

That was the first time Mara shut herself down. She made herself feel blank. No anger. No tears. No feelings at all.

This just isn't happening, Mara decided. None of it was real. The posters of hairstyles her mother pointed out were nothing but inkblots on paper. She wasn't really walking back to the styling chairs. Sitting there with the misty-wet cape around her neck.

"What do you think, Mara?" her mother asked, holding her hand level with Mara's chin. "This length? You can just run a brush through it and go."

"Sure," Mara heard herself say. "That'll be nice."

"You know," Jill said, still wide-eyed attentive, eager to please. "If you're cutting off more than eleven inches, we can donate it to charity. Make a wig for children who've lost their hair to illness."

"Oh, what a nice thought," Mrs. Gaines said. "How many inches is Mara cutting off today?"

Jill took out a thin plastic ruler and measured. "Fourteen."

"Fourteen." Mrs. Gaines looked at Mara meaningfully.

"Sure, let's donate it," Mara said. "Help someone who's truly in need."

Mrs. Gaines beamed. Mara watched herself in the mirror as Jill made a long ponytail and got out the scissors. She didn't blink once while it was being cut.

"You did the right thing," Mrs. Gaines said, when they got back to the car. "It looks nice too. Very chic. And aren't you proud of yourself, now that you've pushed through? You didn't think you could do it, but you did. Good for you."

Mara blinked now, trying to wish away the same numb feeling that descended on her. Not everyone had been like her mother. Sometimes things were harder for Mara, but it didn't mean she was weak. When she'd gone back to college, back to her roommate Robyn, and Will, they had understood. Will hadn't even been her boyfriend, officially, when she'd first gone back to Adams Morgan. But he had always understood.

Nobody is going to understand this.

She couldn't cut back her hours at work. Couldn't give up driving, either. Mara heard her mother's voice again. *Is that necessary? Can't you push through?*

It doesn't do to take the easy way out.

Krushin' It Together

A personal blog by Klara Krusher

In Defense of Timeline Rectifications
Published March 31, 2011

So I try to stay out of politics on this blog. I do. If you've been following my blog for the last couple of years, you know I like to keep things upbeat. But in light of the protest in DC this week and the bloggers coming out of the woodwork to rage against Deirdre Collins's new reality show—which, come on, isn't reality TV pretty rage-worthy anyway?—I feel like I need to speak up.

Look, I don't like the idea of timeline rectifications any more than you do. I want to say that they're a terrible idea, that there's no problem so big that it justifies mucking around with time. I want to post the numbers to some hotlines and give the websites for some charities and tell you that no matter how bleak life seems, there's always help available.

But you know what? That's not true. The kinds of crimes that qualify for a timeline rectification leave more lasting damage than you can fix with three sessions of talk therapy or a couple months in the slammer. They cause big problems that require big solutions.

I feel like I'm going to lose some readers for this. Maybe a lot of readers. But I feel like there needs to be a point where we stop *talking* ourselves in circles and start *doing* something to help.

I've been really frustrated with the tone of the online conversation surrounding timeline rectification. We're all about raising awareness these days. We throw data and statistics at each other to support our points of view. We get angry and drop friends and lose followers as we passionately stand up for what we believe.

But what are we *doing*?

Because, honestly, if you're so against crime victims agreeing to time wrecks, are you *doing* anything to help them in this life map? If their insurance runs out—or if they don't have any—would you pay for their physical therapy? Their mental healthcare? Give them a job? What if they need help even after you think they should have "moved on"? What if they aren't back on their feet before you're bored of playing the white knight in their story?

And what about the offenders? How many people with a criminal record do you know, really? Are you supporting rehabilitation programs? Would you rent to someone who had just been released from prison? Would you hire an ex-con, or is finding them a job someone else's problem?

Because if not, guess what?

You're the reason why people think timeline rectifications are their best option. You're the reason why people think they have more to lose and nothing to gain by staying. You're the reason people think there's no help for them in this life map.

Because sometimes, *it's true*.

Chapter Eight

....

WILL

Mara barely talked on the way home from the neurologist's office. Who could blame her? Will had thought it would be a simple matter of changing her medication dosage. Hearing that there was nothing more to do for her—on the medical side of things, anyway—had been a crushing blow.

Thank goodness there's something that can make a difference. What if they hadn't signed the papers in Nayana's office this morning? What if they'd gotten that news from the neurologist right after they'd walked out on a real solution?

When they stopped by the pharmacy, Mara got out of the car to drop off her prescription. "You don't have to come in with me," she told him. "I'll just be a minute."

But Will hated for her to go in alone. The scrutiny Mara went through at the pharmacy was almost unbearable, even for him.

"They're trying to protect people," Mara had explained to Will once. "People abuse painkillers. They can get addicted.

The pharmacists have to be on guard."

All the same, Will could see how tense Mara got when the heat of the pharmacist's stare was on her.

"This is an increase from your last prescription," the pharmacist said, pinching her lips together. Her name was Lucy. They had dealt with Lucy before. "Why don't I just consult with my supervisor and see if we'll be able to fill this."

Mara and Will watched as Lucy slipped behind the counter and picked up the phone. She spoke quietly, glancing surreptitiously at Mara every few minutes. Will slipped a protective hand around her waist.

"It'll be a three-hour wait before we can fill it," Lucy said abruptly when she returned. "Do you have any questions about your medication?"

"No, thanks," Mara said. "The doctor talked me through it already."

"Are you sure?" Lucy pressed. "This drug can have severe side effects. Do you understand that you shouldn't get pregnant if you're taking it?" Her eyes slid back and forth, from Will to Mara and back.

"I understand," Mara said.

"What type of birth control are you using? We recommend using two types of birth control to be safe."

None of your damn business, Will wanted to say. But Lucy was the one holding the prescription. Could she really refuse to fill it if Mara didn't answer?

"The pill and condoms," Mara said quietly.

"Good. Remember the pill is most effective if it's taken at the same time each day, every day. Give yourself a two-hour window, at most. If you do miss a pill, use another backup method or abstain until your next period."

Mara's cheeks flamed. "I know. Thanks."

Finally, Lucy seemed satisfied. "Your prescription should be ready today, but it'll probably be late. Six o'clock at the earliest. We can call or text to let you know when it's ready."

"I'll just call at six," Mara said quickly. She turned to leave, and Will followed close behind.

"I hate that," Mara said, once they were safely back in the car and driving away. "I know it's a serious drug and they have to take precautions, but still. I feel like a kid being lectured by the school counselor instead of an adult filling a prescription."

"Hey, don't knock guidance counselors. The one at my school talks to everyone with more respect than that." That earned him a small smile. "What do you want to do with the rest of the day? We've got a few hours to kill. Let's do something fun."

"Honestly, I just want to lie down. I'm so burned out from everything today."

Will waited a beat to be sure she meant it. "You don't want to watch a movie or anything? Maybe go out to dinner?"

"We don't have money for that."

"After a day like this one, we can stand to stretch the budget a little bit. Let's do something fun. I want to make you happy."

"Honestly," Mara said, her voice cracking a little, "I really just want to read for a bit and take a nap."

He could see the exhaustion in Mara's face. She was ghostly pale too. "Okay," Will said. He pulled into their parking spot and guided her up the stairs with one hand at the small of her back. "I'll be around if you need anything."

"Thanks," Mara mumbled. She picked up her book from the nightstand but made no effort to open it. Will softly closed the bedroom door behind him.

Without Mara, the apartment was too quiet. He could hear the footsteps of neighbors going up and down the staircase in the hallway. If he strained his ears, he thought he could hear Mrs. Hiddleston talking loudly to her husband in the apartment below. None of which was enough to drown out the thoughts that now clamored for his attention.

No. Not now. He would delve into the deep stuff some other time, when he wasn't sitting alone in the echoing apartment. When Mara got up, they would talk. They'd deal with everything the way they always did: together.

◆◆◆◆◆

Napping was Mara's domain. Will never napped—not since he was in preschool, anyway. Napping was for people who had a *reason*—like, say, chronic pain. Or terrible news at the doctor's office. Or overwhelming offers from the Justice Department to go back in time. He only qualified for one of those.

All the same, Will was surprised when his phone startled him awake, buzzing insistently on the end table. It took him a minute to get his bearings, adjust his glasses, and wipe the thin line of drool that connected his cheek to the couch cushion. Ew.

The phone had stopped vibrating, signaling that the caller had either given up or left a message. Will checked the screen.

It was Tristan, the one friend—other than Mara—who had stuck with him since college. Pretty much everyone else from Adams Morgan University had quietly faded from now-and-again meet-ups to strictly Facebook friendships. Will yawned and tried to keep the sleep out of his voice when he called him back.

"Oh, good. Glad I caught up with you. What are you up to tonight?" Tristan asked.

"Nothing much," Will said noncommittally.

"Awesome. I have a favor to ask."

"You know, come to think of it, I do have a pretty busy

schedule . . ."

"Uh-huh. Our pianist got the flu. Is there any way you can sub for the choir rehearsal tonight? She should be better by Sunday so it would just be tonight. I promise."

Will wavered for a minute. He wanted to get out. Everything about the apartment reeked of loneliness and tiredness and pain. On the other hand, he didn't want to leave Mara here, to wake up alone and discover he was gone.

Will briefly considered waking up Mara to ask her to sit in on a choir rehearsal for the New Life Community Church tonight. He already knew how she'd answer to that.

"Of course, we'll pay you for your time," Tristan added hurriedly.

That cinched it. "When should I be there?"

"You're a lifesaver. Five o'clock if you can, so you can look over the music. Rehearsals are usually pretty short. Everyone comes after work and wants to be home by six-thirty or seven for dinner."

Which meant he would be home around seven-thirty or eight, by the time he got all the way back from the other side of the District. Not so bad. He could probably stop and pick up Mara's prescription for her on the way home, assuming the pharmacist didn't put him through the Spanish Inquisition. "Tell you what. I'll come at four-thirty."

"Why's that? You forget how to read music?"

"Nah. Last time we played pool, you beat the crap out of

me. I'm challenging you to a rematch."

"You're on."

♦♦♦♦♦

Tristan's break shot sent the pool balls all over the table. One ball rolled straight into a pocket. "I'm playing stripes," Tristan said.

Will chalked his cue, more to give himself time to strategize than anything. The last time he'd played pool was a month ago—with Tristan, actually. Since the New Life Community Church had added a pool table to their Youth Center, Will guessed that Tristan played every week at least. It showed.

Back in college, he and Tristan could have been mistaken for brothers. Tristan's hair was bleached blond back then, though, and now his naturally dark hair was cropped short in a buzz cut. He'd pierced one ear and gotten more fit too. Tristan looked the part of a youth pastor in an up-and-coming church.

Will looked down at his tightening waistband and dad jeans and wondered if he looked the part of a middle school band director. Probably.

Will made a bridge with his left hand and aimed for a solid red ball. He scratched it to the right and sighed.

"Nice," said Tristan. "Is this what you came early to show

me? Or is something else on your mind?"

Was it okay to tell a pastor to shut up—and in a church, no less? Will decided not to risk it.

"Who's doing who the favor here?" he said instead, as Tristan shot a striped yellow ball solidly into the pocket.

"You are," Tristan said. "But you never ask to play pool unless there's something you want to talk about."

"Completely untrue." Will finally managed to get the red ball into the pocket. Not bad.

"Last month, we met up for pool and you asked me if I thought Mara was getting in over her head taking the new job."

"That came up naturally."

"In December, you wanted to talk about your brother. Right before Thanksgiving, you were talking about all the stuff going on at your school—how's that going, by the way? Some of the kids here go to your school. They say there's been some more violence."

"Nobody's actually shot anyone, if that's what you mean," Will said. "And you're forgetting that we met up in January and played pool at the bar. No heavy talks, no burning questions, just pool."

Tristan pointed his cue stick at Will. "I suggested that one."

Will slipped and barely avoided hitting the eight ball. He was off his game today.

"So?" Tristan asked. It was his turn, but he just looked at Will, eyebrow quirked.

"So what?"

"Are you going to tell me?"

Will sighed. "Mara and I got these letters"—he tried to ignore Tristan's triumphant smirk—"from the Justice Department."

Tristan instantly looked serious. He and Will had been roommates the first year of college and every year since. Tristan was all too familiar with the legal gymnastics Jason had put them through. "Is Jason appealing his sentence again?"

"No. Well, kind of. He's applied for a time wreck."

"Huh."

That was it. One syllable. Tristan's face was unreadable—the kind of face that would invite parishioners to keep talking.

Except Will wasn't a parishioner. "So you think it's a bad idea," he said.

"I didn't say that."

"But you do."

Tristan appeared to be weighing his response. "I'm not sure how I feel about it, to be honest."

"See, here's what I don't get." Will laid his pool cue down on the side of the table, lining it up with the edge as he spoke. "The whole time I was growing up, the pastor preached about forgiveness. Had a fight with your friend? Gotta apologize and forgive each other. Kid brother took your allowance? Talk it out and then let it go. Everything was just repent, forgive, move on. And now we've got this totally clear-cut case of letting someone apologize for their crime and taking back what they did, and everybody's judging whether it's really a good thing or not."

Tristan frowned. "You lost me. Who's everybody? Who knows about the letter?"

"Just Mara. And you."

"So Mara thinks this is a bad thing."

Will shrugged. "She seems to be open to the idea." *Especially now that we know there's nothing else we can do for her shoulder.*

"So only you, Mara, and I know about the time wreck letter. You say everybody's judging whether a time wreck is a good thing or not, but Mara seems open to it and I'm not sure how I feel." He sighed. "Wanna go ahead and cut to the chase?"

Will couldn't think of anything to say.

"Okay," Tristan said. "Your church back home did a number on you. You've talked about it, I get it, you don't have to go over it again if you don't want. But look—is your focus on what your old pastor or your mom or your church back home would think, or is your focus on what God thinks?"

I have no idea what God would think. Will felt hot all over, as if he were about to hear the real answer. He was a sinner. It was blasphemy to even consider it. He was going to hell.

But when he looked up at Tristan, his friend didn't look angry or anything. Just kind, and a little sad.

"I don't have an answer for you on this one, if that's what you were hoping for," Tristan said. "The church hasn't voted to take a position on time wrecks one way or the other. Some denominations have denounced it and some say it's moral as well as legal. Last time the topic came up in the synod, we were still praying about it."

"I wish I could be sure what the right thing to do was," Will said.

"You and everyone else."

The heat faded from Will's chest and he started to feel almost normal again. "You sound like a real pastor or something."

"Shocking, isn't it?" Tristan laughed and made a bridge with his right hand. "Ten in the pocket."

The striped blue ball shot forward and landed in the pocket with a solid *thunk*.

◆◆◆◆◆

Mara was still asleep when Will got home. He'd figured she would be. She hadn't responded to the text he sent on his way home, telling her that he was picking up her prescription.

Will put the paper bag down on the nightstand and sat on the edge of the bed. He watched the book on Mara's chest rise and fall in time to her breathing. She'd been sleeping just like this the first time he saw her. Will didn't count the shooting as their first meeting. He hadn't really known her then. True, he hadn't been able to get her out of his head after the shooting—but he'd held her bleeding shoulder. Called 911. You didn't just stop worrying about someone after you met like that.

Will had called the hospital every few days, checking on her status. For a while, she'd been listed as "critical." Then her condition was only "serious."

When the hospital said she was out of ICU and in her own room, he'd gone to visit her. It seemed right, just to see for himself that she was okay.

Mara's hospital bed had been half-reclined, with four or five of those thin hospital pillows arranged behind her back. Her head was nodded back, eyes closed, looking peaceful despite all the medical equipment surrounding her.

She was beautiful. At first, Will thought it was just relief when he was standing in the doorway. She hadn't died. There were a lot of dressings and bandages around her right side, but she looked a lot better than she had lying on the floor of the Student Union. Much, much better.

Mara had opened her eyes then, making Will forget everything he'd planned to say. "You look good," he'd said.

"Excuse me?" She seemed to jolt upright, wincing as she did. "Who are you?"

"I didn't mean it like that! Sorry!" Will said. He held up both hands. "I'm not a creeper, I swear." He glanced down for a moment, trying to retrace his steps. "I'm Will Sterling. I was in the Student Union with you. I mean, I'm not the shooter. I just saw what happened. I called nine-one-one for you and I came by today . . . to see if you were okay."

She was going to call the nurse. Or security. Will started to back away a little when suddenly, Mara laughed.

"Hi, Will Not-the Creeper," she said. "Ow. Oh my God. I have to stop laughing."

"Does it still hurt?" Will said. Another idiot point for him. He hoped she wasn't keeping score.

Mara had stopped laughing, but she was smiling. "Well, yeah, but don't tell anyone that. And for the record, I wasn't asleep just now, either. I'm trying to convince them to let me go home."

"What's wrong with sleeping? Didn't you just have surgery?"

"The last one was about a week ago. But every time the doctor comes in, she says words like *fatigue* and *pain management* and *convalescence* and I end up staying here longer. So the party line is: I'm doing great, I'm not tired at all, and I'm ready to get out of here."

Will looked around the tiny room. It was good that she had the room to herself, at least, but the atmosphere was still pretty darn depressing.

"I can't blame you for wanting to go home," he said.

"I want to go back to normal," Mara said.

The truth of it made them both look away for a minute.

Will spoke next. "So since you definitely weren't asleep when I came in, what're you reading?"

"*The Hitchhiker's Guide to the Galaxy*," Mara said. "Have you read it?"

Will eyed the cover. "I don't really read science fiction."

Mara didn't seem put off by that. "You'd probably like it anyway. It's funny. What do you usually read?"

"Thrillers, true crime, stuff like that. I like Jack Reacher."

"I read the first one of that series. *The Killing Floor*, right?"

"Yeah." Will perched on one of the molded plastic chairs. He wondered if he was overstaying his welcome, but Mara smiled at him. Will settled back in the chair. "What else do you like to read? Just sci-fi?"

"I read everything. I like historical fiction a lot too, a little fantasy—"

"Oh! Have you read *Harry Potter*?"

"Yes! I can't wait for the next book to come out."

"Have you seen the movie?"

"I loved it. The second movie is supposed to be out in

November, right?"

"November fifteenth," Will said.

"I can't wait."

Then, without thinking, Will said, "Me neither. We should go see it as soon as it comes out."

Had he said *we*? He had. He'd just asked out a girl he didn't know within minutes of talking with her. Will never did things like that. He tried to think of a way to backpedal.

But then Mara smiled and said, "I've got to get out of the hospital first," and Will thought maybe he hadn't made a mistake after all.

No, Will thought now, looking down at his sleeping wife. *It definitely hadn't been a mistake.*

He touched her hand. Mara's eyelids fluttered open, and she smiled.

"You're back," Mara said. "I saw your note. How was the rehearsal?"

"It went all right. Played some pool with Tristan beforehand."

Mara smiled and wiped the sleep from her eyes. "I figured you would. Did he beat you?"

"Hey!"

"Sorry. Did you win?"

"Of course not."

Mara squeezed his hand. "Next time."

"I feel bad, leaving you here all alone after the day we've

had."

"Don't." Mara yawned. "I wasn't even awake. To be honest, I may just keep on sleeping until it's time to get up for work tomorrow."

"You should probably eat something," Will said. "And take some of the painkillers you had to jump through hoops to get."

"No wonder I'm so tired," Mara said. She yawned again, wider this time. "All that hoop-jumping."

"Come on. Get up. Just for a little bit. We'll eat some dinner and then tuck in for the night."

Mara sat up slowly and swung her legs over the side of the bed. She got up as if every movement hurt. It probably did. Mara often said she felt like a twenty-six-year-old trapped in an eighty-year-old's body. She took a deep breath and then shuffled off to the bathroom.

She shouldn't have to feel like this. A stab of guilt prodded Will. *And she shouldn't have to stay home and sleep while I go out and have fun.*

Tomorrow, he vowed. He'd plan something special for her. She deserved that much, at least.

Is Time Wrecking the New Forgiveness?

By the Right Reverend Peter Lancaster

Much has been made in recent years of the role of the Church on the issue of timeline rectification. Some congregations have declared themselves wholly in support, while others are staunchly against. In many other congregations—including my own—the issue of timeline rectification has been a source of division and contention.

I differ from some of my brothers and sisters in that I don't see timeline rectification as inherently wrong or sinful. The procedure itself requires that the offenders apply for a rectification, complete a rehabilitation program, prepare to make amends to the victims, including obtaining their consent, and indeed change their actions for the betterment of all. In this way, we can see that timeline rectification accomplishes the very essence of repentance and forgiveness: the offender recognizes his or her wrong, chooses to change, makes amends, and "goes forth and sins no more."

Rather, the Church's concerns should be in the implementation of timeline rectifications. Our concern is one of moral rightness, and in that case, God's justice—which requires no government to administer—is more than enough. The government's concerns involve other issues: the safest and best recourse for society's greatest victims, the efficacy of prison and parole, even the costliness of the procedure itself.

The largest source of my concern is in the efficacy. Laypersons, such as you and me, are unaware of any timeline rectifications that have been committed. Our consciousnesses have moved seamlessly from the original life map (or life maps) to the current one. But surely, someone must be watching to ensure that offenders have indeed changed? Surely the government has some record of these offenses that have been erased, some tracking that ensures that, even in the new life map, the same offenders are not slipping back into their old ways?

The government itself tells us that it does. Each year since 2000, the Department of Timeline Rectification has released a report on completed timeline rectifications. Consider this report from 2010:

- In 2010, the total number of prison releases (711,125) exceeded prison admissions (703,798). Of these prison releases, 2,448 were timeline rectifications.

- The number of total timeline rectifications had increased from 2009 (2,331) to 2010 (2,448). This continues a trend in steadily increasing numbers of timeline rectifications since 2000.

- Of the 2,448 timeline rectifications in 2010, 24 percent were re-arrested in the new life map. Eighty-one percent of these arrests were from the same crime that was rectified, while 19 percent were for a different crime.

As a pastor and a Christian, I am heartened that the government is, at least, ensuring that these former offenders are being given a second chance at life in society, while also being monitored to ensure that change is a real and present force in their lives. On the other hand, as a citizen, I have growing concerns about the amount of data that the government may be gathering about myself or others without our knowledge or consent. These are issues that merit ongoing conversation, not argument. It is my hope that, with time and patience, we will all be able to speak to each other about this and all concerns as brothers and sisters, not as enemies.

Every Last Minute

Comments:

TRU4U says:
Amen, brother.

LittleLovely says:
EXACTLY the point I was trying to make this morning!! We're getting sidetracked on the issue of whether we should allow time wrecks. They've been allowed since 1999/2000. Meanwhile, the government is keeping records on which of us have committed crimes and whether we've repeated them, EVEN IF WE DON'T REMEMBER OURSELVES!!!

Mark says:
Big brother is watching.

> **AprilShowers** replied:
> I love that this is news to you. That's so cute.

> **Lourdes** replied:
> Well, it's better than if they weren't keeping track, isn't it? Would you really want ex-cons released back into society with no follow-through? All this "Big Government" phobia has gone a little far. We need to keep track of some things. You know. For safety.

RealTalk411 says:
But don't we, as God's people in the world, have a responsibility to speak up to injustice? While I agree with you that there's a corollary between true forgiveness and timeline rectification, I do see "time wrecking" as an injustice. Would be interested to hear your thoughts on the issue of repentance vis-à-vis the "rehabilitation program" conducted for the timeline rectification procedure.

CLICK HERE TO LOAD MORE COMMENTS....

Chapter Nine

....

MARA

The next day at work seemed to drag on for an eternity. It didn't help that it was Friday and the rest of the office had checked out for the weekend already. Meanwhile, panic set in whenever Mara saw the to-do list that had piled up when she was out yesterday. Elliott had helpfully outlined a list of action items and put exclamation points after the most critical.

Jerk.

At the desk beside Mara's, Colleen was spinning lazy half-circles in her desk chair. "Did you have some fun on your day off yesterday?" she asked. "What'd you do?"

"Just doctors' appointments," Mara mumbled. The computer had refused her password twice and now she was in danger of being locked out of the system. Then Mara would have to call the help desk to reset it and wait for approval. Then she would have to come up with yet another secure password with numbers and punctuation marks and capital letters and find another place to write it down for when she inevitably forgot.

Unless, of course, she could find where she'd written down her current password. Mara willed herself to calm down and remember, but her brain was clouded in a thick, gray fog.

"I guess you have a lot of doctors' appointments, huh? Must be tough," Colleen said sympathetically.

"I'm fine," Mara said, rifling through her top desk drawer. Not there. She scooted back in her desk chair and opened the file cabinet drawer that held her purse. There was her water bottle, her lunch bag, her wallet, her book . . . nowhere she would have hidden her password. Mara closed the drawer harder than she'd intended and it clanged shut.

"Sorry," Colleen said.

Mara swiveled around. "Sorry? For what?"

"I shouldn't have brought it up. It was insensitive of me," Colleen said. Her cheeks were almost as pink as her fuchsia fleece pullover.

"Brought up my password?" Mara said.

"What?"

Mara stared at Colleen, trying to puzzle out what she'd said. Colleen stared back, looking equal parts concerned and confused.

Mara pinched the bridge of her nose, hoping it would help clear the fog out of her head. "I'm looking for my password," she said. "I tried typing in what I remember twice, but the system said I had a login error, so I'm looking to see if I wrote it down anywhere."

"It's under your keyboard," Colleen said. "Remember? On your second day working here, you had the same problem and I told you to tape a sticky note under your keyboard. That's what I do."

Mara flipped over the keyboard and was relieved to see a small, folded green square stuck underneath. "Oh my gosh. Thank you!" Mara carefully typed in each symbol with one finger. She'd forgotten the exclamation mark and the asterisk. The login screen welcomed her into the system, and Mara let her keyboard fall back over with a thud. "Thank you so much," Mara said again. "Really."

"You're more than welcome, sugar. Sure you're only twenty-six? People usually don't start having memory problems until they're my age." Colleen delivered her last remark with an exaggerated wink. Mara gave a polite laugh.

Maybe it hadn't been polite enough. Colleen frowned again. "You sure you're okay, Mara? You seem distracted today."

"I'm fine, thanks," Mara said automatically. There was work to do. She opened the first spreadsheet on her list and scrolled up and down, looking for the place she'd left off. Mara was conscious of Colleen's worried stare, but she didn't turn back around.

I wish I could just start the day over. With a sick, sinking feeling, Mara remembered that she could. She'd just have to start the last eight years over too.

◆◆◆◆◆

Spring. Mara could feel it in the warm air that whipped her hair around the second she stepped outside the Metro station. It was warm enough now that she could unbutton her trench coat for the walk home. Once she made it inside the apartment building, a wave of heat blasted her full force. The building manager still hadn't turned off the heat for the building. He hadn't fixed the chain lock on their door yet, either, Mara realized. Another thing to call about.

Mara mounted the stairs up to the apartment as quickly as she could. The indoor stairwell worked like a chimney, pushing all the too-hot air up to the top. By the time she reached the third floor, she was practically sweating. Robyn was there, waiting just outside the apartment door. Based on her purple-lipstick and heavy eyeliner, today must have been Robyn's day off. Her hair was parted severely to the side, sending a cascade of dark curls over the right side of her face.

"Surprise!" Robyn said. "Will texted and said you needed cheering up. I can't believe I almost beat you here. How are you? Long day?"

Mara let Robyn pull her in to a vanilla-scented hug. By the time she pulled back, Mara had managed to force a smile.

"Thanks for coming," she said. From the looks of the canvas shopping bag looped over her arm, Robyn had brought dinner too. It really was nice of her to come. Nice of Will to arrange it. Mara should be grateful.

She fumbled with her key in the lock for a solid minute before she heard footsteps from the inside.

"Hey! Are you surprised?" Will asked. "After yesterday, I thought you could use a friend."

I could use a shower and an antacid, Mara thought grumpily, but she turned her smile up another notch. Judging by the look Robyn gave her, Mara wasn't fooling anyone.

"Geez, are you ever having a bad day," Robyn said. She shepherded them inside as soon as Will unlocked the door. "Go on in and get comfy. I brought wine. And Coke for you, Mara." Robyn laid her tote bag on the table and started unpacking. "I have a frozen pizza for dinner. Plus Girl Scout cookies."

Robyn looks happy, Mara realized. It had been months now since her friend had broken up with Jessica, the one girl Robyn had loved so much that she'd been willing to come out to her parents. It hadn't gone well. Then, when Jessica broke things off, Robyn had seemed cut loose from reality for a while. No girlfriend. No relationship with her family anymore—at least, not a close one. During those long months, it had been Mara visiting Robyn to cheer her up.

Now the shoe was on the other foot, but Mara had a hard time accepting the same comfort from her friend. "You didn't have to bring us dinner," Mara protested, but Robyn waved her off.

"Calm down, it's not charity or anything. It gives me something fun to do on my day off."

"How's work going these days?" Will asked her.

"The stories I could tell," Robyn said. "I have about three clients who are really open to change and working on getting in to rehab. Then I have about, oh, twelve who are still convinced they don't have a drug addiction. One came in high to our last meeting."

"Who shows up to addiction counseling when they're high?" Mara asked.

"You'd be surprised." Robyn shook open the box of cookies. "Anybody want Thin Mints?"

Will reached into the plastic sleeve and took five. "Maybe a couple. I need to head back out to get Mara's prescription. Do you guys need anything?"

"What prescription?" Mara asked. "You got my painkillers yesterday."

Will looked at her strangely. "Yeah, but I still need to pick up the regular refills. You know. That manage the . . . side effects."

Right. Her birth control pills, which the pharmacist had

been so pushy about yesterday. Plus the prescription antacids that only mostly worked and the stool softeners that worked a little too well.

Just what every woman wants to hear, Mara thought. *Be right back, honey. I need to go refill your stool softeners.*

"Thanks," Mara said aloud. "Sorry I forgot. I could have swung by and grabbed them on my way home."

Now Will was really looking at her strangely. "No, we talked about it when I called you at lunch. Remember? I told you I was going to surprise you since I went out last night."

"Oh," said Mara. "Right. I remember now." She didn't. Her brain had been replaced with warm, fluffy cotton. Mara pictured herself diving in and out of the layers of cotton, disappearing into one cloud and then suddenly breaking through and reappearing in another.

Maybe taking the higher dose of painkillers wasn't such a great idea. If she kept feeling this foggy-brained, she would probably have to call Dr. Ricci and see if he could decrease her dose again. Although that might mean another appointment and another day off work. Fantastic.

Will dropped a kiss on her forehead and grabbed two more cookies. "I'll be back soon."

Robyn waved goodbye as Will left. "I need a pizza pan, two glasses, and a corkscrew," she said. "I can get them. You sit down."

"Thanks." Mara retreated to her recliner and pushed the

lever. *Finally.* She closed her eyes, trying to forget that both Will and Robyn were taking care of things while she was sitting here, resting. It didn't matter now. Just a little rest and then she'd get up and be helpful.

Mara counted her way down from a hundred by threes, willing her shoulder to loosen and the pain to stop every time she exhaled. Her shoulder hadn't been seizing today, at least. The higher dose of painkillers was good for something.

By the time Mara had counted down to number thirty-four, she could smell the pizza baking in the oven. It sounded like Robyn was back too. Mara could hear ice cubes clinking in the glasses and the fizz of a soda bottle. She opened her eyes.

"So what's going on with your shoulder?" Robyn asked. She poured Mara's Coke into a glass before getting to work on the wine bottle. "Will said something about you having a neurologist appointment yesterday. Are they going to do another surgery?"

"Can't. The doctor said this was the end of the road, pretty much." Just recalling the conversation sent another wave of exhaustion rolling over Mara. "Another surgery would just make more scar tissue. He increased the dose on my painkillers, but now that's increased the side effects too."

"That sucks," said Robyn. She freed the cork and poured wine into her glass. "Sorry for drinking in front of you, by the way. Is there another medicine they can give you?"

"Nothing we haven't already tried. Dr. Ricci said that at this point, if I need more help, we'd need to start looking at lifestyle changes. Just not doing anything for a while and slowly adding back as much activity as I can tolerate."

"So that's why Will called and said you'd had a bad day. No kidding. I'm sorry, hon."

Mara took a deep breath. "There's more. So, the shooter? The guy who started this whole mess?"

Robyn stopped with her wine glass halfway to her mouth. "What about him? Isn't he still in jail?"

"Apparently he's been rehabilitated. He applied for a timeline rectification, and it looks like it could happen."

"Wow," Robyn said. "I mean, *wow*. That's . . ." She shook her head. "Any chance this is an April Fool's thing?" she asked weakly.

"It's not a joke. The letter's in the kitchen. Somewhere. I think." Mara squeezed her eyes open and shut, willing her head to clear. "Yesterday, Will and I went to talk with the corrections specialist."

When Mara opened her eyes again, Robyn was staring at her. "That's a good thing, isn't it?"

Mara took a sip of the Coke, delaying her response. She could tell Robyn. Robyn would understand.

"I don't know," Mara said. "We signed the papers to move forward with the process, but now I'm thinking maybe we should call it off."

"Why would you do that?" Robyn asked. It was the way she said it—matter-of-factly. As if a time wreck was the obvious choice.

Mara tried to gather her fuzzy thoughts. "When the corrections specialist was talking, I kept feeling like—I don't know, like it would be cheating for Will and I to do it. I meet so many people at work who really have traumas, people who lose everything, and they keep going. And look what Will and I have," Mara said, indicating the apartment with a wave of her good arm. "We're managing just fine. I feel like time wrecks are for people who have bigger problems. People who really need help. Not us."

She wasn't explaining it well. Robyn was still sitting on the arm of the recliner, frowning at Mara as if she'd started speaking another language. "Mara, it's okay to admit that things are hard for you."

Clearly, Robyn was missing the point. "But things aren't that bad," Mara said.

"I'm going to try to say this as nicely as I can," Robyn said. "You were shot in your freshman year of college. You've had multiple surgeries. You still can't fully use your right arm. You have chronic pain that apparently isn't going to get any better. You somehow managed to graduate from college with amazing grades, and you couldn't find a job for years. Why not fix that stuff? Seriously."

"Well, when you say it like that, it sounds bad," Mara said.

"But I did find a job. I did finish college. And I have Will." She said the last part hesitantly. Was it okay to talk about that with Robyn, or was it still too soon after the breakup with Jessica?

Robyn didn't flinch. "Yeah, and what about Will? You're not the only one who was hurt in the shooting. You told me before that Will has PTSD, and I'm guessing it's a lot worse than either of you guys let on."

"I know Will was hurt too," Mara said, feeling stung. "I even said that in the meeting with Nayana yesterday."

"Nayana?"

"The corrections specialist. Or rectification coordinator— something like that. But I've always been really up front that Will's PTSD is just as bad as my injury. I just wish he'd let me help him as much as he helps me."

Oops. Mara didn't usually talk about Will's struggles. It felt disloyal somehow. But Robyn continued on, unfazed. "Maybe this is a way you can help him."

"How do you mean?"

"What better way to cure post-traumatic stress disorder than to go back and not experience the trauma?" Robyn spread her hands out, as if the answer was obvious. "I can't imagine Will would ask for it. He's too busy playing white knight for you."

"Hey!"

"You know I mean it nicely. But you say yourself that he

won't let you help him. Maybe this is a way that you could. Go through with the time wreck and un-traumatize him."

Mara ran one finger over the edge of her soda glass. She could already feel her indigestion bubbling up. It was nice of Robyn to bring her a Coke. It was her favorite. Mara should have just said thanks and stuck to water, though. Or ginger ale.

I'm so tired of ginger ale.

"There is one other thing," Mara said. "I feel selfish even saying it."

"I doubt it's anything that bad. Come on. Lay it on me."

"The first time Will saw me was after Jason shot me. He's the one who called nine-one-one for me. He held me while I was bleeding . . ." Mara cleared her throat twice. The bubbles in the soda were getting to her. Her stomach was starting to twist and turn. "The EMT said Will saved my life."

"Right, right. I know."

"That's what started things for us. He came to visit me in the hospital and, I don't know, we clicked. But it all hinges on that one night. What if we don't meet in the next life map? What if I walk one way through the Student Union and he walks the other and we never even glance at each other?" Mara felt horrible as soon as the words left her mouth. "That's awful. I know. I wouldn't really want Will to have PTSD so that we would meet and fall in love, and he wouldn't want me to be shot for his sake either. That's sick. I just . . . I love him. I don't want to lose him."

Mara was grateful when Robyn didn't brush it off. "You really think you guys could miss meeting each other?"

"I mean, Adams Morgan is a big school. There were over a thousand people just in our freshman class. I majored in psychology, he majored in music education; our dorms were on different sides of campus—what if we don't meet?"

"I wouldn't worry about that. At all." Robyn seemed even more sure of herself as she warmed up. "You're forgetting all the other stuff you guys have in common. You both like music. You both like to read. You both like crappy TV."

"Hey!"

"You know it's true. It was never just about the shooting with you guys. You're a lot alike. Most of the rest of your time at college was messed up because of the surgeries and recovery time, but imagine if you hadn't had to deal with all that. You and Will probably would have met at the library or the dorky little café that held all those poetry slams. There were thousands of people on campus, but not thousands of people like you and Will."

"That actually makes me feel better." Mara took another sip of her Coke. The bubbles fizzed and tickled her nose.

"Glad I could help. Honestly, Mara, this time wreck deal seems like the best thing that could happen for you guys. Seriously." Robyn passed the sleeve of Girl Scout cookies. "Stop thinking up things to worry about. This is your lucky break. Just be happy."

♦♦♦♦♦

Much later, after Robyn left, Mara had tiptoed down the hall to the bedroom. Will was already asleep—as usual, Mara and Robyn had talked long into the night. Quietly, Mara got ready for bed and slipped under the covers next to her husband. She settled back into her bank of pillows and tried to measure her breathing against Will's long, slow snores.

She was almost asleep when she realized Will's snoring had stopped. Mara was instantly alert. "Will?"

No answer—not to her, anyway. He was muttering something in his sleep. Mara watched him frown and flinch.

This was the beginning of a nightmare, and watching him go through it made Mara's heart speed up too. Should she try to wake him up? Mara was never sure. Gingerly, she put a hand on his shoulder.

Will jolted straight up in bed, sweating hard and breathing in terrible, short bursts.

"Are you okay?" Mara asked, at the exact moment that he asked her the same thing.

Will wasn't himself when he was having a nightmare. He seemed to be looking through her instead of at her. He darted glances all over the room as if he were sure someone was hiding behind the door.

"I'm okay," Mara said. It was easiest that way. "I'm okay. See? We're in bed, in our apartment in DC. I'm right here."

She repeated herself until he finally seemed to see her. "Sorry," he mumbled. "Guess I had a bad dream."

"Don't worry about it. Go back to sleep."

Thankfully, he did. Other nights, he'd had to get up and change his sweat-soaked shirt. Mara would hear him walking around the apartment, watching TV, even doing the dishes. Anything to ground him in the here and now. Mara was glad tonight was easier.

For him, anyway. Mara stared up at the ceiling. Her shoulder was throbbing again. It wouldn't be time for another painkiller until six in the morning, but maybe if she changed position, it would help. Slowly, she eased herself out from under the covers, checking to be sure Will wouldn't wake up. He didn't. She dropped a kiss on the top of his head and quietly opened the bedroom door.

Her heartburn was worse now too. Mara walked down the hall to the kitchen and found the bottle of chalky antacids. It had been long enough that she could take two more. She dug out two—purple for grape, pink for strawberry—and popped them in her mouth. *Whoever named these flavors does not know what real fruit tastes like.*

There was no point trying to go back to bed now—it would take time for the antacids to kick in, and then she'd want to wait a bit before lying down, anyway. Mara flicked on the living room lights and settled in the recliner. Too bad the book she'd been reading was in the bedroom—she wasn't about to risk waking Will to go get it. That meant it was time to see what was on TV. Maybe *Engaged or Enraged* was on.

It wasn't, but *Déjà Deirdre* was. The premiere must have aired earlier that week. The TV guide showed the episode would be replaying on loop all night.

Mara had just missed the beginning of the episode, but that was okay. Onscreen, Deirdre was walking down a side street of New York City. She looked pensively at the camera while New Yorkers jostled past her on either side, seemingly unbothered by Deirdre Collins on her quest to recall her past life map.

"I've always felt a connection to this city, even though I've never lived here," Deirdre said. "When I started to feel that I'd had a timeline rectification, I paid attention to all the little things that were familiar to me, even if I didn't know why. Who knows? Maybe it's a sign that's connecting me to my forgotten life. Whoever I was, whatever may have happened—I feel like my journey starts here."

If Will were watching this with her, he'd be making sarcastic comments. *So, she wanted to move to New York City and have a reality show film the experience. Never seen a B-list actress do that before.*

Even though it was the middle of the night, Mara's eyes

were alert as she watched Deirdre sigh over making a deposit on a tiny apartment. Mara and Will's one-bedroom looked like a castle in comparison. Deirdre took the cameras on a melodramatic tour, pointing out the view of the fire escape and the kitchenette she could span with her outstretched arms.

After a loud, well-timed knock, Deirdre flung open the door without even checking the peephole. It was her new next-door neighbor, offering a bottle of wine to welcome her to New York City. They immediately sat down on Deirdre's couch to sip wine and have a lengthy, personal discussion about what types of crimes they would go back in time to rectify.

That's not even well-rehearsed. If any of their neighbors had turned up on moving day with a bottle of wine, Mara and Will wouldn't have been able to find a corkscrew, much less clean glasses. They definitely wouldn't have started a conversation about philosophical what-ifs.

After the staged conversation was over and the neighbor left, Deirdre addressed the camera head-on. "It was so great to meet Saoirse today—I have a feeling we're going to be best friends! Plus, she gave me some ideas about where to start my search. I've always felt like I was born to be a chef. I'm going to take the cooking class she recommended and see if I don't uncover a forgotten talent! Who knows? Maybe in my first life, I was a chef after all!"

Mara rolled her eyes. *This is unbelievable. Do people think time wrecks really work like this? That people just wander around having déjà vu moments because they have secret, forgotten lives?*

Some people probably did, actually. It was hard to believe that all their memories of their current life—their post-Jason Mann life—could really be erased.

Thinking about it sent shivers up Mara's spine. If they really did this, she and Will wouldn't remember anything about the day they'd just had. Sure, it was just a normal, boring day—but it didn't deserve to be erased into oblivion. Their home, their marriage, their whole lives for the past eight years were worth remembering.

But Will's nightmares. Those deserve to be erased.

How many times since they'd been married had Mara wished that she could help Will the way he helped her? He could get heating pads for her shoulder, fill her prescriptions, even brush her hair and button her shirt if it was an especially bad pain day. But she couldn't take away the night that had etched itself on his memory.

Until now.

American Scene Magazine

EXCLUSIVE: Interview with Deirdre Collins

Former nineties TV star opens up about timeline rectification, her new reality show, and the successes and failures that shaped her life

In the early nineties, you'd be hard-pressed to find a magazine cover or TV show that *didn't* want to feature Deirdre Collins. Everything about Deirdre was larger than life: the bouffant blonde curls, the wide brown eyes, the personality that seemed to jump off the TV screen and join us right in our living room. Many of us grew up feeling that we *did* know Deirdre. Her disarming, self-deprecating approach on *The Deirdre Collins Show* helped launch the "confessional" TV program.

Now, Deirdre's image seems locked in time for many of us: an icon of the nineties that somehow faded away when we entered the new millennium.

"Forget that," Deirdre laughs. "I'm a washed-up has-been."

Her easygoing laugh reminds me of why she rose to stardom in her early career. There's something about Deirdre that makes you feel like you're talking to your best friend.

Deirdre is equally straightforward and unassuming as she talks about her new reality show, which is the reason behind my visit today. We're meeting in her New York City loft, which she's occupying for the filming of her new reality show, *Déjà Deirdre*. As we talk, it's easy to see that Deirdre is just as comfortable filming her life in the loft as she once was performing in front of a studio audience.

"Easy come, easy go," she says airily, whenever I mention her former stardom. "But the truth is that it was a much longer, much more complicated journey."

American Scene: At one time, you were the queen of confessional TV. What led you to the reality scene?

Deirdre Collins: Well, you know, entertainment has evolved so much in the past twenty years. And really, that was why I disappeared from the industry for so long. I didn't change with the times. I had to really reinvent myself, in a way, before I could come back and be relevant in today's world.

AS: What did reinventing yourself look like? What had to change before you were ready to, as you say, be in today's world?

DC: For a long time after the spotlight moved off me, I thought, "That's it. I'm done. My career is over because nobody is interested in what I have to say." It was a very lonely feeling. And then I would see these entertainers still, you know, getting roles in movies or performing or signing book deals and think, "Why not me?" It took me several years to understand that if the entertainment industry was changing, I was going to have to change with it or else I'd be left behind. These other entertainers were staying true to themselves, but they were also changing their platform to reach the modern audience.

AS: In your opinion, how has the entertainment industry changed over the last few decades?

DC: We've gone from regularly scheduled programs on TV to watching our shows on our computers or recording to watch the next day—it's not a bonding thing, for everyone to have to watch a certain show at seven o'clock on Tuesdays. And so much of what I did in the nineties was about conversations—I wasn't just interacting with the studio audience, I was trying to encourage people at home to turn to each other and have those same conversations. But now we watch

TV differently and interact with each other differently, so I needed to change the way I shared my message.

AS: And that's what brought you to reality TV. Tell us what inspired you to start *Déjà Deirdre.*

DC: Well, it was really two things. First, it was that awareness of people tuning in and following reality shows the way they once bonded over talk shows. So I was really looking for a way to incorporate that into my career and reach that audience. And second, in around 2003, 2004, I remember that I started having these overpowering feelings that I didn't really belong in this life path I was on. These years were really at the height of my personal crisis, so at first, I thought these feelings were simply about that . . . but then I was reading articles about timeline rectification, and I was like, "That's it." Finally, I had an explanation that resonated with me, but I still didn't know anything about the life I'd left behind. I was talking with my agent about it and he just looked at me and said, "Deirdre, that's a show. Let me pitch this."

AS: Some people have claimed that you're misrepresenting timeline rectification in your show. Do you feel you're challenging the Department of Timeline Rectification or taking on the justice system with this show?

DC: No, no, not at all. I don't. And if you remember from my original show in the nineties, I never tried to push anyone to a particular point of view or a certain conclusion. I just showed up and said, "Hey, this is what I'm dealing with. Anyone else? How do you handle it?" And then the audience would respond and there would be this great dialogue. So in that sense, I'm doing what I've always done. I'm just being real, and I'm saying, "Look, this is what I'm experiencing. Come join me for the ride."

AS: Where do you see *Déjà Deirdre* going? Do you think you'll eventually discover whether you did have a timeline rectification? Do you think you'd ever be able to find out the details of that?

DC: Well, for the last two questions, you'd have to take that up with the Department of Timeline Rectification. They don't unlock those records for anyone, not even reality stars. (Laughs) But I can say that the big question in my show is one that everyone deals with: What makes me the person I am? Is it the sum of my experiences? Or is it all determined by what I choose to do with my life now? I think those are really essential questions and I hope that [*Déjà Deirdre*] can start some conversations about that.

Chapter Ten

....

WILL

Clarity. The more time passed after their appointment with Nayana, the more Will flip-flopped about the time wreck. Of course it was the right thing to do. Anything that allowed a person to take back their sin had to be right.

But it was a little wrong too. What gave anyone the right to decide which crimes could be taken back and which ones couldn't? How did anyone really know Jason wouldn't do the same thing again, given the chance? And Mara. Why should they give up everything they'd built together over the last eight years just to give Jason another shot?

"Giving Jason another shot" wasn't a phrase Will liked to think about. It felt somehow ominous.

Mara hadn't been much help in talking it through. The higher dose of painkillers seemed to be helping her shoulder, but she'd been asleep or foggy-brained all weekend. Will had found himself reading and watching more TV than usual just to occupy himself while Mara rested.

This was why Will had accidentally stayed up half the night, reading articles and opinion pieces about time wrecks. Some of them sent him straight back to his days at Deer Hill, with titles like,

Time Wreckers: The Unoriginal Sin

and

Don't Be Fooled: Time Wrecks Aren't about Grace. They're about Convenience.

He could feel his ears burning as hot as if it were his old pastor saying the words. Of course, time wrecks were just another example of people playing God.

Then, when he was convinced that timeline rectification was wrong, no question, he'd read another type of article:

Timeline Rectification: Finally, a Healing Space for Criminals

and

Dispelling 5 Myths about Time Wrecks: Why They Aren't Illegal, Immoral, or Even Ill-Advised

Those made sense too. Will had read and read until he

looked up at the clock and realized it was two o'clock in the morning.

Now it was Monday, and Will wondered if his headache was God trying to punish him for questioning His authority.

Assuming there was a God.

Will wandered half-asleep through his first three classes of the day. He introduced the new sheet music for their spring concert. Listening to his middle schoolers sight read each piece was worse than he'd predicted. It couldn't have helped that at least five of his students had forgotten their instruments. The rest were no more awake than he was.

"Let's go back to the top and start again," he said, after one particularly bad read-through. "Trumpets, watch for my beat. You're galloping ahead of the rest of us. Flutes, take a minute to tune, please." He thought of the old joke his own band director used to tell—*how do you tune two flutes? Shoot one.* He glanced up at the Against School Violence banner hanging over the door and decided not to share that joke.

A cymbal crash from the back row showed that the percussion section—mostly snare drummers—were horsing around while the flute players tuned up. He leveled them with a glare, satisfied when the percussion line fell quiet. Good. He still had a knack for discipline. All was not lost.

When the flutes were finally ready, Will lifted his baton to give the downbeat. "From the top. Watch me." He began to count aloud, "One, two, three, and—"

The intercom crackled and the principal's voice came on the PA system. "Code red. Students and teachers, be advised. We have a code red."

For one long second, Will's baton hovered in midair. The entire band room was still and silent, all eyes focused on him.

This can't be happening.

A terrible calm settled over him. This was a moment straight out of his nightmare, but now that he was actually in it, everything felt surreal. The sick feeling of panic that usually rose in his stomach was gone, replaced by . . . nothing. It was almost comforting, letting himself go numb like this.

Will heard his own voice take over. "You know what this means. There are over sixty of you in here, and I need all of you away from the windows. First row, file into my office and close the door. Second row, sit along the wall outside my office. Third row, sit in front of them. Last row, bring a chair over with you and turn it over like we've practiced. Quickly and quietly, please. I need to turn the lights off and I don't want people tripping over each other."

The students had already started moving into position. Will had practiced this drill before, but had he practiced it with this class? He had seven class periods and they'd had plenty of emergency drills. Tornado, code blue, code red, code yellow. Had Cliff said it was a drill this time? Will tried to remember . . .

The last row of students finally found their places and pulled their chairs over. The seats and backs of the chairs now covered the front and tops of the huddled students. *Like shields,* Will thought grimly. He turned off the light and knelt by the door to the hallway. He jammed a music stand under the doorknob too. That should keep anyone from getting in—or at least delay them for a while.

A familiar knot of panic was rising in Will's stomach. He forced himself to quash it back down. *Go numb again. You cannot lose it now.* Will looked back at the rows of students quietly bracing themselves against the wall. He was going to protect them. No matter what.

For three long minutes, the only sound in the music room was the ticking of the wall clock and the hum of the emergency light, glowing faintly in the back of the room. Then somebody let out a fart, and a few other somebodies shrieked "Ew!" and a lot more somebodies started laughing.

"Quiet!" Will ordered. The room fell silent again.

He heard footsteps coming down the hall. Quiet ones, but in the echoing school building, they were making their way closer to the door. He tensed.

Cliff. When Will saw the principal's face appear in the window of the door, a mixture of irritation and relief settled over him. So it was just a drill. Not that he'd doubted it. Now the principal was making his rounds, making sure all the teachers remembered what to do in case of a real emergency. Through the window, Cliff motioned to him with one finger and Will slid the music stand out from under the doorknob.

When Cliff edged his way inside, though, he didn't look like he was doing a routine check. He crouched down by the floor, so Will did too. "There was a report of a student sighted with a gun on campus," Cliff said under his breath. He hadn't been quiet enough, because the students nearest them immediately started whispering.

"Shh!" Will hissed. The whispers didn't stop. Cliff kept talking anyway.

"The sighting was out by the basketball courts, outside the school, but of course we all need to remain on lockdown until the police come and clear the building. It may be a while. Ignore the bells, ignore everything, keep your students where they are."

Will nodded. He wondered if everyone else in the room could hear his heart pounding inside his ribcage.

"Are any of your students in this period diabetic? Any medical concerns that you might need help taking care of? The nurse and aides are on standby."

Will forced himself to think clearly. "Three with childhood asthma. One with an allergy to bee stings."

"That should be fine. If anyone needs an inhaler, push the button to the main office and a nurse will come as soon as it's safe."

The whispers among the students were getting louder. Will turned and issued another, "Quiet!"

"I need to keep checking in with the other classrooms," Cliff said. "Hang in there."

He slipped back out into the hall. Will replaced the music stand under the doorknob.

"What's going on?" someone asked. Will debated for a full minute before answering.

"We're on lockdown for a while, guys," he said. "There's something that needs to be checked out and it might take some time. But you're where you're supposed to be, everyone's quiet, everyone's out of sight, and you've got all the teachers and staff in the building looking out for you. Just keep doing what you're doing."

"Someone's got a gun over by the basketball courts," announced one of the students closest to Will. Was that Phineas? It sounded like Phineas. Even in the dark, Will quickly picked him out and gave him a withering stare.

"*That*," Will said, "was not helpful."

"We have a right to know," Phineas said.

"Right now, you need to worry about staying quiet. I will tell you what you need to know, when you need to know it." Will hoped he sounded authoritative. Panic was rising in his chest again. If someone with a gun wanted to get in the orchestra room, would a music stand really be enough to hold the door closed? Would he honestly be able to keep the shooter at bay?

Don't think about it. Don't.

It was a long time before Will finally stopped kneeling and let himself sit down on the floor. It would be harder to get to his feet this way, but he had no choice. His legs were aching. A quick glance at the clock revealed that it had been almost twenty minutes since Cliff left, and still no sounds from the hallway. The students were getting restless. He heard more murmurs than whispers now, and the occasional squeak of a chair or music stand. He thought he heard the quiet chirp of a cell phone or two, which students weren't supposed to have during school hours. Will weighed the importance of trying to find the phones against keeping his post by the door. He stayed put.

This is going to be okay. Will clung to that thought as hard as he could. It was all going to be okay. Nobody was going to get hurt.

After another minute, Will felt his own cell phone vibrating in his pocket. Technically, he wasn't supposed to have his phone on during school hours, either. Will looked back at the students and then felt his cell vibrate again. *Screw it.* He pulled it out of his pocket and looked at the screen.

It was a long string of text messages. The first two were from Mara:

Just saw your school on the news! You okay?

I love you ♥ Come home safe today.

The next one was from his mother:

Just saw ur school is on lockdown. Some1 with a gun?!?! What is going on?

Then his sister Becca had texted two minutes later:

Praying for u.

Another one from his mother:

It says the kid is suicidal?!?! R u ok? Pls text me back!!!

And then the most recent one, also from his mother:

R U OK?????

Will glanced up suddenly. The hallway was still silent, but who knew what might have happened when he was staring at his phone? He pocketed it again, ignoring it when it kept buzzing. He would worry about texting back after they got the all clear. He had a class to watch over.

"Are those choppers?" a student asked.

Will listened to the *whip-whip-whip* sounds coming closer. Maybe it was Air Force One, just doing a routine flight. Will knew that was a stupid thing to wish. It was probably the news, getting an aerial view of whatever was going on outside.

Or the police, maybe. Will tried to remember whether they'd sent in police via helicopter during the bomb threat months ago. He remembered filing his students out of the building to the football field while the police swept the building. He'd carried the red emergency bag, shifting shoulders as he walked because it was so heavy. A few times, he'd almost lost a student from the line and panicked until he recounted and found everyone was there.

That had been a long day.

Whip-whip-whip. The helicopter, whatever it was, seemed to be coming closer. Will's heart constricted. Maybe someone was being life-flighted. Will tried to push away the images of Mara, the first time he saw her. The ambulance had pulled up, lights flashing and siren wailing, while the first responders strapped Mara to a gurney. Will had caught a glimpse of her as the police officers approached him for questioning. Her face had been as white as the sheet.

Will glanced back at the clock. Thirty-five minutes now since Cliff left. How long was this going to go on?

"Mr. Sterling?" The voice came from farther back, closer to the emergency light. "What if we have to go to the bathroom?"

Great. Will looked at the silent hallway, as if maybe it

would give him answers. "Try to hold it," he said, trying not to sound hopeless. "If it's an emergency, I can try to ring the office and get someone to escort you."

The cell phone in his pocket buzzed again. At the same time, another student spoke up. "It's an attempted suicide. The police got the guy."

"Did he really kill himself?" asked someone else.

"He said *attempted*, idiot. Otherwise, he would have just said *suicide*," said a third.

"Watch the name-calling," Will said. "How are you finding out all this stuff?"

Silence.

Of course. They were on their cell phones. Will sighed and pulled his out. If his students were reading what was up online, he'd better see it too.

He had to scroll through five increasingly desperate texts from his mother before he saw a news link Mara had texted.

BREAKING:

WASHINGTON, DC—An area middle school is still on lockdown, although the situation appears to have been resolved, sources say.

An ambulance was seen departing the school campus, where police and first responders were called on the report of an armed teenager outside the gym.

The school has been on lockdown since approximately 1:00 p.m. Although the teen was outside the school and no direct threats to other students or staff were reported, the principal made the decision to lock down the school because the student was armed.

The incident comes only months after the same school was evacuated for a reported bomb threat. The threat was found to be unsubstantiated. However, the school has engaged in an anti-bullying program to decrease school violence and promote healthy conflict resolution.

Staff writers A. N. Jacobsen and O. Manzinelli contributed to this report.

"So when are we going to be able to get up?" a student asked.

"Yeah. I really do need to go to the bathroom."

"Me too!"

Will sucked in a frustrated sigh. "Hold tight, guys. This isn't anyone's idea of a good time, but the person in that ambulance is having the worst day of all of us."

That quieted them down for a few more minutes, although the tension seemed to have dissipated. It was almost over.

Five minutes later, Cliff's voice came back over the PA system. "Staff and students, the code red has been lifted. You may return to your regular classroom routine. Students, at the bell you will skip your fifth period class and go to sixth period.

"A few announcements are in order. First, the code red

was called because a student was experiencing a medical emergency. There was no threat posed to any other students or staff. I want to be very clear about that. At this time, the situation has been resolved, and all school and after-school activities will resume as normal.

"Second, I understand many of you are on social media and that you may find out more about this situation after school hours. I want to remind you that we have an anti-bullying policy at this school and that harassing or demeaning messages about anyone involved will not be tolerated.

"Finally, I want to congratulate all students and staff for the speed and seriousness with which you responded to the code red today. I am very proud of our community and very proud of each and every one of you."

The PA system clicked off, and Will turned on the lights. "I'm going to need everybody to go back to your places. Anyone who needs a bathroom pass, meet me here at the door. Everyone else, chairs where you found them, take your seats, and please, please, please be careful of the instruments. I don't want anyone or anything getting stepped on."

Will scribbled out three bathroom passes as the rest of the room immediately came alive with noise, scraping chair legs, and chatter. They were okay. Will looked out into the hallway and watched as it swelled with students and teachers, scurrying to the bathroom, to the copy room, to the front office. Things were already going back to normal. They really were okay. The relief of it almost bowled him over.

"Be right back, guys," he said, over his shoulder. "Try to keep it to a dull roar."

Will retreated to his office and closed the door behind him. He made a show of opening and bending over a filing cabinet as if he were searching for sheet music, just in case someone was watching through the frosted glass door. He braced his hands against the side of the cabinet just as his knees started to shake. *Here it comes.*

All the emotions he'd turned off during the code red came rushing back. He let the cold edges of the cabinet dig into his palms, just to ground himself in the fact that he was here, that it was over, that no one, thank God, was hurt.

The memory of a pale, unconscious Mara returned, full force this time. He remembered watching her being rolled into the ambulance on the gurney, surrounded by a grim-faced team of first responders. *I almost lost her. I almost lost her before I even knew who she was.*

"Mr. Sterling?" The door behind him cracked open. "Can I have a bathroom pass?"

Will took a deep breath. It wasn't enough to steady himself. It was going to have to be enough to fake it.

"Sure," Will said. He whipped out a file folder of music as if he'd just found something he'd been searching for. "Meet me up at the front."

Will signed four more bathroom passes on the way out of the office and back to the director's stand. He almost tripped on the felt-covered platform but recovered quickly. No one had noticed. He sat down on the chair just as he overheard someone say, "Thank God we get to skip fifth period today. I hadn't studied for my math quiz at all."

Will had to look away for a minute to compose himself before he turned back around and faced the class.

"I want to address what happened today," Will said. He leaned forward against the podium, as much for support as to get a better look at his students, all seated now, in their properly aligned rows with their instruments on their laps. "Put down your instruments. Let's talk."

"Ever notice how when a teacher says, 'Let's talk,' they mean, 'Listen to me talk'?" someone muttered, not quite quietly enough. Phineas again. Will bit back a frustrated sigh.

"Good point. Did everyone hear Phineas? He's absolutely right. I did not mean 'Let's talk.' I did indeed mean, 'Listen to me talk.' And what's the rule I told you on the first day of school?" Will brandished his baton. "The baton rules. He who holds the baton makes the rules. It's true in music as well as in life. Now listen up."

If Phineas didn't look exactly repentant, at least he was quiet now. "You all already know that the medical emergency the principal was talking about on the announcements was an attempted suicide. Yes, a student had a gun at school. Yes, we were on lockdown because there was a gun on campus. You already know this, so I won't pretend you don't. And maybe that's not the right thing for me to do."

That got their attention. A few of the students sat up straighter, while others frowned a little. Will wondered if they could tell his heart was racing. He was in too deep to stop now, so he continued: "I honestly don't know. See, some people tell teachers that we should address the big issues with our students head-on. No holds barred, we should tell you whatever you want to know. Other people say we need to hold back the stuff you don't need to hear. Don't burden children with information they aren't prepared to handle." Will tapped the edge of the podium. "I think either way of doing things might be right and might be wrong. Maybe a little of both."

For once, Will wished someone would come out with a smart aleck comment. He was sinking in deep. "Here's what I do know: whatever your problem is, whatever is going on in your life, people are here to help you. We have guidance counselors in the front office, we have a resource officer in the hallways, we have peer support counselors and lunch bunches if you want to talk with another student. And there's me. Your teachers care about you. We want to help you. Whatever it is, whether it's your grades or your friends or your parents or any problem, big or small, we don't want you to feel like you have to handle it alone."

"Aww. Thanks, Mr. S. We love you too," said someone in the second row. She meant it sincerely, Will thought, but a couple of the students snickered anyway.

"Quiet," snapped a self-righteous French horn player. "He would know. Wasn't there a school shooting in your class when you were in college? My mom told me."

And there it was. Will wondered what it would have been like to be a teacher before everyone was searchable on the Internet. "Kind of. I wasn't in class. My wife and I were in the Student Union, and there was an active shooter." How much should he tell? How much could he stand to tell?

"You were married when you were in college?" someone called out.

"No. My wife and I didn't know each other at the time. That's how we met. She was shot—" Will's throat constricted. Better pull it together. "And I found her."

"You saved her life? That's how you met?" cooed the French horn player's buddy. "That's so romantic!"

In an instant, Will felt as if he were back there, holding the body of the girl he didn't know, trying to press down against the blood that squirted out of her blouse like a fountain. He could still smell the coppery scent of her blood and see her eyes roll back in her head. Feel the weight of her sinking into his lap.

"No," Will said. "It wasn't. It wasn't romantic at all."

3 Reasons I Wish I Could Have a Time Wreck
and 4 Reasons I Know I Can't

By Brian Kendall

Long ago, before timeline rectifications, before the Internet, before reality television or answering machines or any of the other modern-day annoyances that have come to plague my life, there was a young man. He was sixteen years old and his name was Johnathan.

Johnathan was five-foot-eleven, played basketball at his high school, and was dating a girl named Becky. Like most high school boys, he aspired to many things: becoming an astronaut, visiting his uncle's ranch in Wyoming, passing his geometry class.

Johnathan did none of these things, because on one warm spring evening, he was riding his bicycle home from Becky's house. He was out later than he was supposed to be and was pedaling home as fast as he could; trying, I expect, to make curfew. He was not wearing a helmet, as children often didn't back in the seventies. He was not watching the road, and thus he did not see the car coming around a sharp bend up ahead. The driver of the car also did not see him.

Johnathan was killed immediately on impact.

I was the driver of that car.

In the nearly forty years since that horrible night, I have heard many young people talk about this concept of "justice." Of late, the most heavily debated iteration of criminal justice is timeline rectification, and, if you'll permit me, I'd like to give you the perspective of one old man who wishes more than anything that he could be a time wrecker. These are the top three reasons I would gladly take a timeline rectification:

1. **Johnathan's death was easily avoidable**.

   Those of you who have grieved are doubtlessly familiar with the "if only" game. I'll share the highlights of mine:

   - If only I had waited five minutes to go to the store. Alternatively: if only I had gone five minutes earlier.
   - If only he had reflectors on his bicycle, I might have seen him.
   - If only I had taken that turn more slowly.
   - If only he had been wearing a helmet.

   That a person should die due to factors as small and easily rectified as these adds an additional level of horror and injustice to that night.

2. **His passing cast a pall on all who knew him . . . and many who didn't**.

   I have never claimed to grieve at the same level as those who knew Johnathan: his parents, his friends, his schoolmates. I can only imagine the burden of grief they carry and the hole that his loss has left in their lives. Despite never having laid eyes on this young man until the accident, after his death I became somewhat obsessed with trying to honor the life that I had, wholly unwittingly, brought to an end. I read his obituary, the memorial in his school's yearbook, and every article the newspaper printed about the accident. It was his death and my role in the accident that caused me to descend into alcoholism, which additionally cost me my wife, my house, and my job. I went from being a full-time father to an every-other-weekend parent—that is, when I was sober enough to pick up the kids. After a hell of a fight and two years of sobriety, I have now regained a job, an apartment, and a strained relationship with one of my children.

3. **Johnathan deserved to live**.

And don't we all? Whether Johnathan had continued to play basketball or date Becky, whether he ever became an astronaut or passed that geometry class, he deserved to live.

However, timeline rectification is a tricky business. The government does not simply turn back time for every sad old man who wishes he'd lived differently. There are four reasons that I will never be able to take back that night.

1. **Legally, the accident was not a crime**.

Certainly, I have felt the weight of my role as a killer each day of my life. Legally, however, no charges were ever filed, and none were ever sought. This was an accident. According to the rules and statutes of the justice system, there can be no rectification for events that were not criminal.

2. **There was a fatality**.

Timeline rectifications are not performed for incidents that resulted in a pregnancy or a death. I understand, in principle, why the Department of Timeline Rectification would make such a stipulation. In my heart, I think those of us who have seen crimes result in loss of life wish for the opportunity to turn back time even more earnestly.

3. **The accident occurred before 2000**.

The technology for timeline rectification has existed since 1999, when the Supreme Court ruling was made. Presumably, Dr. Bennington had invented it before that, earlier in the nineties. However, partly due to the ruling and partly due to preventing some type of time paradox, we cannot change events that occurred before timeline rectification was first enacted under law.

4. **The accident involved a minor.**

One of the facts I ruminate on the most is that Johnathan was killed in the prime of his life. Sixteen years old, with years of school and career and love stretched out before him. As much as I wish I could give that back to him, the law prohibits rectifying crimes that involve a minor, either as the perpetrator or the victim.

Often, people who are perhaps well-meaning or perhaps not will claim that there is a good and worthy reason behind every tragedy. Some will press me to believe that Johnathan was an angel meant to be called home early or that his death must surely have inspired some new law, some spiritual awakening, some good act that made this tragedy understandable. There is none. From one man who wishes he could change his past, to those who could change theirs: seize the opportunity you have. Nothing is worth a lifetime of regret.

Chapter Eleven

....

MARA

Mara resisted the urge to text Will again on her walk home from the Metro station. Of course, he would be fine. He'd already called twice today to check in, and texted her in between each class.

"I know yesterday scared you. I don't want you to worry," Will had said each time, but his voice gave him away.

"I'm just glad to hear you're all right," Mara would respond. *And I wish you'd tell me that you're the one who's scared. I wish you'd just let me comfort you.*

Will hadn't opened up to her last night, either, even when he woke up three different times with nightmares. Each time he'd gotten out of bed to drink a glass of water, or use the bathroom, or check all the windows and the chain on the apartment door. He was so quiet and moved so slowly, as if he wouldn't wake her up. As if Mara could sleep.

Each twinge of her shoulder had felt like a condemnation. It had been pure chance that she had been the one to cross paths with Jason Mann. What if it had been Will instead? Mara flinched whenever she imagined Will in her place. Could she have helped him, the way he had helped her? Would she have had the presence of mind to press on the wound, or call 911, or hold him until the first responders arrived?

"Of course you would have," Will had scoffed, the one time she'd spoken about it to him. "Weren't you thinking about being premed when you were a freshman? Hell, you probably could have taken the bullets out, cauterized the wound, and made me a sling out of your jacket or something."

Right. He probably wouldn't have let me help him back then, either.

Thank goodness the workday was over now. Mara quickened her pace when she saw their apartment building ahead. Will had promised he was coming straight home, no staying late for a meeting. They would have dinner and then Mara was going to go to bed early, even if she couldn't convince Will to rest. Just knowing he was safe at home with her would help.

Mara wasn't having a great day herself. Her shoulder was twinging horribly, sending wave after wave of pain rolling down her arm. It was probably from insisting she could carry a stack of files by herself—something that counted as "exertion" even though it was such a simple task. Now that she thought of it, Mara hadn't wanted to ask for help, either. She guessed that made her and Will even.

Mara's stomach gurgled, reminding her that she'd taken her last pill dry. She'd need to eat something soon. Plain bread, maybe. A few more antacids.

Mara pushed open the door to the apartment building and was immediately hit by the wave of heat. *Why couldn't the building manager turn down the heat already?* Mara's stomach started doing backflips. She stopped and closed her eyes. Swallowed.

I am not going to throw up in the lobby. I am not.

She swallowed again.

"Mara? Are you all right?"

Mara recognized Mrs. Hiddleston's voice. Usually, her downstairs neighbor was saying things like, "Would you all mind just walking a bit quieter?" or "Does your husband need to practice that instrument during the dinner hour?" Since the Hiddlestons' dinner hour seemed to be any time from 3:00 to 7:00, it was a bit hard to avoid.

Mara opened her eyes. Mrs. Hiddleston didn't seem irritated today, just concerned. The short gray curls that framed her face stood at attention, like miniature question marks. "Mara, dear, are you ill?"

"My stomach isn't so good," Mara said. She had to swallow three times.

"Let me walk you up," said Mrs. Hiddleston. "Come along.

Is the heat bothering you? Let's get that coat off."

For a minute, Mara's neighbor had morphed into Grandmary. Mrs. Hiddleston fussed over her, carefully pulling off her coat and helping her up the stairs. She smelled a little like beef broth and carrots. She was probably making another pot roast, which meant Will and Mara's apartment would smell like it for the next three days.

Mara tried not to think about food.

She concentrated on keeping her steps even with her breathing. They turned on the landing and started the last flight of stairs.

"That's a girl. Watch your step now, honey," Mrs. Hiddleston said, just like Grandmary would have. Only Mara's grandmother had always smelled like Old English lavender lotion instead of pot roast, and she would have been six inches taller than Mara. Mrs. Hiddleston barely came up to Mara's chin.

I wish Grandmary really could be here. Mara was horrified to feel her eyes watering. Now was not the time to let down her guard. She let Mrs. Hiddleston guide her around the final turn of the stairs and up to her door.

"Thank you," Mara said with all the grace she could muster. Her keys were in the pocket of her trench coat, which was folded over her neighbor's arm. Before she could ask, Mrs. Hiddleston had already started knocking on the door.

"Mara?" Will answered the door barefoot, in sweatpants and a T-shirt. "Are you all right?"

"She's a bit sick to her stomach," Mrs. Hiddleston said. She gave Will a knowing smile and winked as she helped Mara inside. "You take care of yourself, dear." She bustled off and the door swung closed.

"She thinks I'm pregnant." Mara realized it as soon as she said it.

"You'd think she'd be pissed. If she can't handle hearing us tiptoe around the apartment, why would she be excited about having a baby upstairs?"

"Who knows. Besides, there's no baby for her to worry about." Mara closed her eyes and swallowed again.

"Mara?"

"Can you get me some bread, please? Or crackers?" Mara had to stop and swallow again. *As soon as I can stand to lie down, I'm going to bed.*

Will returned with a stack of Saltines. She crunched through them slowly, waiting for relief.

"Better?" Will asked, after a few minutes had passed.

"Better." Mara walked over to the recliner and sat.

"Okay. Um, I've got something to tell you. But before I do, I'm really, really sorry."

Mara's heartbeat sped up. "That doesn't sound good."

"I forgot to tell you a social worker called yesterday. Someone named Traci Bryant. Apparently, she's the social worker assigned to our time wreck case and she needs to check in on us and see how we're doing."

A brief glimmer of hope. Had she called, or had Will called her? Talking to someone about the code red yesterday would probably help Will, even if he didn't want to admit it. "That's fine," Mara said, trying not to sound too enthusiastic. "It's good she wants to check in. Nice of her to call to see how you're doing after the code red."

Will frowned for a moment, as if he was confused. "No, it's not about the thing at school yesterday. She didn't mention it, anyway. I guess a social worker has to come meet with us over the time wreck stuff to be sure we understand and know all our options. She said 'community support' a lot while we were talking."

Disappointment flooded through Mara, followed quickly by a hot flash of irritation. "How many people are we going to have to meet over this stupid thing? Don't we have to see that psychiatrist on Friday? Isn't that enough?"

"I guess they want to be extra cautious. Anyway, I was going to tell you yesterday when you got home, but . . ."

"Well, it's not like you had anything else on your mind." Mara waved off his apology. "Right. So did you make an appointment with her?"

"Yeah . . ." Will said. "It's tonight. I forgot until she called with a reminder, and that was right before you got home."

Mara bolted upright in the recliner, sending shock waves

of pain down her arm. "Tonight? When is she going to be here?"

"In an hour. I'm so sorry."

"Don't be," Mara said, trying to hide her annoyance. Her nap would have to wait.

At least Will handled all the last-minute clean-up, probably spurred on by his guilty conscience. Mara tried to help put the clean dishes in the cabinets and move the dirty dishes into the dishwasher, but Will shooed her away. "Go sit down for a minute. You look"—Mara shot him a look—"like you could use a rest."

Well, at least he hadn't said she looked terrible. Or tired. Or grumpy. All of which were true, but it was nice not to be reminded of it. Mara settled back into her recliner. She wouldn't bother changing. She'd just wear her work clothes through the social worker's visit, and then she'd get ready for bed.

Mara had only met with a social worker once before, back when she was in the hospital. She didn't remember much about it. That social worker had a soft voice and said some things about trauma and coping. Beyond that, Mara's memory went fuzzy. Most of her memories from her time in the hospital were like that.

Today, everything seemed to be happening in painful detail. The lights seemed extra bright and every sound seemed to echo. *Am I getting a migraine?* With all the medicine she'd taken today, she wouldn't be surprised. Mara closed her eyes again and tried to doze off. She might have succeeded, because the next thing she knew, there was a hefty knock at the door.

The social worker had arrived with a cracked leather briefcase and a wide smile. "So nice to meet you!" she exclaimed, walking in as if she were an old friend coming for a visit. "Traci Bryant. Pleasure to meet you both." She shook Will's hand enthusiastically before turning to Mara.

Please don't, Mara thought, holding her right arm tight against her side. Traci only paused for a minute before shifting her briefcase and shaking Mara's left hand instead. "So good to see you. Thank you for making time to see me."

Mara couldn't help smiling back. Something about this Traci Bryant was infectious. She was a large, comfortable-looking woman dressed in black slacks and a purple-and-green patterned top. Her hair was coiled in bleached, coppery curls that stood out against her dark, almost-black skin. Mara led Traci to the couch and sat beside her. *She's wearing cologne,* Mara thought. It probably wasn't strong to anyone else, but with her pounding head, it felt like she'd taken a bath in cinnamon and spices. Mara's stomach turned again. *Don't think about food.*

I wonder who she usually meets with? Mara wondered instead. At work, Mara met survivors of every kind of trauma, from every kind of life. She usually made up a picture in her head of who a participant in the study might be after reading the file, and she was usually surprised when she met them in person. Maybe social work was like that too.

If Traci Bryant found anything about Will and Mara surprising, she certainly didn't show it. She opened the briefcase like she was Mary Poppins getting ready to pull out a hat stand.

"Well, you've probably heard all you can stand to hear about timeline rectification at this point, so I'm here to talk you through your thoughts on the process." Traci pulled out a manila file and a handful of pamphlets from her briefcase. Mara recognized half of them from the display stand at work. *Living with Disabilities, Recovering from PTSD, Trauma Resources* . . .

"What are these for?" Mara asked.

"Just some information on local resources. We're fortunate to have a lot of nonprofits that support crime victims and trauma survivors. Lots of fantastic community partners."

Mara's shoulders dropped . "So you think we shouldn't have a time wreck."

"That's not for me to decide, either way. My job is to make sure that participants make the choices that are best for them. I'm not here to push you toward a timeline rectification or away from it. I just want you to know all the options you have."

A deep sigh escaped. *The only options I'm interested in are a hot shower and a long nap.* Her stomach gurgled again.

"I appreciate where you're coming from," Will said, taking up the cause. "But we've been living with this for eight years. My wife works with trauma survivors. We've seen all the doctors and all the specialists. There really isn't any resource we haven't tried."

Mara slid a sideways look at her husband. *For me, maybe. You're still convinced you can handle PTSD on your own.*

Traci nodded. "I was reading through your file before I came, and you've both done an impressive job of handling some very trying circumstances. Why don't you tell me what that's been like for you?"

The longer she talked, the more it sounded to Mara as if she were underwater. Her ears throbbed and her cheeks reddened. *Not now.*

Will was saying something. Mara tried to focus on his words, but she started to feel the rising warmth again and felt bile in her throat. *No. Don't.*

Too late. Mara lurched down the hall to the bathroom. She barely managed to slam the door behind her before she started to throw up.

When she was done, Mara curled up on the bathroom floor with her back against the cool fiberglass tub. Her right shoulder was seizing, probably in response to how fast she'd had to move. Mara closed her eyes and breathed through each spasm. She'd clean up later. She'd do everything later. She just wanted to rest. At least her stomach, now empty, was starting to untwist.

I don't want this to be my life anymore, Mara thought. *I'm so tired. I just want to feel better.*

In the back of her mind, the usual thoughts bubbled up. *Maybe after I sleep, I'll feel better. Maybe if I just remember to eat something plain with my pills . . . or if I stop eating anything dairy . . . or if I give up soda for good . . .*

Or maybe the time wreck is exactly what I need.

She realized that someone was knocking on the bathroom door. "Mara," Will called. "Mara, I'm coming in now if you don't answer." He pushed open the door.

"I'm sorry," Mara whispered.

"What are you sorry for? Come on. Let's get you to bed."

Will helped her up and gave her a paper cup of water to rinse her mouth. Mara's head pounded, but at least sipping the water didn't make her want to throw up again. That was something.

"Is Traci still here?" she managed.

"No. She left her card and said she hopes you feel better."

"I'm going to clean up."

"Nope. You're going to bed. Let's go."

No point fighting, Mara thought sleepily. *I'll get up and help in a few minutes.*

Her shoulder seized as she leaned back on the bank of

cool pillows. Mara breathed in and out through her nose until finally, mercifully, sleep came.

Chapter Twelve

....

WILL

Date: April 7, 2011
To: Staff
From: Cliff
Subject: Update on Student

Dear Teachers and Staff:

I want to thank you all again for your quick response to our code red on Monday. The student's family has contacted me to let me know that he is still in the hospital receiving psychiatric care and will likely be discharged soon. I am working with the family to determine how we can best support this student's educational needs during his recovery. The family also wanted to share their thanks for quickly recognizing their son's needs and getting him help while also keeping the other students out of harm's way, so I wanted to pass that on to all of you.

—Cliff

Date: April 7, 2011
To: Will Sterling
From: Cliff
Subject: Assembly

Will:

Just wanted to thank you again personally for your calm and collected response to Monday's code red. I heard that you shared a bit about your own experience at Adams Morgan with your class. Bravo on opening up to your students about the real-life ramifications of these difficult situations. Hopefully some of them will take your words to heart.

On that note, do you have any more thoughts on sharing your story at a school assembly next week? Particularly after Monday's events, I think it's critical for our staff to come together and remind our students of our core values and why we work so hard to be a safe space. Let me know.

—Cliff

Will left the email checked as "unread," even though he'd looked over it dozens of times. He should have known that his little speech to the students would get back to Cliff. Will had managed to avoid bumping in to him in the halls throughout the day on Thursday, so Cliff hadn't been able to corner him to follow up. And now it was Friday. A day off, even if it didn't feel much like a vacation at all.

Will braced his foot against the seat in front of him. He

wished there was more legroom on the Metro. More shock absorbers too. The ride to the Bennington Building today was bumpier than usual. Beside him, Mara was sitting straight at attention, cradling her right arm in her lap. Her face was impassive, but Will noticed that she closed her eyes briefly with each shudder of the train car.

She had barely managed to wake up from her nap in time for them to make it to the Metro stop. This week had been hard on Mara—harder, Will suspected, than it had been on him. Each day she'd seemed to eat less and sleep longer.

I wish there was a medicine that could help. I wish there was a surgery or a treatment or anything.

Then Will remembered where they were going. *Oh, right. There is.*

"Two more stops," Mara announced suddenly. "Do you have everything?"

"Everything like . . . what?" Will asked. "I thought we just had to show up."

Mara was already checking her jacket pockets and slinging her purse around her good shoulder. "I just meant make sure you have your Metro pass and your jacket and whatnot."

She was such a mom. The thought made Will ache a little bit. If the appointment went well today, maybe she could be a mom. Maybe in their new life map, they'd already be parents at this point.

The train lurched to another stop, and Mara closed her eyes again.

"Hey," Will said, reaching over and touching her knee. "It's going to be okay."

"Of course it is," Mara said, without opening her eyes. "We always make it through. No matter what."

◆◆◆◆◆

If Will had thought Nayana's office was impersonal, the waiting room of the psychiatrist's office was downright cold. There weren't even magazines on the tables or abstract art on the walls. Just a room full of uncomfortable maroon chairs. Will practically had to fold himself in half to sit down. That was the problem with being so darn tall.

Without anything to distract him, Will couldn't find a way to stop his heart from racing. Will knew about psychiatrists. There was the one he'd seen in college that diagnosed him with PTSD. What if this psychiatrist said the other one was wrong? What if he thought Will was just oversensitive? Imagining things? Even if the main motivation was healing Mara's shoulder, surely his PTSD factored in. What if he wasn't crazy after all?

What if that blew it for both of them?

Chill, Will told himself. He and Mara would probably get called in together, like they did to Nayana's office. This appointment was just a formality, anyway. Nothing to it.

The door to the waiting room opened, revealing a middle-aged woman with a deep voice and a deeper scowl. "Sterling?" she called.

Will jumped. "Yes?"

The woman pointed to the hallway behind her. "Second door on your left."

Will and Mara both stood. The receptionist shot a glare at Mara. "*Mister* Sterling first, please."

"We're doing different appointments?" Will asked.

"You have different appointment times, don't you?" The woman looked annoyed. "Second door on your left."

Will glanced back at Mara. She smiled encouragingly. If she looked as worried as he felt, it didn't show.

The second door on the left was marked with a laminate wooden nametag engraved DR. AARON HENDRIX. Will was surprised to see a man standing just inside the doorway, hand already extended for a handshake. For once, Will didn't have to look down to make eye contact. Dr. Hendrix was easily as tall as he was. About three times as wide too. Glasses, like him, but Dr. Hendrix's kept sliding down his nose. It was probably sweat. Dr. Hendrix's pale skin was pink and blotchy, as if he'd just run up the stairs.

"Mr. Sterling," the psychiatrist said, pushing the glasses back up with his index finger. "I'm Dr. Aaron Hendrix. Pleased to meet you, although naturally I wish we were meeting under different circumstances."

Did everyone in the Bennington Building say that?

"I've read through your complete mental health evaluation," Dr. Hendrix began. He shut the door behind Will and gestured him toward a chair. "It was completed by one Dr. Rodriguez approximately seven years ago." Dr. Hendrix plopped down behind the desk, rolling back slightly in the desk chair as he did.

"When I was in college," Will said. "Yes."

"I want to commend you for seeking help so soon after the incident. Many people have difficulty admitting that there is a problem and try to handle it themselves. They want to 'tough it out,' so to speak."

Dr. Hendrix's tone was complimentary, but Will still felt stung. *I got help because it was the right thing to do. I'm not weak.*

"I see you have a documented diagnosis of post-traumatic stress disorder and a detailed analysis of how the shooting contributed to your condition."

"It caused the condition," Will said.

Dr. Hendrix pinched his lips and nodded shortly. "I just want to do a quick assessment to bring us up to speed. Are you seeing a psychiatrist currently?"

Will cracked a smile. "Yes. You."

Dr. Hendrix didn't laugh. *Okay. Not the time for humor.* Will cleared his throat. "No. I saw Dr. Rodriguez for six months or so. He worked for the university I went to. He mostly just wanted to make sure I understood what PTSD was and to help me learn some ways to handle everything."

"Do you take antidepressants?"

"No," Will said vehemently. "I'm fine." Too late, he realized that this wasn't the time to put on a front. Mara needed this rectification. "I mean, I didn't feel that they would help," Will amended. "I don't always have nightmares. Just sometimes. So I didn't want to take medicine every day for a problem that only crops up from time to time." Will was making it worse, he was sure.

Dr. Hendrix jotted down some notes. "It looks like you've had stable employment since graduation. Any issues at work?"

This was not the time to be a hero. Still, Will couldn't make eye contact with the psychiatrist when he answered the question. "We've had some issues with school violence this year. There was a bomb threat a few months ago where we had to evacuate the building. Earlier this week, a student had a gun on campus. Suicide threat. We were all on lockdown for that." Will slid his eyes up to meet Dr. Hendrix's. "I guess it's been a trigger for me."

"I see," Dr. Hendrix said, jotting down some notes. "I want to talk you through the realities of timeline rectification for your situation. There are certainly ways in which a timeline rectification would be helpful for you, but it's still important to carefully weigh this decision. There are some benefits to the events in this life map that you will not receive after a timeline rectification."

Here we go. Despite himself, Will let out a sigh.

That seemed to pique the psychiatrist's interest. He scribbled down more notes. "You seem resistant to the idea that there have been benefits from the shooting."

"No, it's just—" Will sighed again. This was much easier when Mara was here. "At first, right after the shooting happened, everyone was shocked and upset too. And then, I don't know, after a few weeks, people started pressuring us to find the bright side to what had happened. They kept talking almost like the shooting was a *good* thing. Like if we looked hard enough, we'd see that it was really a blessing in disguise. And I just don't feel that way."

Dr. Hendrix nodded thoughtfully. "Give me an example, please."

Will was surprised at how easily the answer came. "Like the issues I mentioned at the school where I teach. My principal's all up in my face trying to get me to share my story and share my perspective with the students, as if I have some big, overwhelming 'life lesson' to share." Will used his fingers to make quotation marks in the air. "And I feel like, did I do this wrong? Because I don't feel wiser or more grateful than I think I'd be otherwise. I don't have an incredible perspective to share to help people 'choose the right path,' or 'appreciate the little things,' or 'remember what's important."' More air quotes. Will was embarrassed by his own dorkiness.

"No," Dr. Hendrix said. "It doesn't sound like you're doing anything wrong. Everything you've said sounds perfectly normal to me."

Perfectly normal. Will relaxed a little. *Wait. If I'm normal, will he say we don't need the time wreck?* Will was about to speak up again—*no, really, we're not doing that well, trust me, I'm a mess*—but Dr. Hendrix had another question.

"You say everyone was pressuring you to find the bright side or to feel grateful because of your experience. Then you mentioned your principal. Are there any other people who specifically pressured you over this?"

"No, no. That was just an example. People in general is what I meant."

Dr. Hendrix didn't write down anything. "No one at all? No one else specific?"

"Well, my mom, I guess," Will said. "My whole family back home."

Now Dr. Hendrix was writing. Will must have said something interesting. "And how many people would that be?" the psychiatrist asked. "Aunts? Uncles? Cousins?"

"No, it's just my mom, brother, sister, and me. No dad in the picture," Will said, waiting for Dr. Hendrix to pounce on that. This was the kind of junk psychiatrists probably liked to hear. *And do you feel you're really seeking a time wreck because you lack a father figure to look up to?*

But Dr. Hendrix didn't seem interested in that at all. "Has your family always been so unsupportive?"

"I wouldn't say they're unsupportive," Will said. "They're religious. They want me to understand the purpose of God in this and how it all works toward the greater good."

"Are you religious, Will?"

Were psychiatrists allowed to ask that? Maybe they could ask anything they wanted. "I like the idea of a God," Will said. "I like the music and the stories—except that one with Abraham and Isaac, that one always creeped me out—but I don't think I feel it. When I shut my eyes and pray, I don't feel what everyone at their church seems to feel. I don't feel like dancing or praising or falling on my knees. I just feel normal."

"So," Dr. Hendrix said. "Do you think that the shooting could have been God doing something terrible to work toward the greater good?"

"No," Will said. "No. I mean, I think God is good, but I think sometimes things just happen. Bad things. Like this, obviously."

Dr. Hendrix nodded. He didn't say anything. Just nodded, like a Bobblehead doll.

"One more question," he said. "Tell me more about your relationship with your wife. How do you think you would have met if it hadn't been for the shooting?"

You Get One Life

By Renee Rasmussen

One life.

One time.

One chance to get things right.

There are so many times that I've waited and wished and prayed for a second chance, only to be denied. Have you read all the articles out there about timeline rectification? I have. Have you looked up an inmate in the system to see if they're nearing eligibility for parole . . . meaning they might have a shot at getting into the rectification program? I have. Have you written personal letters begging an inmate to consider a rectification? I've written over 200—averaging one a week for four years.

I had a perfectly ordinary life until I was thirty-two years old. Not perfect, mind you. Perfectly ordinary. I had a roommate who was friendly and a cat with terrible cat-food breath and a job I liked well enough but wasn't a career.

And then, one day, in the middle of my very ordinary existence, I was knocked unconscious. I woke up in a hospital bed, attached to more monitors than I'd ever seen in my life. My apartment had been broken into by two teens who were high on drugs and looking for anything they could steal and sell on the black market. I didn't know them, and neither did my roommate. Our door was locked. Our blinds were shut. We just had the bad luck to be in the first-floor apartment when these two men got the idea to break in.

They were arrested quickly, did us the favor of admitting their guilt, and are currently serving their sentences. This is where the story gets interesting: at the end of the trial, my lawyer turned to me and said, "Give it a few years. If they qualify for the rehabilitation program, you'll probably get a time wreck. This isn't forever."

This isn't forever. I clung to those words as I tried to rebuild my life. My roommate was too traumatized to consider another apartment in the city. She ended up moving back to her home state to be with family. She took the cat too. I hope they're doing well, but to be honest, the whole experience was so hard that we can't talk without it all bubbling back up.

I don't have my old job anymore. When it reached the point that I'd been in the hospital longer than I'd ever worked there, they let me go—and legally, they had no obligation to keep me for as long as they did. Finding a new job and getting insurance with what are now "preexisting conditions" was a nightmare. I'd like to go back to counseling, but I can't afford it. I think a vacation could be restful, but I have to save up all my days off in case I need another surgery.

For years, the only thing that kept me going was the chance that someday, I might get a timeline rectification. Believing that all my struggles were temporary helped me handle every challenge.

At last, the time came when the criminals could qualify for the rehabilitation program. They both signed up.

They both dropped out.

I felt like I was going crazy when I found out they'd left the rehabilitation program. What happened? Why did they change their minds? Could they try again? Finally (after I wrote many, many letters), one of them wrote back. He had been willing to put forth the effort to rehabilitate, but his partner in crime wasn't. Prison was working for him. He was powerful there, respected. He didn't want to change. The other criminal—the one who had written to me—was very sorry, but unless they were both willing to rehabilitate, a time wreck would be impossible. He was working toward his own parole, apologized again for his actions, and wished me well.

This is forever. It took me one letter to realize it, but much, much longer to believe it. For over a year, I devoted myself to the cause of convincing these two men to change their minds.

But after a while, I began to realize that I simply couldn't change people who weren't willing to change. The only person I could rehabilitate was myself. And so—slowly, painfully—I began the long, hard process of accepting my reality.

This is the problem with time wrecking: it lets victims focus on changing the past instead of shaping the future. At some point, we all must decide whether we're going to keep looking back or start moving forward. My journey has been full of stops and starts and many, many backward glances, but I am finally moving forward. At last, I'm starting to heal.

This is forever—this one broken, beautiful life. We're only guaranteed one chance to do it right.

Let's make it count.

Chapter Thirteen

....

MARA

Saturday was a sleeping-in kind of day. It was warm but overcast, tucking in the city with a snug blanket of humidity.

Or smog. It was probably smog, Mara reflected as she went for a second glass of water from the kitchen. She'd been up since six o'clock, when she'd taken her first round of pain pills for the day and stopped to eat a little breakfast. She didn't want another repeat of Tuesday, that was for sure. Ever since, she'd been careful to eat her crackers, drink her water, and take antacids at the first sign of a stomach gurgle.

She still didn't feel all that well. Mara's shoulder ached more as the week wore on and taking off work for the appointment Friday had been a welcome relief. Welcome until she heard what Dr. Hendrix had to say, anyway.

Don't think about that now. Hold it together a little longer.

Mara glanced up at the clock. It was nine o'clock in the morning, and Will was still asleep. *Let him,* Mara's intuition told her. Will had been up with two nightmares last night, even though he wouldn't tell her what they were about. Mara scribbled out a note and left it on the kitchen table, just in case he woke up and noticed her missing.

Going out to run a few errands this morning. Try to get some more rest. Love you!

—M

Not that the errands Mara had in mind would take very long. She liked to get fresh flowers for the end table, especially when they'd had a bad week. It made their cluttered little apartment feel more like a home. Grandmary would have approved.

Granted, Grandmary always had a vase of flowers somewhere in the house because she had maintained an enviable flower garden. Thinking about that garden—that house—made Mara's heart start hammering. She tried to talk herself out of it for the whole walk to the Metro, but she still boarded the train heading toward Arlington.

There's nothing wrong with it. It's just a little visit. But Will would be hurt she hadn't asked him to join. He probably would have tried to talk her out of it.

"Why are you torturing yourself?" That's what he'd say. "Leave the past in the past."

On the other hand, maybe he wouldn't have said that, now. Ever since they'd gotten the letters about the time wreck, leaving the past in the past was impossible.

Mara's heart thumped faster when she got off the train at the familiar stop. There weren't many passengers getting off here on a Saturday morning. Most people were going the other way, into the city for a day of sightseeing or shopping. It hardly took any time at all for Mara to go through the turnstiles and up the tall escalator to the street.

Emerging into the sunlight brushed off the last waves of guilt. Arlington was still a part of her, even if she didn't live here. She belonged here.

The breeze picked up a bit, and Mara walked extra slowly to take in every detail along the route. The deli where she used to stop to pick up soda had changed management. There were new neighbors in the house at the corner, people who parked their cars outside of the garage and used the space as a potting shed. Mara heard them arguing over whether it was too early to plant tomatoes and peppers. She walked on, head bowed, until she was directly in front of the house.

Grandmary's house had always looked like a little storybook cottage to Mara. It had red brick along the bottom and white siding on the second floor, with little green shutters surrounding every window. The front window had leaded glass. When she was little, Mara used to trace her fingers along the diamond pattern and pretend that she was Rapunzel looking through her tower window. Other times, she pretended to be Goldilocks, testing out the furniture before the three bears came back home. It was strange to look at the house now and know that other people thought of it as home.

The new owners hadn't replaced Grandmary's stepping stones, thank goodness. Mara had helped her lay them when she was still in elementary school, which was why they were a little crooked. There was still some semblance of a garden, even though it was nothing like Grandmary's had been. Just the rosebushes and a few tulips. Nothing special. A red plastic toy car with a yellow roof was parked haphazardly in the mulch. No wonder the new owners didn't have much time for gardening. They had little kids.

Good. It was the kind of house that needed a family.

Mara's heart sank even lower.

She'd spent most of her summers and school breaks here, so her parents could work. When Mara had gone off to college, she'd come back to visit Grandmary here in Arlington just as often as she'd gone to visit her parents in Alexandria. Maybe even more often.

And then it had been her house.

Mara and Will had only been married for a few months when Grandmary died. Knowing that she'd planned to leave her house to them—even used Mara's married name in the will—showed that although the stroke had been sudden, Grandmary might have felt that the end was near. Mara hoped so. Imagining that Grandmary had felt a sense of closure for herself helped.

It would have been a beautiful home for them. A single-family house in a good neighborhood, with good schools, already paid off. It should have been perfect.

In another life, maybe it would have been.

Mara had cried for two hours straight after they decided to put the house up for sale. "We don't have to," Will had said. "We can find a way to make it work." He hated it when she cried and here she'd lost her grandmother and had to list her house all in the space of a month. Mara had thought she could see the wheels turning in Will's head, trying to find a way to keep the house, at least.

But it wasn't practical. Mara hadn't been able to find a job and they were barely surviving on Will's salary as a first-year teacher. Besides, living in Arlington added a full thirty minutes to his commute, each way. At twenty-two, Mara was both a new college grad and a new wife, which meant she wasn't covered under her parents' health insurance anymore. The insurance from Will's job with the school system was good, but Mara had to spend hours arguing with them over each treatment her doctor recommended for her shoulder. If the pain was manageable with painkillers, did she really need another revision surgery? Acupuncture wasn't covered, and only ten sessions of physical therapy a year were considered necessary. Mara had watched their bank account sink lower and lower as the doctor's office and the insurance claims department battled it out.

Selling the house and renting a little apartment in the city had helped. They hadn't gone into debt during the years Mara was unemployed. They'd been able to pay ten thousand dollars in deductibles the year she had the revision surgery. Selling the house had been the right thing to do.

Besides, we knew we wouldn't need a house like this. It had been fine to imagine that someday, maybe, they could have had children. People in worse circumstances than theirs had done it. If she'd been able to go without the painkillers for nine months, she could have been pregnant. There were ways to work around the physical things she couldn't do.

But she had never been able to decrease the painkillers she was on, only increase. And they had never—would never—be able to afford adoption. They'd only just begun to be able to add to their savings account again when she'd gotten the job as a researcher. It wasn't much. Not enough to even upgrade their one-bedroom apartment and rent a two-bedroom instead. They couldn't even apply to foster or adopt unless they had a two-bedroom home.

A curtain on the second floor of the house fluttered. Mara started walking again. Now she'd probably creeped out the current owners of the house, standing and staring at their home like she owned the place. Which she didn't.

Anymore.

Someday, she and Will would run out of the money they'd gotten from selling this place. It was already getting dangerously low before Mara had seen and applied for the research job. Now, hopefully, they'd be able to hang in there. As long as she could keep working.

Or maybe it doesn't have to be this way.

Mara put one foot in front of the other, heel to toe, trying to balance just as if she were walking a tightrope. She'd done gymnastics one summer. Grandmary had watched her practice with endless patience as she turned every surface into a balance beam. Mara had probably done it right on this sidewalk, just like she was now.

Except now she wasn't an eight-year-old with the balance of a cat. Now she was twenty-six, tilting dizzily from her painkillers, imagining a conversation with her dead grandmother.

Am I crazy for considering the time wreck?

She imagined Grandmary, standing tall despite her elegantly sloped shoulders. She would probably be wearing those green canvas gardening gloves and squinting underneath her straw hat.

I couldn't say, Mara. Never imagined myself in a situation like yours.

But if you had to. Mara started walking normally again, even as she carried on the conversation in her head. *If you had to choose, would you go back and change things?*

Grandmary would have been quiet for a while before answering. Unlike Mara's parents, Grandmary had always seemed unhurried. How Mara's father could have been raised by this woman was a mystery Mara had never quite figured out.

I believe there are situations that could warrant a timeline rectification. So if it was necessary, yes, I believe I would.

The thought of Grandmary's measured response was only comforting for a moment. *And this circumstance? If you were me, would you do it?*

That's a decision you'll have to make yourself. You and William. What does he want?

That was the question Mara didn't know how to answer.

What exactly did Will want?

◆◆◆◆◆

Down two blocks and over one, the farmer's market was in full swing. Mara abandoned her daydream and walked in lazy circles around the stalls. It was early in the season for produce, but a few people had managed to scrape together offerings from their gardens and greenhouses. One couple was selling gallon-size plastic bags filled with salad greens. Another woman was proudly displaying handicrafts she'd made with her sister. Little ceramic boxes and wood carvings, mostly.

Mara stopped by a table with bunches of flowers. Even though she couldn't pick from Grandmary's garden anymore, smelling the heady, earthy scent of the farmer's market helped to make up for it. Mara counted out enough change to pay for a small bundle of pink peonies. There were only six, but the large, fluffy heads filled out the bouquet. They bobbed and nodded on the weak stems as she started the long walk back to the Metro station.

Mara liked to think that she would have learned to garden if they'd kept the house. Truthfully, she hadn't exactly inherited Grandmary's green thumb. Transferring seedlings to larger pots, pruning, and other once-a-season tasks had been easy enough. It was the daily upkeep that she fell behind on. Grandmary plucked weeds the moment they appeared instead of waiting for them to grow thick stalks and to weave their roots under the flower beds. She knew when the soil was too dry or when aphids were beginning to invade her rosebushes.

Mostly, Mara had spent her summers and weekends reading on Grandmary's front steps while her grandmother tended to the garden. Mara would sit so still that passersby sometimes thought she was a little garden statue. Neighbors would come by to chat with Grandmary, not registering Mara at all until she coughed or turned a page.

"Who's that?" they would exclaim.

"My granddaughter Mara," Grandmary would answer

with evident pride.

"Ah. Adopted?"

"She looks like her mother. Isn't she a beauty?" Grandmary would say firmly, stopping any further comments with a coldly polite stare. Mara's cheeks would burn anyway.

Once, there had been a neighbor who didn't let it go. "And where's her mother from? China? I went to high school with a Chinese girl. Nice girl. So polite."

Grandmary had waited an extra beat before responding, "Mara's mother is originally from Los Angeles."

"But *her* parents are from—"

"Los Angeles."

After that neighbor left, Grandmary had taken off her gardening gloves and sat on the porch step beside Mara. Grandmary was never the first to talk. Mara liked that.

After a minute, Mara had leaned on Grandmary's shoulder. It smelled like Grandmary even perspired perfume. "I don't look like anyone," Mara had said. "I don't look all-Japanese like Mom and I don't look white like you and Dad."

"You look like Mara Elizabeth Gaines to me," Grandmary had said.

"I don't want to look like me," Mara said, warming up and feeling sorry for herself. "Mom says I should just tell people I'm American, but they keep asking. You heard."

"And what does your father say?"

"He says to ask Mom about this stuff."

Grandmary chuckled a little at that.

"Everyone thinks I'm different. Everywhere I go. If I'm around white people, they think I'm Asian; and if people are Asian, they say I'm white. It's like no one can agree on who I am."

"Other people don't get to decide who you are," Grandmary had said. "Only you do."

♦♦♦♦♦

The Metro ride back into the city was long and bumpy. Mara sat straight, bracing both feet and her good arm to keep her injured shoulder still. It didn't help much.

Even after the train plunged into the dark underground tunnel, Mara still felt lighter. More relieved. This was what she'd needed—a little trip down memory lane. Not a jump back, like the time wreck would be. Just a short visit to help her get her bearings.

The tissue-wrapped bundle of peonies almost tumbled off her lap when the train came to a stop. Mara rescued them and tucked the bouquet securely under her elbow.

When she got home, she and Will would talk. They hadn't spoken much about the psychiatrist appointments yesterday. After her own appointment with Dr. Hendrix, Mara understood why Will hated seeing psychiatrists. The man kept hammering on about that one question. "If it hadn't been for the shooting, how do you think you and William would have met?"

It was like he was trying to make her say that maybe they wouldn't have met. Maybe they would have passed each other in the Student Union without even making eye contact. Maybe they wouldn't have ever been at the library at the same time, or at Al's sub place, or at the little café and bookstore in the neighborhood that surrounded Adams Morgan. Maybe they would have just kept missing each other and would have never known the love of their lives had been so close by.

But what were the chances, really? Even Robyn had said that they would have to have run into each other at some point. Sure, Adams Morgan University was a big school, but she and Will had both been there for four years. They had a lot in common. It wasn't like they'd had one chance in a lifetime to meet.

Dr. Hendrix had gotten more impatient the longer she'd talked like that. He was trying to look calm and professional, but she could see the irritation building from the set of his jaw.

"But do you understand that this isn't a guarantee?" Dr. Hendrix had said, finally. "We cannot promise that you will definitely meet your husband in some other way at some other point in your college career. We can only say that the offender is prepared to relive that point in his life and choose not to shoot. What happens after that . . ." He spread his long arms as wide as they could go, as if to demonstrate how many possible ways their lives could go.

Mara felt a little impatient herself. "I understand that," she said. "I know. It's a big risk we're taking."

"And are you willing to take that risk? If the timeline rectification is approved, will you go through with it, knowing that there is no guarantee you will meet William in the revised life map?"

When he put it like that, Mara wanted to say no. No, of course not. Of course she wouldn't risk losing Will. Not for anything.

What did Will say? Mara had wondered, and at that moment, she'd remembered Will coming back to the waiting room after his session with Dr. Hendrix.

"How'd it go?" she'd asked.

"Fine," he'd said. "He was easy to talk to. Nothing to it."

The realization hit Mara like a sucker punch. She had thought Will was trying to make her feel better—putting on a brave face, as usual. But maybe—maybe Will did have an easy time answering that question.

Maybe the idea of a life without the shooting was worth risking a life without her.

Mara was sure Will didn't think that. No. He had probably told Dr. Hendrix that he was sure he and Mara would meet again. That he wasn't risking anything because he was positive that somehow, in some way, he and Mara would find each other. That was what Will had been saying from the beginning.

But Dr. Hendrix hadn't given her time to think through all of that. He had kept staring at Mara, prompting her to answer. "Are you willing to take that risk?"

Will had come back to the waiting room, after all. Will hadn't come back and told her not to bother, or that the time wreck was off, or that he couldn't ever risk losing her. And if he were that miserable—and the last week of nightmares seemed to indicate he was—was it fair for her to keep him locked in this life map?

"Yes," Mara had said. "I'm willing to go through with a time wreck."

Now, as the train picked up speed, bringing her back to Will, Mara wished she hadn't said that. But it was okay. Nayana had said they could stop the process at any time, hadn't she? It wasn't too late. She and Will would talk and get it all sorted out, and if a time wreck wasn't for them, they simply wouldn't do it.

Easy.

Chapter Fourteen

WILL

"Will? I need you."

The second Will heard his sister Becca's shaking voice on the phone, he wanted to run to his car and drive straight to North Carolina. She was twenty-four now, but in Will's mind, she always seemed like a little kid. Looking up to him for help tying her shoes or making a sandwich.

"What is it?" Will said. He rolled out of bed and grabbed his glasses off the nightstand. Ten o'clock in the morning. Mara's side of the bed was cold. Of course, she would be up early, even on a Saturday.

Over the phone, Becca sounded like she was barely holding back tears. "Ben and I are fighting. I think he's going to break up with me."

Maybe it was a good thing he wasn't in North Carolina. Any guy who made his kid sister cry deserved whatever Will could dish out. He'd never been in a physical fight in his life, but he was willing to amend that. "What did Ben do? Did he hit you? Did he hurt you?"

"No-o," Becca said softly.

"You don't sound sure." Will felt the heat rising in his chest. Maybe he wouldn't even have to drive down to North Carolina. Will might just fly straight down there, powered only by outrage and caffeine.

"He got so mad," Becca said. "He wanted to hit me, I think. He looked like he was going to. But he stopped himself. That's good, right?"

"Not good enough," said Will.

"I need to move out," said Becca. "He'll be at work all day today and tomorrow, and he'll probably sleep at his buddy's tonight. He's really mad."

"Where are you?"

"I'm at Mom's. When he said to get out, I just left. But I need to get my stuff. I need my clothes, some of my furniture. Can you help me?"

So Becca was safe. Scared, but safe. Will breathed in and tried to sort out his jumbled thoughts. "Becca, I'm in DC," said Will. "I can't get to you today. Where's Mom? Where's Chris?"

"Mom's working. And you know Chris. He just said I shouldn't have moved in with Ben in the first place."

Will sighed. Now that he knew Becca was out of Ben's apartment—for now, at least—the first rush of adrenaline was starting to wear off. He stuck his head out the bedroom door to see where Mara was. The bathroom, maybe? Kitchen? Neither. The entire apartment was silent and dark. Will frowned and made his way down the hall. "Well, thinking about the past doesn't help anyone now," he said into the phone. "What about a friend? Can't you get someone from church to help you?"

"I don't want to tell them," Becca said. "They don't know I was living with Ben."

Will sighed again.

"Please, Will? Please, can you come? Tomorrow? I know it's a lot to ask. I just really need you."

Tomorrow. A ten-hour drive to Deer Hill, North Carolina, to move out his sister, followed by another ten-hour drive back to DC. Plus time to get Becca's things and take them back to their mom's house, not to mention time to eat or sleep. *There's no way.* On the kitchen table, he saw a piece of notepaper leaning up against the salt and pepper shakers.

Going out to run a few errands this morning. Try to get some more rest. Love you!

—M

So that's where Mara was. Will sat down in one of the kitchen chairs and tried to focus on his sister.

"Becca, I can't," Will said. "You know I'd help you if I could. But I'm all the way up here—I'd have at least twenty hours of driving to do before work Monday morning. It's too far."

Becca sniffed. "Couldn't you take off a day? Please?"

It wasn't like Becca to beg. *She must be really upset.*

"I only have a few vacation days left for the school year. I've got to save them in case they schedule the trial soon."

Becca was quiet a moment. "What trial?"

Crap.

Will rubbed his suddenly sweating temples as he tried to figure out how badly he'd screwed up. It couldn't hurt to tell Becca, could it? She was different from their mom and Chris. Becca went to the church once a month or so, maybe less—probably less, if no one there knew she'd been living with her boyfriend. Of the three siblings, Becca had always been the one most open to questions from an early age. She'd refused to attend Sunday school for a whole year after the teacher said animals didn't go to heaven. Becca had also done a little drinking in high school—Will knew that for sure—and he thought she'd smoked some pot before too.

Maybe she wouldn't be against a time wreck.

Maybe she'd understand.

"Will?" Becca prodded. "What trial? Did something happen?"

Will and Mara had already told Tristan and Robyn. Maybe it would cheer Becca up to hear that they were going to get a second chance. It could be a little reminder that there was always hope or something. Becca liked that kind of thing.

"Why aren't you saying anything?" Becca asked, voice rising. She was starting to sound panicked again. "What aren't you telling me?"

"Calm down, calm down. It's okay. This isn't exactly out in the open, but I guess I can tell you. Mara and I might get a timeline rectification."

"A *what?*"

Now Becca really sounded upset. Something was wrong. Maybe she hadn't understood what he meant. "A timeline rectification. You know, where a criminal gets a chance to go back and relive the moment of the crime, only they make a different choice? They undo their crime, basically."

"I know what a time wreck is."

Will had a horrible sinking feeling. "Okay, wait. I know you might not approve, but it's really not as bad as it sounds."

"I can't believe you guys," Becca said. "I can't believe this at all. What are you thinking?"

"Um. That life might be better if Mara hadn't gotten shot?"

"Will, listen to me. I know you think of me as your baby sister, but listen. What I'm going through right now? This is *bad*. I don't know what I'm going to do. I don't know how I'm going to get my things, I don't know where I'm going to live—I mean I know I can crash at Mom's for a while, but we all know that can't go on forever. And the worst part of it is that I really loved Ben." Her voice cracked a little, and Will wanted to fly down to North Carolina all over again. "I thought what we had was special. I thought Ben and I were going to get married and have kids and be together forever. And I know I can tell you that because you won't be like, 'Well, then you should have waited for the ring instead of moving in with him,' and giving me the lecture about how a farmer won't buy a cow if he can get the milk for free."

"To be honest, I didn't like you moving in with Ben," Will said. "And not because of that stupid saying about the cow or whatever. I just didn't think he treated you as well as he could've. You deserve better."

"Thanks. That's very helpful now that we're breaking up." Becca sighed. When she spoke again, the sarcasm had disappeared. "Most people don't get to have what you and Mara have. You two are so lucky and you don't even see it. And you're willing to throw all that away to give a criminal another chance to stumble through college without shooting anyone?"

"It's not just for his benefit," Will said. "And we're not throwing anything away. We went to the same college. We were bound to meet sooner or later."

"Are you sure? Maybe here in Deer Hill, that would be true, but you could multiply our town by ten and still not fill up that college you went to. What happened was terrible. Really. I know it's been bad for you guys. But honestly, Will, I'd take a bullet for a chance at the kind of love you and Mara have."

"You have no idea what you're talking about," Will said, gritting his teeth.

"Neither do you."

◆◆◆◆◆

Something was up with Mara. An hour passed, then two, and she still wasn't home.

Lunchtime came and went. Will made himself a sandwich and debated about texting her again. What kind of errands was she running? Usually, she went to the grocery store or the pharmacy around the corner. Had she gone off to a bookstore to blow off some stress? That would explain why she'd been gone so long, but why wouldn't she have asked him to go with her?

Because she needs a break from me.

Well, why wouldn't she? Their lives were in limbo and it felt like they were in limbo too. Ever since the shooting, it seemed Jason Mann would resurface every few years to throw everything back into question. Whatever lawyer his father had hired must have been very, very good at his job. Half the evidence had been thrown out before they even made it to trial.

Will in particular had been called into question for identifying the shooter. Holding his memory under that level of scrutiny had shaken Will's confidence. What had been so certain in the aftermath of the shooting seemed like a guessing game at the trial years later. Under the heat of the lawyer's scrutiny, Will even started to wonder if he'd just imagined the whole thing. Thank goodness the trial hadn't hinged on his testimony. It was a good thing the college had security cameras.

Once the lawyer ran out of ways to question whether Jason was the shooter, he'd changed tacks and started listing all the reasons Jason wasn't truly responsible for the crime.

Jason was too young—only eighteen and bearing the intense stress of failing out of a prestigious college.

Jason was naïve. He had bought the gun for protection because he was scared of going to a big school in the city.

Jason was privileged. He had no understanding of the consequences of his actions, since he'd never faced the harsh realities of the world before.

Jason lacked intent. It had been impulsive.

That was the argument that had finally nailed Jason's conviction. Jason may not have intended to shoot anybody. He may have had the bright idea to shoot out some windows and cause some damage to the Student Union, just because he was mad. He probably hadn't intended to do it—who planned to shoot up a building with a gun that only held six bullets?

But he had shot Mara twice. The first time he shot her, he had been surprised. He'd panicked.

But then he shot her a second time. Mara's lawyer had no trouble arguing Jason's intent to kill.

Will and Mara had been seniors in college before Jason was finally, finally sentenced. That had started off another round of appeals from Jason's lawyer. Certainly Jason couldn't be expected to serve time in prison. Not for a one-time, spur-of-the-moment crime. No. Bearing his family name and the immense wealth that came with it, Jason would surely become the target of the other inmates.

The decision came shortly before Will and Mara graduated—twenty years in prison. If Jason had shot anyone else—Will, for example—he was pretty sure Jason would have been let out on house arrest. Being the daughter of a lawyer and a congressman had its benefits.

And now here Jason was, eight years later, declaring he was rehabilitated and mucking up their lives again. Will felt a surge of anger. *How dare Jason Mann do this to us?*

Better question: why are we letting him do this to us?

Maybe the time wreck wouldn't be granted, anyway. A judge had seen through Jason before and given him a real sentence—jail time and everything—instead of letting him off easy. Maybe it would happen again. And then he and

Mara would be back where they'd always been. Making the best of things.

So why not do that now?

They had a good life together, he and Mara. They didn't have to stop enjoying it while they waited to see what would happen at the trial. *That's probably why Mara's been out so long. She just needs a break from all this time wreck stuff.*

When she came home, Will was going to show her he understood. They'd take a break together. Becca was right—he didn't appreciate what he had with Mara. Not as much as he could.

So tonight he'd cook dinner—scratch that, they'd go out. Maybe they couldn't afford any place fancy, but Mara liked chicken fingers and fries better than steak and lobster, anyway. They'd go have dinner and hold hands across the table and talk about everything real instead of everything that might have been.

It would be a good night.

Will felt his cell phone vibrating in his pocket and answered it without even checking the caller ID. "Mara?" he asked breathlessly.

"No, just your mother," Bonnie Sterling huffed. "So I was talking with your sister about why it is you can't be troubled to come down and help her."

Will's stomach clenched. And here he was again, with the subject of the time wreck creeping back up on him. *How could Becca rat me out like this?* "Mom, I know what you're going to say, but just hear me out."

"I'm your mother. I don't hear you out, you hear me out. Listen, William. Your sister looks up to you. For you to go and pull something like this—"

"I'm not pulling anything," Will snapped. "Mara and I didn't ask for this. This is Jason Mann's doing and no one else's. He said he wanted to rehabilitate. He said he wanted a time wreck. *He* did."

The silence on the other end of the phone was profound.

"Did you say time wreck? Do you mean to tell me that that ingrate has gone and tried to loop you into more of his shenanigans?"

No. No no no no. "I thought you knew. I thought Becca told you."

"Becca told me you weren't able to make the drive and for some reason, you couldn't see yourself taking a day off work. What's really going on? What are you doing Monday that's got to do with a time wreck?"

"Nothing! Nothing. I was just saying I needed to save my vacation days in case there was a trial. That's all I meant." Will felt like his words were still hanging in the air. *If only they offered time wrecks for stupidity.* He'd give anything to rewind now and take back what he'd said.

Finally, Bonnie Sterling spoke. "Well. I have to confess I'm a bit confused. Why would you need to show up at the trial? Wouldn't you and Mara just say you're not interested? I hear all this talk about the victims being offered time wrecks and turning it down so they could keep living in the Lord's time. We had one of them come speak to our women's group. Very empowering."

Will felt his mouth suddenly go dry.

"Does this mean you and Mara are considering it?"

He couldn't lie to his mother. Couldn't find a way to tell her the truth, either. Eventually, the fact that he'd paused spoke for itself.

"So that's what you told Becca about. And neither of you had the simple respect to clue me in to what you were thinking," Bonnie said. Will could picture her skin getting flushed and patchy, the way it did when she was really angry.

"It's the best thing for us," Will said. "Really, if you look at it. I thought you'd understand." *Stop talking.*

"No, Will, I don't understand," Bonnie Sterling said. Will could hear her voice rising. "This isn't a mistake. You're *planning* this. You're *considering* whether to sin, and you're deciding to do it anyway."

"We're not sinning, Mom," Will said. "We're doing the right thing."

"You're turning back time," Bonnie said. "You're rejecting all the lessons and all the blessings God's given you through this crime. You're tampering with God's time and you're tampering with God's will."

"Mom," Will said. "Mom. It's not like that. We're making things better for everyone. We're doing the right thing."

"I'll pray for you," said Bonnie Sterling. Will listened to the dial tone for a full minute before he hung up too.

Time Wrecking: The Latest Injustice in Our Justice System

By S. Elizabeth Llewellyn, Esq.

As a civil rights attorney, I've had the opportunity to represent a variety of special interest groups. Often, I'm asked by friends and family to describe the biggest problem facing our justice system today. I'm not trying to be humorous when I respond: "The system works beautifully. The only problem is that humans are operating it."

All the injustices that I fight against in the courtroom are issues outside of the courtroom too. The system is prejudiced because people are prejudiced. We fail to hold some criminals accountable because we fail to hold some people accountable. We throw the book at other criminals just as we, in society, over-punish those who fall outside our constrained view of social norms.

There is one great hope that keeps me going as I tirelessly advocate for those who society seems to have forgotten. I've seen, firsthand, that change is possible. I know that people can learn from their mistakes. I believe that we can create a more just and egalitarian society, one person at a time.

Surprisingly, the biggest obstacle to social progress that I'm seeing within the courthouse is the concept of timeline rectification. Although many of my colleagues tout it as a wonderful, redemptive alternative to parole or jail time, particularly for new and nonviolent offenders, I think it's had the opposite effect.

Computers often work better if you shut them down and power them back on. Computers benefit from having a bad application deleted. However, we in the justice system aren't reprogramming computers: we're attempting to reprogram people and their lives.

That's a much more difficult task. Additionally, humans learn by recalling and choosing not to repeat their past mistakes. Removing the original crime, along with the memory of the crime itself, removes the opportunity for offenders to learn and grow.

In my practice, I've begun refusing cases from clients who are interested in pursuing timeline rectification in the future. I hope my colleagues will begin to do the same. We're in the courtroom to promote progress, and to do this, we must allow our clients to live and learn through their mistakes.

Chapter Fifteen

....

MARA

When Mara arrived back at the apartment, she half-expected Will to be waiting for her at the door—she'd been gone longer than she'd imagined—but the apartment was empty. Mara frowned and looked around for a note while she tried to remember where she'd put the vase. They only had one. It was a green-tinted glass vase that her Valentine's Day bouquet had come in. Mara finally found it under the sink and filled it halfway with water and one packet of flower food.

Grandmary was right. Fresh flowers really did make the world look brighter. Mara put the arrangement on the end table between the sofa and the recliner, and that was where she saw Will's note.

Just in case you get home before I do—I'm going out for a run. Be back soon. Call if you need me.

XOXO

—*Will*

So that's where he was. When Will went out for a run, it definitely meant he was stressed. With as much pressure as they'd been under, it was amazing he hadn't been running all week. He'd probably be out for a while.

Mara sank back onto the couch and turned on the TV. Nothing was playing on Saturdays, other than movie marathons and home-decorating shows. Mara opted for a Harry Potter movie. It was the *Deathly Hallows Part I. Part II*—the last movie—was supposed to be out this summer.

I wonder if we'll still be in this life map when it comes out.

She and Will had gone to see the second Harry Potter movie as their first official date. *Harry Potter and the Chamber of Secrets.* Will had paid for her ticket, she remembered. He'd sat on her left side during the movie but hadn't tried to hold her hand right away—not until she moved her arm along the armrest, silently giving him permission.

Maybe that had been the real moment of choice in their relationship. Dr. Hendrix had made it sound like Jason Mann had decided their whole lives when he pulled the trigger, but hadn't she and Will had a lot to do with it?

Mara tried to focus on the movie. Her shoulder throbbed but at least the painful seizes seemed to have stopped. Maybe the higher dose was working. If only it didn't make her so sleepy and foggy-brained.

Nothing's perfect.

As soon as she heard the key in the lock, Mara lurched forward. It was Will, leaning against the door with such force that the chain lock pulled straight out of the frame when he walked through.

"Crap," Will said, examining the damage. Perspiration dripped down the center of his chest and down his back. His gray T-shirt clung damply onto him.

"Guess you don't know your own strength," Mara said, jokingly. "How long were you out running? I wasn't gone that long. Were you trying to find me?"

Instead of laughing, Will let the door swing closed with a sigh.

"Will?" Mara asked, suddenly alert. "What's wrong? Don't worry about the chain lock, okay? It's been partly broken for ages and maintenance hasn't called me back once. Maybe now they'll fix it."

He sat down hard on the recliner, making it screech. Will rested his elbows on his jutting knees and buried his head in his hands. "I think I screwed up."

This felt big. Mara sat on the end of the sofa nearest him, feeling suddenly dizzy from the scent of the flowers. "Okay. Just tell me. Whatever it is, it can't be that bad."

Finally, Will looked up. Behind the silver frames of his glasses, his eyes looked smaller than usual. His blond hair stood at attention, a sure sign he'd been running his hands through it the way he always did when he was stressed.

"What happened?"

"I told my mom."

"About . . ." Mara had a sinking feeling she already knew the answer.

"Becca and her boyfriend broke up. Becca called me to ask if I could help her move out. I said no—since we live ten hours away—and she asked why I couldn't take a day off work to make the round trip."

Despite herself, Mara rolled her eyes. "Because it's not like there's anybody in the entire state of North Carolina who could help her instead."

"And when Becca asked, I told her that I had to keep my days off free in case they scheduled a trial date and told her what for . . ."

"And Becca told your mom."

"No, actually. Mom called after that to bug me about not coming down to help Becca, and I thought Becca must have told her why."

"Oh, Will."

"Turns out she didn't know." Will rubbed both his temples. "But she does now."

"I'm guessing she wasn't happy about it."

Will wiped more sweat from his face. "I'm so sorry. It just popped out. I had just talked to Becca and the time wreck was on my mind, and then before I knew it, it just—popped out." Will gestured as if the words had literally jumped out of his mouth.

"It was a mistake," Mara said. "What did she say when you told her?"

"Oh, you know. We're sinning. We're going against God's time and God's will. She'll pray for us."

Mara felt her head swimming. She knew Bonnie Sterling wouldn't like the idea of a time wreck, but she thought they'd be able to avoid her finding out.

"Sounds like it was a rough day," Mara said. She walked over to the recliner and rested one hand on his shoulder. Will didn't seem to register her touch.

"I'm so sorry," Will said. "I really thought Becca had already told her. Please don't be mad at me."

"I'm not," Mara said, at the exact second she realized she was.

•••••

He made one mistake. One. Mara reminded herself of this all through the afternoon. *He feels terrible. There's no point being angry at him. What's done is done.*

Mara was sure that Will could tell she was upset. He had a sixth sense about these things. That made it even worse. *Will is so patient with me. He doesn't get upset when I'm grumpy with him, or tired, or when I don't feel like going out, and the one time he needs me to be understanding, I'm not.*

"What can I do?" Will asked, late into the afternoon. "I want to make it better. Please."

I want to call off the time wreck. Except then I can look forward to living the rest of my life listening to my mother-in-law make digs at us for almost ruining God's plan.

Would it be terrible to do a time wreck just to avoid having anyone find out? After the time wreck, no one would know a crime had ever been committed—much less the lengths they'd gone to undo it. But if they didn't do the time wreck, this life map would continue.

This crappy life map. The one where her shoulder hurt and her husband ran his mouth and her in-laws knew they were sinners who wanted to play with God's time.

"Do you want to talk about it?" Will asked. "About the time wreck, I mean?"

"No," Mara said finally. "I think we should get out for a bit. Try to have some time where we don't even have to think about it."

There it was—a solution. Mara could see Will's eyes light up. There was something he could do to make things right again. "I was thinking that too. This morning, before Becca called. I'll call up Tristan and you call Robyn. Let's all go out tonight. It'll be like old times."

Sure it will. Mara didn't believe it. She was pretty sure Will didn't, either.

♦♦♦♦♦

The little bar in Adams Morgan was smaller than Mara remembered. Louder too. The neighborhood surrounding their alma mater was the same as it always was, but somehow, it felt different. Was this what it was like to get old? The four of them had been here hundreds of times throughout college, although they'd come less and less every year since.

Robyn, sporting hot-pink tips at the ends of her flat-ironed hair, was closest to looking like she still fit in. Judging by the way she hung back, Mara guessed even Robyn felt like an outsider here.

"Look how young everyone is!" Robyn said, leaning close to Mara's ear so she could be heard over the noise. "Is it college night or something?"

"I'm pretty sure every night is college night here," Mara answered. Will lagged behind them, looking out the window for Tristan. Luckily, he wasn't far behind. As soon as they saw each other, Tristan grabbed him up in a wrestler-style bear hug, complete with three loud thumps on the back. Mara thought it looked painful, but Will seemed to feel better.

Tristan grinned. "I just want to be clear: no matter what kind of day you've had, I'm gonna show no mercy at the pool table. Don't start a game if you're not prepared to lose."

Robyn rolled her eyes. "I love how they talk about pool like it's ice hockey or something."

Mara giggled, and Tristan pointed his finger at her. "You laugh, but I've won every game of pool I've played for six months straight."

"Yeah, too bad your winning streak ends tonight." Will looked to the girls for support. "Anyone? Mara? Back me up here."

Mara patted him on the shoulder. "Love you, honey."

"Ouch."

Robyn waved to the guys and pointed to the bar. "We'll be over there. When you guys are done, come join us." She led Mara to a barstool while Will and Tristan wandered off to an empty pool table in the back of the room. "One beer, and a Coke for my friend," she said to the bartender.

"Club soda, actually," Mara said. The bartender smiled as she filled their glasses, but she didn't stop for a conversation. Thank goodness.

"So," Robyn said. "Bonnie went bonkers, huh?"

"Something like that."

Robyn whistled through the tiny gap between her front teeth. "Dang. Poor guy."

"He didn't have to tell her," Mara said, more viciously than she meant. Robyn looked a little stunned. "I mean," Mara added. "We kind of knew she'd react badly, right?"

"I thought you said it was an accident."

"It was. He'd been talking to his sister Becca about the time wreck, and then his mom called him about something else, but he just assumed that Becca must have spilled the beans. Which she hadn't."

"Well, the beans are spilled now," Robyn said pragmatically. "Are you going to tell your parents?"

Mara rolled her eyes and reached for the club soda. She wished it tasted like something, at least, but it just felt like a mouth full of bubbles. "Please. I could write it on a bulletin board and my parents wouldn't even notice."

Robyn ran a finger through the condensation that was already building on her glass. "What do you think your grandmother would have said?"

Mara shrugged, as if she hadn't been wondering the same thing herself. "I wish I knew. Did I tell you I walked by the house again?"

"Why do you torture yourself with that?"

"You sound like Will," Mara said.

"I bet. Did he go with you?"

"I didn't tell him," Mara said. When she said it like that, it sounded like she'd kept it from him on purpose. It wasn't like that. She just . . . hadn't told him.

Oh, who was she kidding. Mara hadn't told Will about it because she knew he'd try to talk her out of it, or make her feel better about it when she came back. She didn't want to be comforted.

Robyn raised her eyebrows. "It's not like you guys to keep things from each other."

Mara one-shoulder shrugged.

"Anyway," Robyn said. "I think your grandmother would have been on your side. She wouldn't have liked the idea, but she wouldn't have wanted you guys to suffer. Not for anything."

"I miss her," Mara said.

"So do I. Not like you do, of course, but Mrs. Mary Gaines was a class act. I felt like she was my grandmother too."

"She would have liked that." Mara took another sip of her club soda. *I wish I could have a beer.*

Mara had never had alcohol, really. She'd been on pain meds since she was eighteen, and she'd been too much of a good girl to drink underage. By the time her twenty-first birthday hit, she'd just put ginger ale in a beer stein and called it a night.

Mara felt a tap on her elbow. There was Tristan, looking grim and handing her Will's cell phone. Someone was calling—it was ringing up and down a five-note scale.

"Do you want me to answer it?" Mara asked.

"It's his mother," Tristan said. "Will doesn't feel like answering it just yet. Can't say I blame him. Can you watch it for him while he just chills out for a bit?"

Mara hesitated. "Do you think it'd be better to just answer now and get it out of the way? She's probably not going to stop calling until she gets through."

"It wouldn't be a productive conversation. He talked to her just a few hours ago and they both said their piece. If there's something more she wants to add, he's got a voicemail."

"Wow," Mara said, taking the still-ringing cell. "You sounded like a real youth pastor just then. Laying down the law."

Tristan smiled. "It's almost like that's my job." He turned and walked back to the pool table, dodging a group of giggling college girls as he did. Will was still making his bridge, lining up the cue to take his shot. He scratched it. Mara grimaced in sympathy and turned back to Robyn.

"I think you can go ahead and mute that," Robyn said. "He has a point. Maybe Will and Bonnie both just need to cool off a bit, and then in a day or two, they can talk it out. I can't imagine she'd really be against it, if she stopped to think. What kind of mother would choose for her son to get shot at if there was a choice?"

"Technically, he wasn't the one who was shot at," Mara said without thinking. "It might not be as personal for her."

"Okay, really? Your mother-in-law loves you. I'm sure she wouldn't want you to get shot, either. It's just—it's a new technology. It's different. There's some moral ickiness around some of it, but it makes sense for you guys."

The phone was silent for a minute. It had gone to voicemail. Bonnie must have hung up and dialed back, because her caller ID flashed across the screen and the phone started ringing again.

"Seriously, just silence that. Good grief," Robyn said. Mara pushed the mute button on the side of the phone. Now it just flashed and vibrated, moving slightly across the bar counter as it did.

"Can I have another one of these?" Robyn asked the bartender. "Thanks."

"You already finished it?" Mara asked as the bartender took the empty glass.

"It was kind of a crappy day for me too," Robyn said.

"I'm sorry. I didn't even ask when I called you to vent earlier."

"It's fine. I just, I don't know," Robyn said. She sipped the foam off the new beer as soon as the bartender placed it in front of her. "I think I met someone."

"Oh?" Mara waited for more, but Robyn didn't say anything. "Girl? Guy? Where'd you meet? Details, please."

"Guy," Robyn said. "Met him at work. Not one of the patients or anything."

"Good. That'd be a little unethical, hooking up with the clientele."

"Yeah," Robyn snorted. "Picture that. 'Hey, you came for

Narcotics Anonymous and some group therapy. You left dating the counselor.' Not good."

"So who is he?"

Robyn ran one finger in the wet ring her first beer stein had left on the counter. "He's a counseling intern, actually. Not in the drug rehab program, specifically, he's just shadowing another counselor who does some stuff with our program and some with a general community therapy program."

"Okay," Mara said. If alcohol was supposed to loosen lips—and it usually loosened Robyn's—it wasn't working tonight. Mara felt like she was dragging it out, piece by piece. "So, what's the problem? Is it because he's an intern?"

"No, ethically it's fine. He doesn't work for me or even with me, really. We had lunch a few times, flirted a lot, he asked for my number and called it."

"And . . . ? This sounds like a good thing."

"It is," Robyn sighed. "It just makes me wonder—okay, I don't know if this will make sense to you. But it makes me kind of wonder, is that what happened with Jessica?"

It took Mara a minute to put together what she was saying. "You're wondering if you and Jessica broke up because maybe you're not really bi? Is that what you're saying? I'm confused."

"Exactly. I mean, obviously I know I'm bi. I like men, I like women." Robyn suddenly looked around her and lowered her voice. "Didn't mean to announce that."

"I think you're fine."

"You never know. Sometimes people are—" Robyn shook her head. "But I really thought Jessica and I were it. I could see myself spending my life with her. I never felt like that about anyone I went out with before. And then when it fell apart, I thought, you know, maybe I'd missed my chance."

Even though the words weren't meant for her, they hit Mara hard. *No one should have to miss their chance.* "But now you've met a new person. Maybe he's the one, and if you and Jessica hadn't broken up, you wouldn't have met him. You know?" Mara's purse buzzed on her lap. "Hold on." She dug out her cell phone. "It's Bonnie."

"Then who's calling Will now?" Robyn frowned at the caller ID. "It says Chris. Isn't that his brother?"

"Of course he had to get involved," Mara said. She pushed both of the vibrating cell phones to the side. It looked like they were slow dancing across the counter until one— Will's—knocked into her glass. "Anyway. Yeah. So maybe this new guy is the forever one. Or even just a for-fun one. It'd be good to see you happy again."

"It just makes me wonder. Is everything I did for Jessica for nothing now? Should I really have been with her if I could have fallen in love with someone else?"

"Oh!" It finally clicked. "Because you came out to your parents when you met Jessica."

"Right."

"And . . . everything that happened with that."

"Yeah."

Mara looked down at her club soda. It had stopped fizzing now, unless she moved the glass. When it was still on the counter, it just looked like a glass of plain old water. "I mean, I don't know what to tell you about that. You are bisexual, you did fall in love with a woman, and I think it was good you gave your family a chance to be supportive of that." She spun the glass with her fingers, causing it to erupt in a flurry of bubbles. "Even though they didn't take it."

"Right. But now I have no girlfriend, no family, really—I mean I still see them at holidays, but it's not like it was before—and if things get serious with this guy, I know my parents will be like, 'I told you so! I told you it was just a phase!'" Robyn took a long drink of her beer. "I kind of knew they'd react that way, but I also kind of wish I didn't know that for a fact."

"Yeah." Mara looked down at her cell phone buzzing alongside Will's. "I know exactly what you mean."

Chapter Sixteen

....

WILL

The weight of his family's anger hung over Will like a black cloud. On Sunday, it was metaphorical, but on Monday, the sky was overcast and a few cold, wet rain showers obligingly reflected Will's mood. The fact that this was the beginning of the week before spring break did nothing to cheer up Will. The kids were already counting down the days until their mini-vacation. There wasn't going to be a lot of learning going on this week.

So far, Will had managed to avoid Cliff and his persistent questioning about the assembly. Speaking out to his class on the day of the code red had been a mistake, Will was sure. Now he fit the image of the troubled survivor, anxious to share his experience and ruminate on life lessons. Nothing could be farther from the truth. After accidentally outing himself to his mother last weekend, Will just wanted to stay under the radar and out of the spotlight. If only he could keep out of Cliff's sights, he might just succeed.

The charade ended by his first planning period of the day, when Will was making the long trek down the hall to the mailboxes. "Mr. Sterling." Cliff's voice boomed down the hallway after him. Will turned slowly on his heel.

"Yes?"

"I'd love to put you up on stage during our assembly next week. Given any more thought to it?"

"No," Will said. Cliff looked briefly confused. "I mean, no. I'm not up for that."

"Okay," Cliff said, in a tone that said it wasn't. "If you're not comfortable, of course we won't force you to speak."

"Thanks," Will said. "I appreciate it." He started walking again, backward for a few steps until he was brave enough to turn his back. "Lots of work to do this morning. Catch you later!"

Will felt Cliff's eyes watching him all the way down the hall.

Great. For once, Will had an uninterrupted stretch of time to work—and on a Monday morning too—and now he couldn't concentrate. He retreated to his office and banged the door closed.

He needed music. Will logged on to his computer and turned to the local rock station. It was on commercial now, advertising another grand opening for another local business. That was DC, all right. Something was always changing.

Back home, nothing ever changed. If he had driven down to help Becca over the weekend, he probably could have gone the last five miles of the drive with his eyes closed.

"Y'all should think about moving down here," his mom would say, every so often. "You could probably get a job at the high school or lead the church music on Sundays. A dollar goes a lot further down here than in the city. Mara might not even have to work at all."

Thinking about his mom made his stomach hurt. She and Chris had finally stopped calling at ten last night. No message since. Maybe they were calming down now.

I wish. More likely, they were strategizing how to get through to him and Mara.

The rock station was still on commercials, so Will typed in the radio station from back home. Was it really his home anymore, now that he had said—out loud, even—that he was willing to be a time wrecker? Maybe it was naïve of him to look for comfort in his hometown. Or sadistic. Maybe both.

Then Sings My Soul, Deer Hill's hometown radio station, came on in the middle of a laugh track. It was some talk show—Will thought he even recognized the voice of the announcer. It sounded like Joe, the same kid that had copied off his math homework and set the frogs loose in biology lab. Will checked the profile on the station's website. It was Joe, all right. All grown up, with a goatee and a picture of his smiling family. A beautiful wife, two little boys, and a baby girl. Life had been good to him.

Good for Joe.

Will cracked open the top drawer on the left filing cabinet. He was pretty sure he had some sheet music in here for an exercise he wanted to do with his eighth graders today. Needed to find it soon in case he had to make copies. Will was only half-listening when Joe announced the next segment of the radio show.

"We're taking callers to share some Monday Miracles this morning," said Joe, over the radio. "Do you have a special blessing in your life that you'd like to share? Did you have a God moment today? Call in and share it with our listeners."

I wish.

A thin, reedy voice came on the air. A mid-thirties woman, Will guessed. "Hi, this is Shelley. I've got some good news to share."

"Yes! Hi, Shelley, we're glad to hear from you. What's your news today?"

"Today marks the fifth anniversary of the day I walked out of an abusive relationship. It was the lowest moment of my life. I thought there was nothing out there for me and if I left him, I had nothing, because that's what my boyfriend had been telling me all those years."

Will felt a stab of guilt. Had he even called Becca to see how she was? Just to see if anyone had helped her? No. He got wrapped up in everything with Mom and Chris and forgot about her.

He would make it right. At lunchtime, he'd give Becca a call to check in. Will sliced his thumb on the edge of a file folder and winced as the cold air drew out a thin line of blood. That paper cut was going to take a while to heal.

Over the radio, Joe sounded suitably impressed with Shelley's story. "Wow. I bet it took a lot of courage to leave."

"It did. And my best friend, she convinced me to get out, she helped me get my things, she let me live with her for six months while I got back on my feet, and five years later, I want to go back and tell myself that it's the best thing that ever happened to me. You know, if that hadn't happened, I wouldn't be where I am today. I wouldn't have met my husband, I wouldn't have these wonderful friends who have showed me how kind the world can be. I think every moment of my life is a miracle, good times and bad, and I just wanted to call in and tell everyone that no matter what your life is like right now, it's a miracle. It's a miracle! Be grateful for every minute because you never know where it could be leading you."

"What a great perspective. All the best to you, Shelley, and congratulations on your new life! We have another caller on the line. Hello?"

"Hey, I'm driving into my shift at work and I had to pull over and call in to say thank you to that last caller. Shelley, whoever you are, wherever you are, God bless you for sharing your story. I wish everyone realized what a gift each day can be."

I'm hallucinating. Will felt his heart beating double-time. *Can guilt cause auditory hallucinations?* He couldn't really recognize this caller. It wasn't really who he thought it was. Couldn't be.

"I agree. It's such a great message to hear in the hustle and bustle of today's world. What's your story? Do you have a miracle to share today?"

"I wish I did, you know. I really wish I did. I just found out someone I know is getting a time wreck."

That son of a— Will thought, before he remembered that he and his brother had the same mother. *What is Chris thinking, calling into a radio station with this?*

"Wow. That sounds intense. Is this someone you're close to?"

"Yeah. My big brother."

It was Chris, all right. Will knew that voice anywhere.

Dear God. What if Joe recognizes Chris's voice too?

Chris had been two years behind them in school. Why would Joe need to know who Will's kid brother was? Then again, it was a small town.

"And how did you feel when you found out?" Joe asked.

"Honestly, it really hurt. I mean I know their lives aren't perfect, and mine isn't either, but if things were that bad, I wish my brother would have called and asked for our help. I remember when everything first happened, but I thought they'd moved on."

"You're saying 'they'—are there more people than your brother involved? Can I ask if he was the perpetrator of the crime, or is he a victim?"

"He's a victim. He and his wife. We thought the whole business with the crime was settled years ago, and now the government's going to make it like none of it ever happened."

Shut up, Chris, Will thought. *Just shut up and mind your own business.* His hands were itching to throw something. If he could reach through the radio waves, wrap his hands around Chris's neck, and strangle him, he probably would have.

"Well, to me, that sounds like it might be a good thing. Depends on the crime, you know? Can you sympathize with your brother at all?"

Thank you, Joe.

"Well, sure. If someone offered me a chance to go back and get rid of something bad that happened to me, I'd probably be tempted too."

"You said you'd be tempted. So you don't think you'd go through with it?"

"No, no. I don't think I could ever do that."

"So you're saying you could rise above the temptation," Joe said.

"Yeah, I mean, that's what you have to do. Everybody gets

tempted to do the wrong thing sometimes, but you're supposed to rise above it."

That was one of their mother's sayings. Will gritted his teeth.

"I just want to quickly remind our listeners here: timeline rectification is legal. None of this is against the law. So when you're saying that you feel this is right versus wrong, is that a religious standpoint, or do you think it should be illegal?"

"I do think it's wrong from a religious standpoint. So yeah, I do think it should be illegal. Maybe in some circumstances, I could see making an exception. But for most people, no, I don't think this is right."

"I've got to move to commercials now, but thanks for calling in, Chris. After the break, we'll hear from some more listeners. If you have a miracle you'd like to share, be sure to call in!"

Will listened to the music start. It was a pop-country kind of song. Something his mom would probably sing along to while she cleaned.

The thought made his stomach twist into another knot.

Had it been his imagination, or did Joe say his brother's name? There at the end. Will walked back through his memory. *Thanks for calling in, Chris.*

Will sank into his office chair and laid his head down on his desk. There were probably millions of germs lurking on there. Will inhaled the strange scent of pencil shavings,

Lysol, and cork grease. This desk had probably smelled like this since the first music teacher sat here in the seventies. It was nice to know that some things never changed.

How am I going to tell Mara?

Will pulled himself up. Dr. Hendrix probably hadn't even written his evaluation from their appointment yet. They didn't have a trial date—and if it was anything like past appeals and sentencing hearings, they might not have a date for a long time.

For the first time, Will found himself truly hoping, 100 percent, that the time wreck would be approved. If it wasn't . . . well, now things were even worse than before. Now the news was out on the radio. Someone could put the pieces together. If this caught on . . . if Chris's stint on the radio put him and Mara into the spotlight . . .

Mara would never forgive him. As if growing up as Congressman Gaines's daughter wasn't enough, now she'd have to live through another scandal.

How had everything gone so wrong? Will buried his head on the desk again, breathing in the smell of Lysol and cork grease. At this rate, Mara might not even want to end up with him in the next life map. He doubted she would be able to tolerate him for the rest of this one.

Chapter Seventeen

....

MARA

Mara was wrapping up an interview when her cell phone vibrated in the pocket of her cardigan. "Excuse me," she said quickly, reaching down to silence it. *Good thing Dr. Olivier didn't see that. Or Elliott.* Hopefully it wasn't her mother-in-law, starting her phone call campaign again.

"What support do you wish you had received immediately after the trauma?" Mara asked, hand poised over the keyboard. The client was a forty-year-old man. Combat veteran.

"Well, I was offered therapy and didn't take anyone up on it. Thought I could handle it on my own, you know?"

Mara smiled, encouraging him to get to the point. *Yes. I do know.*

"But now it's been a year and I still haven't been . . . coping. I just got involved in a support group. I wish I'd done it sooner. None of that touchy-feely, feed-your-spirit crap. It's all accountability, all about being there for your brothers."

Mara's cell phone buzzed again, and she hurried to silence it.

"Do you need to get that? I don't mind," the man said.

"Oh no, thank you. We've wrapped up our interview for today. Thank you for coming in. Your responses will help us greatly with our research."

Mara walked him out, her heart hammering the whole time. She was going to turn her cell phone off as soon as she was alone. The last thing she needed was something else for Elliott to poke her about. Mara had barely returned to the office when Dr. Olivier called out to her.

"Mara? Your mother is on line one."

My mother *is calling?* It had to be an emergency. Maybe something about her dad. A heart attack? A car accident? *Was he hurt or was he . . .*

Mara ran to pick up the phone at her desk.

"Mom?" Mara said breathlessly into the phone.

"Mara. Excellent." Mrs. Gaines spoke with the kind of brusque, authoritative tone she used as a lawyer. "Obviously, your father needs to prepare a statement. His office will issue one tomorrow, but I thought he and I should release a personal statement tonight. It's always good to get ahead of the press. Are you and Will planning to release one yourselves, or shall we include you in ours?"

"A state—" Mara stopped herself when she realized that

Dr. Olivier could probably hear her end of the conversation. Thank goodness Colleen wasn't at her desk. Mara lowered her voice. "What do you mean?"

"So you haven't heard," Mrs. Gaines said disapprovingly. "Mara, tell me you at least have Google Alerts set up for your name. You can't afford to be the last to know what's being said about you. I thought we'd taught you that."

"What's . . ." Mara struggled to get out the words. "Wh-what's being—"

"And don't stutter. Very unattractive. There's a rumor that you and Will have been approved for a timeline rectification. It was only a matter of time, with timeline rectification getting so much attention from the press and your father's office taking a stance against it. Really, I'm surprised it took eight years after the shooting for someone to make the accusation."

Mara closed her eyes. So her mother knew. Knew, but didn't believe. Of course not. Time wrecks were probably beneath the dignity of a Gaines. "This really isn't a good time to discuss this. I'll give you a call on my lunch break." There. Professional enough in case Dr. Olivier overheard, final enough for her mother.

"Mara, we can't afford to wait on issues like this. You know that. I'll email you a copy of our draft statement, but I'll need your approval within the hour at the latest. Once the public decides something might be true, they're not going to let it go. We need to shut this down and shut it down hard."

"Mom." Mara felt as if all the air was being squeezed out of the room.

"Within the hour, Mara." Her mother's voice turned conciliatory, almost tender. "I know it's difficult to see your name in the press. It's humbling for all of us, no matter how many times we've been through it. Chin up. We'll get it under control. You'll see."

Mara could hear her pulse throbbing in her temples as she hung up the phone.

"Everything okay?" Dr. Olivier called from her office. Her smile was warm, inviting. She probably imagined that there had been an accident of some sort, or that Mara had a sick relative.

The kinds of problems normal people have.

Mara put a hand on the doorframe to steady herself. "Just some troubling talk at home. I'm sure it'll be fine." She tried to take a deep breath. "May I take an early lunch today? I think I should call Will."

"Of course," said Dr. Olivier, smiling with an understanding Mara knew she didn't deserve. "Take all the time you need."

◆◆◆◆◆

Mara walked three blocks down to a small park. It wasn't

much of a park, really. Just a few benches tucked between three buildings. There were a few potted plants and trees in concrete barriers to add a touch of green to the gray-and-brick city.

Mara tapped open a text to Will. He should be at his planning period. Or at lunch. Hopefully, she wouldn't have to wait long for a response.

11:55 a.m.
Mara: My mother knows.
11:58 a.m.
Will: Oh no.
Will: Chris called in to the radio station back home and was talking about it.
Will: Us, the time wreck, everything.
Mara: He said our names???
Will: No, but I didn't figure it would take long for anyone to guess.
Will: People around there know his voice.
Mara: When was this??
Will: Before school this morning.
Will: I can't believe your mom found out so fast.

Mara remembered the days when her father's name was splashed across the local papers. Her mother always knew what was being said about her family, long before it made it to print. She briefly closed her eyes before typing the next part.

12:02 p.m.
Mara: Mom said she and Dad are going to release a statement.
Mara: Can't let this affect his career.
Will: When?
Mara: We have to approve their draft within the hour.
Mara: Unless we tell her we're going to release our own statement.
Will: ...

The ellipses appeared and disappeared three times, showing that Will was typing something and then deleting it.

12:05 p.m.
Will: Wouldn't it be better not to say anything?
Mara: Yes. YES IT WOULD HAVE BEEN.

She stuffed the phone down deep in her pocket and stormed across the makeshift park. She would walk as far as she could go during her lunch break. Anywhere, as long as it wasn't her office or her apartment or anywhere else someone might know her. She didn't want to talk. She just wanted to think.

No one so much as glanced her way as she thundered through a crosswalk and powered her way up another block. Everyone was busy. Everyone was focused on their own lives and their own problems. No one was interested in the Asian-American woman with the limp arm and the stormy expression.

For now.

◆◆◆◆◆

Mara felt only slightly guilty when she called Dr. Olivier and asked for the rest of the day off. She couldn't possibly focus on anything now. She didn't offer much of an explanation, and luckily, her boss didn't ask for one. She would know soon enough. Mara didn't want to be in the same room when Dr. Olivier found out that she'd been considering a timeline rectification while she'd been working on a research project about helping trauma victims heal. Talk about a conflict of interest.

There goes my job.

Mara was barely at the Metro station when her phone dinged. There was a new email from her mother. Mara guessed over an hour had lapsed. Of course, her mother wouldn't want to wait around any longer than that.

Her mother had emailed her the bare link—no subject, no message. Just a hyperlink to Congressman Gaines's webpage, where he categorically denied the truth.

Well, at least her father didn't know it was the truth. Why would he? No Gaines would ever turn down an opportunity for character growth.

Mara read the press release three times while she waited

for her train.

Statement of Congressman Gaines regarding Timeline Rectification

Press Release — April 11, 2011

Congressman Gaines released a statement regarding unverified reports that his daughter, Mara Gaines Sterling, plans to participate in a timeline rectification and shares his personal views of this controversial technology.

"In response to unverified reports that my family is or will be involved in a timeline rectification, I deny any knowledge or participation by myself or any member of my family.

"While I personally disagree with the use of timeline rectification, I respect the many patriotic Americans who have worked hard to regulate this technology and ensure that it is made available to rehabilitated convicts. I urge citizens on both sides of this controversial issue to work together toward a mutual understanding of timeline rectification and the potential legal and moral ramifications."

Mara kept her head down for the entire ride home. No one was looking at her—yet. But it was coming. The day the news broke about her father's embezzlement scandal—*supposed* embezzlement scandal, she corrected herself—it had taken hours before it hit the news channels. But this was different. Now there was the Internet. Who knew how long they had until the entire world started talking.

Every Last Minute

Not long, Mara found out. By the time she got to the apartment and checked her email again, she had another message waiting in her inbox.

Date: April 11, 2011
From: Dr. Olivier
To: Mara Gaines Sterling
Cc: Dr. Chen, Dr. Young, Dr. Zimmerman, Ms. Poole
Subject: Your employment

Mara:

I would have appreciated being told that you were pursuing a timeline rectification before the research center director called to discuss it with me. He believes that we cannot afford to be associated with someone who doesn't uphold the study's mission, and frankly, I agree.

As you know, my research involves tracking long-term data on the effects of traumatic events. It is a clear conflict of interest for my research assistant to be gathering data on the effects of trauma while privately pursuing a timeline rectification for herself. Given your lack of transparency on this issue and your quick exit this afternoon, it is obvious to me that your involvement in a timeline rectification is not merely a rumor.

You are dismissed from my research team and your employment has been terminated with prejudice. Furthermore, you are banned from the research center property effective immediately.

Dr. Francine Olivier

Chapter Eighteen

....

WILL

Mara hadn't texted at all since their lunchtime argument. Will had the presence of mind to stop at the grocery store for flowers. Peonies. The little bouquet Mara had bought on Saturday were already wilting and turning brown on the table in the dim living room. Truthfully, he was also dragging his feet about going home. It was going to take a lot more than flowers to make this up to Mara.

The florist was a little too eager to help him. "One dozen or two?" she asked.

"That depends. How much are they?"

The florist tsked as she pointed to the price in the book. "You want my advice? You better make the bouquet match the apology."

"Who says I'm apologizing?" Will said, feeling a bit stung.

The florist put a hand on her hip. "Are you planning a wedding?"

"No."

"Funeral?"

"No."

"Is it her birthday?"

"No."

"Get two dozen."

The pink, fluffy blooms made his car smell like a perfume ad. Well, it was worth it. Will didn't know how many flowers it took to apologize for accidentally outing them as time wreckers, but he hoped two dozen was a good start.

Mara was in the kitchen when Will arrived at the apartment. He could hear her banging around in there. "Hello?" he called. "Mara?"

"In *here*," she singsonged.

That was new. Will walked into the kitchen, holding the flowers in front of him like an offering. "Everything okay?"

Nope. Wrong thing to say. He had a knack for saying exactly the wrong thing at the wrong time lately.

Mara swirled the ice cubes in the bottom of her glass. It looked like she was drinking a soda. That wouldn't be any good for her heartburn.

"Thought I'd pour myself a drink after my last day of work. Want one?" Mara asked. Her voice was bright, but her eyes looked like she'd been crying.

On the counter behind her, Will saw the two liter of Coke and a half-full bottle of rum.

"What are you doing? You aren't supposed to drink with

all the meds you're taking."

"I'm not supposed to do a lot of things," Mara said.

"Mara." Will put the peonies down on the counter. How much rum had been in that bottle? He couldn't remember. "How much have you had to drink?"

Mara took another sip from her glass. "Just a little less than not enough," she said. She smiled at her own joke.

"What's going on with you?" Will asked. "Why are you doing this?"

"Why am I doing this?" Mara asked. "Why am *I* doing *this*?" Her brown eyes snapped and sparked in the middle of her too-pale face. "I am doing this," she said, drawing out each word, "because I have just been fired." The F in *fired* whistled between her teeth.

Will stepped a little closer. How did alcohol affect the painkillers she was on, exactly? He wasn't sure he wanted to find out. "Okay. Let's just talk about what happened. What did Dr. Olivier say?" Another step forward.

"She emailed after I left today. I have been dismissed from her research team and terminated with prejudice." Mara took another drink and repeated herself. "Terminated with prejudice." The second attempt was actually a pretty good imitation.

Note to self: drunk Mara can pull off a decent French-Canadian accent.

Gently, Will put his hand around the glass and took it

from her. She let it go without much of a protest.

"See, what happened was," Mara said, pointing a finger at him. He could smell the rum on her breath. "What happened was, I spent the last eight years doing exactly what I was supposed to do. If I had physical therapy exercises, I did them. If I had a doctor's appointment, I kept it. After the shooting, I only took off part of a semester from school and I still graduated on time. And then, when I couldn't find a job, I kept applying and searching until I found one. And since I've been at the research center, you know what? I do everything I'm supposed to do. Every. Single. Thing." She poked his chest three times, emphasizing each word. It didn't hurt.

Mara continued. "I get everything done right, done on time, and I don't make excuses. I don't even take half the accommodations I'm technically allowed to have, and Elliott still breathes down my neck, waiting for me to prove that I'm a freeloader. And *now*, I get *this* email. See this? *They found out about the time wreck.*"

Mara thrust her smartphone at him. It was already open to her email browser. Will read the email and sucked in his breath.

"She just fired you over email? She didn't even try to have a conversation about it?"

Mara's head sagged. *Obviously.*

Will put the phone down on the counter and reached for

Mara's empty hand. "You're going to be okay. If the time wreck goes through, none of this will have happened. It won't matter. And if the time wreck doesn't happen, you can probably sue over this. I don't know if this is a case for wrongful termination or not, but I would bet—"

Mara was already shaking her head. "I was an at-will employee. I already looked it up. It would be really hard to make a wrongful termination case. And now I can't even get a reference for my next job."

"Hey," Will said. "I know. But you're so smart. You're so good at everything you do. Another employer has to see that. And until someone does, I mean, we lived off my salary for two years. We can do it again if we need to." He shrugged, hoping he looked more confident than he felt.

That made things worse. Much worse.

"It took me two years to find this job," Mara said. She was yelling again, but there was no fire in it. She looked exhausted. "And now I'm going to be back at square one, back to job searching. I barely got two months of employment before the rug got pulled out from under me. Again."

"And that's my fault," Will said. "I shouldn't have told."

There was a moment when he was afraid Mara was going to keep yelling. Instead, she leaned in and rested her head on his chest.

"No," she said. "You shouldn't have told." She exhaled

slowly. "But it was an honest mistake. And it's not your fault how they reacted. You didn't ask for this, either."

It felt like forgiveness. Will wrapped his arms around her tentatively. She didn't pull away.

"Neither of us asked for this," he said. "And neither of us need it, either. Whether the time wreck gets approved or not, we'll be okay."

"Yeah," Mara said. She was quiet now, leaning more heavily on him.

"You really scared me," Will said. "You've never started drinking before. That can't be good for you. There are warnings all over your pill bottles about that."

Mara one-shoulder shrugged, her head lolling a bit on his chest.

"Thanks for the peonies," she said.

♦♦♦♦♦

Will called in sick to work the next day. It had been a long night, watching and worrying over Mara. She'd fallen fast asleep on the couch, giving Will plenty of time to look up "why can't you mix narcotics and alcohol" on the Internet. After the first three search results, he'd called her neurologist. He'd kept calling until the after-hours answering service gave him the doctor's cell phone number.

Dr. Ricci sounded annoyed when he answered the phone,

but his voice quickly became concerned after Will explained. "It's not like Mara to do something like that," Dr. Ricci said. "Do you think this might have been an attempt? Did she seem suicidal in any way? Did she have a plan? Did she leave a note?"

"No! No, she's not thinking like that at all. Mara just said some stuff about wanting to cut loose because following the rules never paid off. I've known her since we were eighteen, and she's never even sipped champagne because of the meds she's on."

"Are you sure?"

"If I wasn't, I'd already have her in the ER."

"It couldn't hurt to go to the ER anyway, just so they can monitor her for any effects from mixing the medicine with alcohol." Dr. Ricci sighed. "How much did you say she'd had to drink?"

"I'm really not sure. There's about half a bottle of rum left, but I don't know how much was in it before she started drinking. I know it wasn't full."

"So it's hard to gauge . . . and Mara's thin, with no tolerance to alcohol. Plus she's on a higher dose of the meds. How is she breathing?"

"Normal."

"And does she usually fall asleep around this time?"

"If she's had a bad day, then yeah. I'd say about fifty percent of the time."

"Does she seem disoriented at all? Have any memory loss?"

"She didn't really even seem that drunk. Just mad."

Dr. Ricci sighed again. "Okay. Here's what I want you to do. Watch her tonight, make sure she's breathing normally, that when she talks, she makes sense. If she seems more tired than usual, depressed breathing, seems disoriented or confused in any way, take her straight to the ER. If not, I'll see her at the office tomorrow morning. Just bring her whenever she gets up. I'll squeeze her in."

"Okay. Th-thank you," Will stammered. Dr. Ricci hung up.

That was the start of a long night—longer even than the ones when Will woke up with nightmares. Mara slept for three hours before she woke up and ran to the bathroom.

"You okay in there?" Will called through the door.

Mara threw up again before answering. "I feel terrible."

"Can I come in?" No answer. Will let himself in and soaked a washcloth in cold water.

"Not that I'm advising you to make a habit of this," he said, wringing out the washcloth, "but in general terms, if a soda makes your stomach queasy, adding rum isn't going to help."

Mara smiled wanly as he gave her the cloth. "Thanks for the tip."

"How are you feeling, seriously?"

"My stomach is awful, my head kind of hurts, and there's

this nerve damage in my right shoulder that just won't go away."

Still sassy. Mara couldn't be too bad off.

"You should eat something."

Mara groaned.

"I'm not going to give you runny eggs or anything. Just toss something down there to soak up whatever's left of your little do-it-yourself cocktail. Bread? Crackers?"

"Okay," Mara said, wiping her face with the washcloth again.

That wasn't exactly a choice, but Will decided to leave it. He went back to the kitchen and made her a plate of white bread and plain crackers. He cracked open a cardboard box of yogurt and took out a cup of vanilla-flavored.

In a few minutes, Mara shuffled down the hall. "Hey," she said, sitting down at the kitchen table. Will moved her laptop and a stack of papers out of the way and put down the plate in front of her.

"Sorry," she said.

Will shrugged. "Everyone does dumb stuff."

Mara bit tentatively into a cracker, chewed, and swallowed. "Most people get away with doing dumb stuff. I don't."

"Neither do I," said Will. "I accidentally outed us as time wreckers to my extremely judgmental, holier-than-thou mother. That's probably not going to smooth over any time soon."

Mara rubbed her temples. "Believe me. I know." She ate another cracker. "I just want to say one thing," she said, and Will's cheeks turned hot. "How come other people can do dumb things and get away with it? If we make one wrong move, we pay for it forever."

Will shrugged. "I don't know. Bad luck, I guess. Or else we're overachievers." He rubbed his chin, as if deep in thought. "Although most people start small. An overdue library book here, a thoughtless comment there—you don't have to jump from perfection to risky drug interactions in one step."

Mara almost laughed at that. Good.

"I'm not perfect," she said. "Even if the shooting hadn't happened. Or if it gets undone or whatever. I still won't be perfect."

"I know," Will said. "But you're perfect for me."

VA Congressman Denies Daughter, Son-in-Law Involved in Time Wreck

April 11, 2011

In a statement earlier today, Congressman Joel Gaines spoke out against "unverified reports" that his daughter, Mara Gaines Sterling, was involved in planning a timeline rectification. These "unverified reports" include a statement to a radio station from Sterling's brother-in-law, Christopher Sterling. Several individuals have come forward claiming to have knowledge that Mara Sterling and her husband, William, have indeed been asked to participate in a timeline rectification, although we have so far been unable to verify these reports.

Timeline rectifications are considered a parole-alternative for rehabilitated convicts, allowing them to return—literally—to the scene of the crime and choose to undo their actions. If Mr. and Mrs. Sterling were indeed asked to participate in a timeline rectification, it is very likely in reference to the shooting at Adams Morgan University, of which Mrs. Sterling was the victim and Mr. Sterling a witness. The offender, Jason Mann, has served eight years of his twenty-year sentence for the crime, making him eligible to apply for parole or a parole-alternative.

Congressman Gaines is doubtlessly eager to squash rumors of his daughter and son-in-law's potential involvement in a timeline rectification due to his own political stance. The congressman has long been "tough on crime," even during his own scandal, when the congressman himself was accused of embezzlement. The charges in his case were cleared, and Congressman Gaines has continued to

273

fervently represent the interests of Virginia's eighth district. Following the shooting at Adams Morgan, the congressman lobbied for harsher punishments for offenders convicted with violent crimes, rather than lobbying for stricter gun laws. His stance at the time drew harsh criticism from anti-gun advocates, while those who support an individual's right to bear arms applauded his decision to "punish the criminal and not the tool."

Whether he is simply denying an ugly rumor about his family or making a calculated statement against timeline rectification, it's clear where Congressman Gaines stands. For much of the country, however, timeline rectification is a deeply divisive issue. In a recent poll, 42 percent stated that they would participate in a rectification if offered the chance, while 46 percent felt that they would never consider a rectification, regardless of circumstance. However, 72 percent of those polled believed that timeline rectification should be legal "in exceptional circumstances," while only 28 percent felt it should be illegal. Nearly 90 percent of respondents felt that timeline rectification "should have more stringent controls," while 10 percent felt the process was already well-regulated.

What do you think of timeline rectification? Why do you think the congressman issued his statement? Let us know in the comments!

Comments:

MissusMarie said:

Not only do I think his daughter is planning to have a time wreck, but I also think the congressman arranged it. Sorry, but I think this is a case of Daddy being against something on principle but moving heaven and earth to get it for his little princess. I remember being shocked that he didn't introduce tighter gun control legislation after the shooting. Now it makes sense. It was probably his plan all along to try to erase the whole thing.

DanTheManStevens said:
Yeah, why would people have timeline rectifications, anyway? Locking people up and throwing away the key totally solves the problem of rehabilitation and reintroducing criminals into society. Oh, and it's just our tax dollars funding the prisons. We like throwing our money into perma-homes for criminals instead of, I don't know, helping them change. /sarcasm.

~~ANGELonEARTH~~ said:
Personally, I can't see myself ever having a time wreck. I just don't feel like I could go that far, ethically. I feel like it's important to take the life you're handed, good and bad. But that's also my choice, and I understand why people who don't feel like I do would want to have the choice to do a time wreck. I don't know. It's tricky. All the best to the Sterlings, whatever they decide ♥

NOLOO5ER5HERE said:
So what, the shooter got put away and that's still not enough for the little brats? Do you know how many shootings and cold-blooded MURDERERS get waved off in this country because of insufficient evidence or mistrial? This case already got prosecuted with a lot more zeal because the victim was a congressman's daughter. Now that's not enough and they want to undo it completely. Meanwhile, people are shot dead in the streets and no one bats an eye . . .

Chapter Nineteen

....

MARA

The neurologist office regularly opened at nine o'clock. At 9:05, Will and Mara had signed in at the front and had been escorted back to a room. Mara sat uneasily on the paper-covered table. Every time she moved, she could hear the paper crunch underneath her.

"You okay up there?" Will asked. "You still look kind of pale."

"I'm so sorry. I feel so bad," Mara said for the fiftieth time. "I'm really embarrassed."

"Look at you," Will said. "You only had one drink and you've already memorized the Battle Hymn of the Hungover."

Mara laughed, which made her feel both better and worse. "I'm sorry you had to take off work this morning."

Will shrugged. "I wasn't exactly anxious to go into the school today. Who knows what people have heard by now."

Mara wasn't sure how she felt about that. They weren't *in*

the news yet, exactly. Not like when her dad had been in the middle of his scandal. That had been bad. Right now, they were on the outskirts. The information was out there, but you had to search for it. When Mara had put her name into a search engine this morning, the first three results weren't too bad:

VA Congressman Denies Daughter, Son-in-Law Involved in Time wreck
April 11, 2011

Mara Gaines and William Sterling Marry, Four Years After the School Shooting That Nearly Ended Their Lives
June 2006

Updated: School Shooting Victims Gaines, Sterling Return to Class
January 2003

Mara remembered how relieved she felt when the updates about her father's scandal had dropped off the evening news report. Then when she and Will had survived the school shootings, they were briefly in the news again. Mostly write-ups following their progress from the college alumni magazine, and a few human-interest pieces in local papers.

Maybe this would go the same way.

Yeah, right.

Mara settled back on the exam table just as the nurse came in. "We don't usually see you until the end of the month," the nurse said. "What brings you in today?"

"Abject stupidity," Mara said. "I did some drinking last night."

"Hmmm," the nurse said, clicking her tongue. She held a laptop open for typing notes on the electronic chart. "Let's get started.On a scale of one to ten, how would you rate your pain level?"

"An eight," Mara said. Unmedicated, her shoulder sent shooting pains nonstop down the length of her arm.

The nurse clicked through to another screen. "Describe your pain."

"Burning under the right shoulder blade. Shooting pains and numbness down my right arm and fingers."

"Does it get worse when you bend your elbow or move your fingers?"

"It's difficult to move my fingers and hurts to move my elbow. My shoulder and shoulder blade hurt if there is any movement."

"So is your pain level an eight at rest? What is your pain level if you move your arm in any way?"

"Nine." Mara never said ten. If she hadn't been living with this for eight years, she would have ranked this kind of pain a ten. She would probably be screaming her head off too. She remembered what Dr. Ricci had told her when they first met: *Chronic pain generally doesn't improve over time, but your ability to tolerate it does.*

The nurse tapped on her laptop as if she were scrolling through different screens. "When did you last take your pain medication?"

"Yesterday afternoon."

The nurse looked from the laptop screen to Mara and back again. "So you're currently not taking anything for pain relief?"

"No." Mara felt heat pricking across the back of her neck. "I figured I should probably check in with the doctor before I took my meds again."

The nurse pursed her lips. "And what time was your last dose?"

"Four-thirty in the afternoon."

"And what time did you drink?"

"Around six o'clock."

"Any ill effects?"

"Just a lot of nausea and a headache."

The nurse typed into the computer. "You and the rest of the planet. I'll let Dr. Ricci handle the lecture, but you realize you aren't supposed to mix alcohol with this medication, right?"

Mara felt like a child being chastised. "Yes."

The nurse finished typing and handed her a paper cup. "You know the drill. Down the hall, leave your urine sample on the counter. The doctor will be in soon." The door swung closed behind her.

Mara balanced the cup between her knees and worked the cap off the pen one-handed. Finally, Will reached over and took the cup and pen. Mara let him. Her shoulder and arm ached so badly she wanted to groan out loud.

"You probably could have taken your pain killers this morning," Will said. "I'm pretty sure it's all out of your system now."

"I'd rather be safe than sorry."

"That sounds more like you." Will finished writing her name on the cup with a flourish. "Your chalice, madam."

"Thanks."

By the time she returned, the doctor was already in the exam room, talking to Will. They both turned to look at Mara. Her cheeks flushed hot.

"Gave us a bit of a scare last night," Dr. Ricci said.

"I'm paying for it now, believe me," Mara said.

"The nurse mentioned you hadn't taken any medication. It's been over twelve hours at this point. It's fine to go ahead and take your pills. Do you have them on you?"

"In my purse," Mara said. She felt gratitude pulse through her system almost, but not quite, as steadily as her shoulder throbbed.

Will pulled the small orange bottle out of her purse and shook out three pills into the cap. Mara tossed them back on her tongue and swallowed them with a paper cup of water Dr. Ricci offered her.

"You really should take that with some food," Dr. Ricci said, frowning.

"She's got some," Will said. He tore open a pack of oyster crackers and passed them to Mara. She'd forgotten she had them in her purse. *Thank goodness Will remembered.*

"Now, of course the meds won't kick in for a bit. Can you stand a brief exam?"

Mara gritted her teeth. "Mm-hmm."

Dr. Ricci slowly flexed each of Mara's fingers, her wrist, and her elbow. When he tested the range of motion on her shoulder, she couldn't help crying out. Dr. Ricci shook his head.

"How is the timeline rectification case progressing?" he asked. "Do you have a trial date yet?"

"Not yet," Mara said. "We just did the psychiatrist evaluations on Friday."

Dr. Ricci's eyes didn't leave her arm as he gently pulled it straight. "I'm sure that won't be a problem," he said. "Your case seems pretty open-and-shut to me."

I hope so. Mara didn't say the words aloud. She wasn't sure if she really meant them.

"How is the higher dose working for you? When you take it on schedule, do you have more relief?"

"A little," Mara said. "But the side effects are awful. I'm

always tired, I'm super-forgetful, my stomach is just—bad."
Will silently nodded, backing her up.

"It was worth a try," Dr. Ricci said. "But since you're here,
I can go ahead and step you back down to a lower dose. That
should help alleviate some of the side effects and make life a
little more bearable."

"Yes," Mara said. "That would really help."

Dr. Ricci jotted down a note on his prescription pad. "Get
this filled today and take the new dosage the next time
you're due for a pill. Don't try to cut up the pills you have,
please. And then, go ahead and keep your end-of-the-month
appointment with me, and we'll see how you're doing." He
ripped off the new prescription and handed it to Mara. "Be
well. And don't pull another stunt like that again. Even on
the lower dose, you can't mix alcohol with these meds."

"I know," Mara said sheepishly. "Thank you."

Usually Dr. Ricci hurried out, but he lingered a little
today. "And who knows, your next appointment may well be
your last," he said. "I confess I don't know much about how
timeline rectifications work. But I do know that they're
supposed to erase the crime and its effects, so I very much
hope that will be the outcome for you." He stood up, sending
his wheeled stool twirling back behind him. "Good luck to
you."

"Thanks," Mara called after him. The door had already
shut.

♦♦♦♦♦

"Everyone's staring at us," Mara whispered. She hung a little closer to Will as they walked into the pharmacy. A woman who was just leaving had done a double-take when she saw them.

"You don't know that. Don't be paranoid," Will said. "We'll just drop off the prescription and go get some lunch."

Mara would have answered, but her shoulder seized suddenly. Will noticed and stopped walking.

"You okay?" he asked.

Tears pricked her eyes. "No."

"We'll just get the prescription filled and go home," Will said.

Mara's shoulder seized again. She concentrated on counting her steps as they walked back to the pharmacy counter.

I wish this really could be the last time we have to do this. They were at the pharmacy counter now. Mara let Will take care of it while she stood still and breathed. If she stayed still enough, focused hard enough on her breathing, maybe the pain would stop.

"You've already filled this prescription this month," the pharmacist said loudly. Mara's cheeks burned. Out of the corner of her eye, she could see the other customers stop their shopping.

"We just came from the doctor's office. He wrote this script an hour ago. We're not early. He stepped down the dosage. See?" Will said.

"You're too early," the pharmacist said. "I can't fill this." She waved her hand to the person behind them in line. "Next!"

Will looked to the prescription and back at the pharmacist. "Call Dr. Ricci. He just wrote this. It's a change in the dosage, that's all."

The pharmacist smirked and waved to the person behind them again. "Next in line, please."

Will snatched the script off the counter and turned. "We ought to complain," he muttered, not quietly enough.

"Will, please," Mara said. "Let's just go somewhere else."

"They should fill this for you," Will said, more quietly, but he quickened his pace. Mara gritted her teeth through another shoulder seize and hurried to keep up.

The next pharmacy over already had a dozen people waiting in line. Mara leaned on Will's shoulder as they inched forward, step by step, until it was finally their turn.

"We don't have this in stock," said the pharmacist immediately.

Mara wanted to cry in frustration. Was it her imagination, or was the pharmacist eyeing her suspiciously?

"Let's try the one around the corner," Will said to her on

the way out. "It's bigger than this one. They'll have to have it there."

Mara sighed. *I'd bet the rest of the money in our bank account they have it here too.*

There were only five people in line at the next pharmacy, but more were starting to filter in. Probably here to do errands on their lunch break. Mara glanced behind her as they waited. The line was snaking halfway down one of the aisles.

Finally, it was their turn. Mara's heart sank as the pharmacist read the prescription twice, then looked up at her.

"You need to leave," said the pharmacist. Behind them, the line fell silent.

"This prescription was written earlier today—" Will began, but the pharmacist cut him off.

"Your regular pharmacy already called us," he said. "You've already filled this prescription this month. You need to leave."

"What the hell is wrong with you people?" Will exploded.

The pharmacist smiled grimly. "Just so you're aware, pharmacists talk to each other. We watch out for prescriptions like this. You need to leave now." Mara saw his hand snake briefly under the counter. He was probably ringing for security, Mara realized.

"Will, let's go," she said.

The man behind them spoke up. "Hey, the rest of us have prescriptions we can fill. Let us through."

The pharmacist waved him forward. "Next in line."

Will rounded on his heel so fast Mara had to grab his elbow. "This is ridiculous," he grumbled. "We've never had to deal with this crap before. Let's call the doctor and get it straightened out."

"It's just a flag in the system. Dr. Ricci gave me a different script for a smaller dose, but since I've already filled a month's supply a few weeks ago . . . it looks bad." Mara kept her head down and hurried to keep up with Will's long stride.

"They could at least bother to read that it's a different dosage," Will grumbled.

"We'll call Dr. Ricci and get him to clear it up," Mara said. They were almost at the door now. It was probably close to lunch time, since a steady stream of customers had started coming in. Already the pharmacy was more crowded than it had been when they arrived. Mara and Will stepped aside to let another group of customers pass. Most of them walked straight past Will and Mara, seeing them but not seeing them.

Except one.

A middle-aged woman did a double-take as she walked past. Someone Colleen's age, Mara guessed, although this woman had none of Colleen's friendliness and compassion.

Mara raised her chin to meet the woman's stare head-on. Completely unabashed to be caught gawking, the woman looked from Mara to Will and back before raising her eyebrows and walking off.

"What was that about?" Will asked.

Mara knew. That was the same look she got when her father's embezzlement charges had hit the news. As soon as it was in the headlines, she'd become a celebrity of the worst kind. The whispers had followed her everywhere: "Isn't that Mara? The congressman's daughter? You know, the one who . . ."

Mara felt her stomach sinking. It was happening again. That woman had recognized her and Will. Which meant she'd heard something. Read something. Word was getting out.

People know we're time wreckers.

FundItUp Campaign
Help Me Stop a Time Wreck!

By Chris Sterling
April 12, 2011

Raised so far: $4,283 out of $250
Goal exceeded!

How far would you go to stop a time wreck? Most of us will never know, since the government is so secretive about these "timeline rectifications." I have a chance to help stop a time wreck before it happens, but I need your help to do it!

My brother and sister-in-law, William and Mara Sterling, were involved in a school shooting at Adams Morgan University on October 18, 2002. Now the shooter, Jason Mann, is eligible to "go back in time and undo the crime," conveniently changing time for the rest of the world too. As soon as my family learned about this, we began praying for Will and Mara and asking them to remember that timeline rectification is a sin. There is no horror so great that our God cannot use it for good. By undoing the original crime and changing time, we all lose the chance to humbly repent of our sins and walk with God in His grace.

However, Satan is a powerful tempter. In the last two days, my brother and sister-in-law have stopped answering their phones as my family has tried desperately to reach them and offer our support. My mother and I fear that time is running out to stop them from agreeing to the time wreck. I've volunteered to drive up to DC and hold an intervention with them, but I need your help to do it. I live in North Carolina. The drive is ten hours away by car, and I'll also need to take at least two days off work. My employer has blessed me by graciously allowing me to take up to three days off unpaid for this journey. I'm trying to raise enough money for gas to travel by car, but if you prayerfully consider our need and can donate more, I could take the Greyhound or even the train and get there even faster.

Please help us do the right thing! Remember my brother and sister-in-law are victims of this crime. They've struggled to overcome so much since the shooting. I know if I can meet them and remind them of their many blessings, they'll choose to walk away from this sin. We can't let Jason Mann victimize more people by changing time for the rest of the world.

Tags: Intervention, Travel, Faith

UPDATE 1 by CHRIS STERLING:
April 12, 2011
1:00 p.m.

Some people are commenting that Mara's father, Congressman Joel Gaines, said on his website that Will and Mara are not considering a time wreck. I don't really want to contradict anyone, but let's just say the information our family has is different.

UPDATE 2 by CHRIS STERLING:
April 12, 2011
3:45 p.m.

Every Last Minute

To those who are saying this is a hoax and we are just looking for money, I just want to say that is absolutely not true! My mother works three jobs, my younger sister is in training to be a veterinary assistant, and I am currently working at a local drug store and getting ready to apply for my trucker's license. We all live in our hometown of Deer Hill, North Carolina, except Will, who works as a teacher in Washington, DC. Our family doesn't have money to just drive for ten hours whenever we want—believe me, if we could, we would already be there!

And if you still don't believe me, honestly that's okay, because there are enough people who KNOW the TRUTH!

UPDATE 3 by CHRIS STERLING:
April 12, 2011
4:50 p.m.

Thank you so much for your generosity! We are in awe of the amazing power of a few good people who seek to do the right thing. I was going to close the fund early, but decided to keep it open with the promise that all the money we don't use will be donated to One Life, One Time and their powerful anti-timeline rectification work. I am leaving soon so will not update again until I return, hopefully with good news! Please continue to PRAY!

Chapter Twenty

....

WILL

Of course it had been Chris. Will had thought Mara was just being paranoid when she claimed a woman at the pharmacy was staring at her. Plenty of people had been staring at them, since the pharmacist had basically accused them of trying to abuse painkillers.

Mara had put in a call with Dr. Ricci's office as soon as they got home. He hadn't called back yet. Will looked at the clock and counted the hours until her next dose. He hoped Dr. Ricci would straighten things out soon.

Now, Mara was huddled in her recliner with a heating pad wedged under her shoulder, eyes focused on her phone. "Chris has raised over seven thousand dollars in fewer than six hours," she said.

"I can't believe he used our Christmas card picture for the image on the campaign," Will grumbled. That was just the first of a carousel of Will-and-Mara images that Chris had posted. Another was their wedding photo, one was a picture of them at Thanksgiving a few years back, and another was a snapshot taken when they first started dating. An actual snapshot, since Will hadn't had a digital camera back then. Chris must have gone to the trouble of scanning in the image of their first happy picture, post-surgery.

The images made them look so healthy. Lucky, even. Just two crazy kids who'd been in love for years. Two people who had just been tempted to follow a bad path and needed a good old-fashioned talking-to to realize how good they had it.

"Three thousand people have shared his campaign so far," Mara said. "Just since this morning. And the comments. Have you read what people are saying about us?"

"Stop checking the updates," Will told Mara. "Seriously. We need a media blackout."

"Mom says it's best to keep on top of what people are saying about you."

"Your mom is a lawyer and the wife of a politician." *Kind of a crooked politician too.* He didn't add that part. "You and I are just regular people, who ran into some bad luck and have a chance to fix it."

Mara bit her bottom lip. She looked so cute when she did that. Usually. Not so much now, when everything was going wrong. "I hate this," she said softly.

Will almost dropped his cell phone when it rang. It was a DC area code. He hovered his thumb over the screen for a minute. It couldn't be Dr. Ricci. They would call Mara's phone. What if it was someone from his school? A reporter? His in-laws?

"Should I answer it?" Will asked.

"Well, don't let it go to voicemail," Mara said. "Then if it *is* a reporter, they'll hear you say your name and know they have the right number."

"Right." Will clicked speaker. "Hello?" he said brusquely, trying to disguise his voice. Mara looked like she was holding in a burst of the giggles, despite herself.

"Yes, hello, is this William Sterling? It's Nayana Patel."

Will didn't know whether to feel worried or relieved. "Nayana! Hi. This is Will. Will and Mara, I mean. She's right here."

"Excellent. I'm hearing there's a bit of an issue on social media about the timeline rectification."

Will tried to read Mara's eyes from across the room. Did this mean they were disqualified? "There's definitely—I don't know what you've heard, but my brother and my mom are really against time wrecks, so when they found out we were considering one, they really—" Will let his voice trail off. She knew. Everyone with the Internet could know that.

"Yes, I see," Nayana said. "I've been in conversation with Dr. Hendrix and Traci Bryant about how to proceed. But first, I need to know—do you want to proceed?"

Will felt his mouth dry out. He looked helplessly at Mara.

"Here's where we are," Nayana continued. "We have all the pieces together from your discussion with Traci during her visit and from your appointment with Dr. Hendrix last Friday. We can go ahead and file for a court appearance with the judge. If the case is approved, things will move very quickly after that. We'll move you to a secure location and we'll begin doing simulations to reenact the event."

"What kind of secure location?" Will asked. "Like, Witness Protection Program?" That didn't feel like such a bad idea.

"Not quite that intense, no," Nayana said. "After the trial, we'll put you and Mara up in a hotel until the timeline rectification is complete. You'll also have a security guard during that time to ensure that you travel safely to and from the area where we conduct the simulations."

"We'll need a security guard?" Will asked, temporarily stunned. Across from him, Mara's forehead creased into a deep frown.

"It's a precaution. Once the timeline rectification is approved, we work hard to ensure the safety of all the participants."

Is the procedure that dangerous? Will started to ask, but Mara waved her left arm to get his attention. With one finger, she made a slicing motion across her neck.

"What? Are you hurt?"

Mara sighed. "No, I was just trying to tell you. They can't

do a timeline rectification if someone from the original event has died. So once the time wreck is approved—"

"They'll do everything they can to make sure we stay alive." Will finished. "But not until the judge gives the approval."

And then we can't back out.

"Until then, we're on our own," Mara said.

"Nobody's threatening to kill us," Will said. "They just want to stop us from . . ."

Mara lifted her eyebrows.

"Chris isn't going to hurt us," Will said. "He would never do that."

"And the three thousand people who have already shared Chris's campaign? The ones who now have pictures of what we look like and know that you're a teacher in DC and I'm a researcher? *Used* to be," Mara corrected herself. "You don't think any of them are fanatical enough to try to keep us from time wrecking?"

Will's blood ran cold. "That wouldn't happen."

On the phone, Nayana cleared her throat delicately. Oops. He must not have kept her from overhearing after all. "Mara is correct that once the timeline rectification has been approved, we do everything possible to offer you protection. However, our department simply doesn't have the resources to offer that level of protection to every participant who is notified of the possibility of a timeline rectification."

So. Chris put us in the crosshairs. We're on our own unless we agree to the time wreck and it gets approved. Will would have appreciated the irony more if it weren't his and Mara's lives at stake.

"Because of the amount of interest in this case, Traci and I can work to try to move up your hearing with the judge," Nayana said. "That is, if you're willing to proceed."

Will looked at Mara. He didn't want a time wreck. He didn't want this life map, either. They had to choose.

Mara let her head fall forward in a single, defeated nod.

"Yes," Will said. "We're willing to proceed."

♦♦♦♦♦

Dr. Ricci's office didn't call them back that day. Mara took the higher dose of painkillers when she was due for her next pills.

So we couldn't get the prescription for the lower dosage filled because the pharmacist thought she was abusing pills. Now, as a direct result, Mara's taking a higher dose than the doctor prescribed.

Will didn't appreciate this round of irony, either.

Mara kept an eye on the Internet while they made dinner. "Four thousand people have shared the campaign," she commented as Will put a frozen lasagna in the oven.

"People will click to share anything," Will said. "Most of them don't really care."

"The campaign got picked up by the One Life, One Time website," Mara said. "Look. They tweeted about it and asked for people to donate."

"Well, it is right up their alley," Will said. "Their whole organization is devoted to stopping time wrecks." He was trying to keep things light. Keep it from feeling so serious. But he couldn't stop looking over at the front door, wondering when Chris would show up.

By the time the lasagna was done, the whole apartment smelled like cheese and slightly burned plastic. Will pulled it out with two oven mitts while Mara set the coffee table with napkins and silverware. As soon as she was done, the phone was back in her hand. "Hashtag YSOLO is trending on Twitter," Mara said.

"YSOLO? What does that mean?"

"It stands for You Should Only Live Once. Apparently One Life, One Time used it as a hashtag and it took off."

"You should put it down so we can eat," Will said gently. "People are going to say what they're going to say. We don't have to read it."

As if he wasn't just as preoccupied with the news. But Mara said, "You're right," and put the phone on the charger. She even carried one of the paper plates, heaped high with steaming lasagna, over to the coffee table. Will followed and sat next to her on the couch.

"Want to watch TV?" Will asked.

"Not really."

The side of his fork made little grooves on the paper plate as he cut apart each mouthful.

"So what are you going to do tomorrow?" Will asked.

"Nothing, I guess. No point looking for another job if we're going to be leaving this life map."

They ate in silence for a few more minutes before Mara caught him looking at the door. "I'm surprised your brother hasn't showed up yet," Mara said. "Hasn't it been ten hours since he raised enough money for the trip?"

"More like seven," Will said. "And who knows if he'll leave right away. Earliest he could get here would be late tonight or early tomorrow morning."

Mara shifted in her seat on the couch. "Okay, don't get mad at me for asking this, but what are we going to do if Chris does make it up here?"

Will shrugged. "Who cares? We don't answer to him."

Mara sighed. Will could tell by her expression that she was choosing her next words carefully, which made his stomach start to knot up. "How are you going to react if Chris does try to have an intervention with you? With us?"

"I'm going to be annoyed and wonder how we came from the same parents. Nothing new there."

Mara rubbed her forehead. "What I mean is," she said, "do you think it's a sin for us to have a time wreck?"

Will waited a beat before answering. "I thought you didn't

believe in God."

"I don't. But you do. Maybe not the way your family does—"

"Most people don't believe in God the way my family does," Will grumbled.

Mara ignored his comment. "But do you think time wrecks are a sin? Because if you do—even a little bit—we don't have to do this. We can call Nayana right now and say the whole thing's off. I don't want it on my hands that I pushed you in to doing something if you thought it was wrong."

Will's cheeks burned. "That's not fair," he said. "If I say it bothers me, then I'm basically making you suffer because of my beliefs."

"But if it bothers you," Mara said, "then I don't want to do it."

She was serious. Will took in her measured gaze and felt guiltier by the minute.

"What if it's not exactly a belief?" Will asked. "What if I'm not sure there's a God and even if there is, I'm not sure He'd object to a time wreck?"

"Then I think you need to figure it out," Mara said. She grimaced. "Sorry, that didn't come out the way I meant. Look. If you come to me and tell me that you just don't feel right doing a time wreck because you honestly believe it's wrong, then I wouldn't even want to do it. It'd be a pain to live with the shoulder stuff and I'm basically going to have to find a new job and deal with all this"—she motioned to her phone—"but I'd do it in a heartbeat." Will felt his stomach loosen.

Then she continued. "But if we just get pressured out of doing this, I'm going to resent it."

His stomach knotted up again. "You're going to resent me," Will translated.

Mara didn't agree, but she didn't disagree, either. "What you believe matters to me," Mara said. "What your brother or your mother or their church or the whole country believes doesn't so much."

"I'm not a pushover," Will said. "And if it was your family threatening to pull an intervention because a time wreck 'looks bad' or 'lacks character' or whatever—which they might, by the way—you can't tell me it wouldn't bother you. Wouldn't you stop and wonder whether all this was really worth it?"

Mara looked like she'd been shocked into silence for a few minutes. "Touché," she said, finally.

Mara crossed the room and picked up her cell off the charger. Will pushed his empty plate aside and took out his phone too. The search results for their names were growing every time he hit "refresh."

He could see that Mara was reading something on her screen. Something bad, since her forehead was creased into a frown. "Hey," Will said. "Don't worry. This isn't forever."

"What isn't?" Mara said sharply, putting down her cell phone.

"This. The stuff on the media and the people talking bad about us online. They'll cool off. And if we get the time wreck, they won't remember anything about this in the new life map. We'll have a fresh start."

"Without each other," Mara said. "Is that what you mean? If we don't meet each other in the next life map, we won't fall in love or get married—"

"Whoa," Will said. "That escalated quickly."

Mara leaned forward now, crossing her good arm over her bad one. "When we were at the psychiatrist's appointments that day," she began, "you came back to the waiting room and said there was nothing to it. Dr. Hendrix was easy to talk to."

"He was," Will said.

"But then when I went in there, Dr. Hendrix kept hammering on how there were no guarantees. You and I might not meet in the new life map. Was I prepared for that? Would I do a time wreck even if it meant we never met or fell in love?" Mara blinked hard, the way she did when she was trying not to cry. "Why was that conversation so easy for you? Why were you so willing to risk our marriage?"

"I'm not," Will said. "I'm not risking anything. We are going to meet in the next life map. No matter what."

"You can't be sure of that."

"It's the only thing I've ever been sure about." Will crossed the room and sat next to her, moving her phone out of the way so he could hold both her hands. "You and me. All the other stuff can change or be rectified or whatever you want to call it, but we're a sure thing."

Mara leaned in toward him then, resting her head on his chest. They fit together perfectly, just like they always had.

"I never want to live without you," Mara said.

"You'll never have to."

♦ ♦ ♦ ♦ ♦

Will drove as slowly as possible to work the next day. Naturally, on the day he really didn't want to get there early, Beltway traffic was light and he pulled into the parking lot with ten minutes to spare.

He wasn't ready to face anyone. If he had enough sick days to call out for the next two weeks, he would have taken them. But what if the time wreck wasn't approved? What would they do if neither he nor Mara had a job?

Will was barely through the main entrance when he heard the principal's voice.

"Mr. Sterling," Cliff said. On the outset, Will's boss looked the same. He was wearing a Hawaiian shirt unbuttoned a little too low and two gold chains around his neck. Cliff threw an arm around Will and whacked him—hard—on the back as he ushered him into his office. And closed the door.

Cliff never closed the door to his office.

"First off, I just want to say we're all behind you, Will," Cliff said. "I saw your name in the news and just really felt for you. You're a good man. No one would blame you for taking action, if the rumors are true."

"I'm guessing we're talking about timeline rectification," Will said.

Cliff's laugh was long, loud, and fake. He gave Will a few more whacks on the back for good measure. "Always the comedian. Yes. Now, as I'm sure you know, news about our educators travels fast. So there have already been discussions about your, er, situation."

Should he admit it was true, or say it was a rumor? Both could help. Both could hurt. Will decided to wait and see if Cliff would keep talking. He did.

"And of course, the school board this term is very conservative. Our school's already under a microscope because of the bomb threat and the situation with the student a little over a week ago. It's been a helluva time, Will. I know I can always count on you to keep your cool. I appreciate that about you."

Will smiled back, nodded slightly. *But.*

"But it's these parents, you know. There have already

been a lot of complaints. If I'm being honest with you, there are already parents calling for your dismissal. Even rumors of timeline rectifications generate a lot of controversy. I was aware of this last night, and then this morning—just before you came in, in fact—the superintendent called me personally."

This wasn't sounding good. Will had a chilling thought. What if the time wreck didn't go through? Could he and Mara both be out of work?

Out of work and looking for someone willing to employ social-pariah, would-be time wreckers.

This wasn't sounding good at all.

Will looked into Cliff's big, forced-empathetic eyes and nodded like he understood.

"Now, I'm not asking you to tell me whether this is a rumor or whether it's true that you and your wife are pursuing one of these timeline rectifications. That's not my business. The superintendent wants to make sure we're handling this, though, so he asked me to talk with you and come up with a solution that works for everybody."

Will swallowed. He was going to get fired. No, he wasn't. He had tenure. That had to count for something. Could he call a union rep? Did the union even help teachers who wanted to be time wreckers? Or would they just get involved and muddy up the whole thing by trying to start legal proceedings?

I should have thought of this. I should have had a plan.

"This is my suggestion, Will. This is what I suggested to the superintendent, and he thinks this sounds like a good plan. The school year's almost over, when you think about it. You've been through a lot with your wife's health issues, and I'm sure the stress of the bomb threat and the code red lockdown have been difficult for you. I can see the stress is getting to you. Just weeks ago, you opened up to your class about your experiences after the code red, but now you're reticent to share again at our school assembly. On top of that, you've got these rumors to contend with. It would be very understandable if you needed to take some time to take care of those issues."

Will's mouth went dry.

"The school board doesn't want to make a statement, and we don't want to invite any controversy from the parents or the students. We can offer you the rest of the year off—with pay." Cliff hastened to add. "With pay. If you are indeed having a timeline rectification, I'm sure you can use the time to, ah, prepare. And if not, you take some time, deal with the personal issues you're facing, and we can discuss your continued employment over the summer, when things will hopefully have died down."

There was something. He and Mara would have insurance and a paycheck until the time wreck. If there was a time wreck. And if there wasn't . . .

If there weren't a time wreck, then he'd be a liability. Who was going to want a middle school music teacher who had been all over the news? Even if Will could convince everyone it was just a rumor, parents would still recognize his name.

I can get the union involved then. If the time wreck doesn't go through, I'll call the union. I have tenure. They'll make sure I keep my job.

Another thought hit Will like a speeding train. *No, they'll make sure I keep a job. They could always put me in a different position ... put me in a different school ...*

Cliff was watching him. His eyes were so wide they might just take over his whole face. *He wants me to say yes. Say I understand. He wants me to make this okay for him.*

But Will just couldn't manage to say anything.

"What do you think, Will?" Cliff asked. He threw an arm around Will's shoulder again and gave it a squeeze. "Have yourself a little vacation. Take care of the missus and take a break. You deserve one."

Don't fight this, Will's intuition said. *Go along with it. Hang on to your insurance.*

"Right," Will said. "Sure." When Cliff still didn't let up, Will added, "Thanks for looking out for me."

"Atta boy, Will," Cliff said, delivering a hard pat on his back. "You know we're all here for you, don't you? We're all behind you."

Will nodded. *Sure you are.*

Kickass Chronic Pain Survivors Web Forum

Admin note: This is a public forum designed for chronic pain survivors to come together and talk about the realities of life with chronic pain: the good, the bad, and the ugly. Feel free to share as openly as you wish, but no hateful, insulting, or bullying speech will be allowed. Voyeurs, sympathy vampires, and all other trolls will be banned.

Date: April 12, 2011
Subject: So WDYT of the Mara Sterling Time Wreck? WWYD?
By: BeautifulRide

Hey all,

Has anyone else been following the news about the supposed time wreck for Will and Mara Sterling? I know "of" them vaguely—my sister was at Adams Morgan University in 2002. I remember being so relieved when I realized my sister was already driving home for fall break when the shooting happened! My parents didn't want her to even go back to the school afterward, but she did anyway.

My sister wasn't personal friends with them or anything, but she had a couple classes with Will and saw Mara around campus. As a fellow chronic pain sufferer, I found myself thinking about Mara sometimes over the years because I remember in one of the early news stories it said she had a lot of nerve pain from her shoulder injury.

Anyway . . . if you were offered a time wreck that could "undo" your pain, would you take it? I have fibromyalgia so there's not exactly an "event" that we could go back and rectify—it's just the way I am—but

309

if it was possible, I feel like I would. I mean, I do all kinds of other treatments trying to manage my pain so I feel like how is this different? But on the other hand, I really like the life I've built and my pain is part of that. I wouldn't have met you guys if we weren't all kickass chronic pain survivors, for example. I'd probably have my same job, but I probably wouldn't be a blogger, and that opened a whole new outlet for me. I dunno. If you were Mara Sterling, what would you do?

Comments:

Abby1010 said:

Honestly, I was so mad when I read about that. I didn't know about the shooting before but just reading her brother-in-law's FundItUp and newspapers from over the years, Mara kind of strikes me as a whiner. I think she's someone who probably could have dealt with things a lot better and been a lot happier if she'd just accepted what happened and moved on instead of being so bitter. Will seems nice, but I wonder if he's the one pushing for the time wreck? Probably wants to unload her sorry butt or at least stop her whining.

> **MissInforMed** replied:
>
> @Abby1010 Geez, Crabby Abby. I read the same articles and I don't get that vibe off her at all. Projecting a little on someone else's situation, are we?

> **Moderator** replied:
>
> @MissInforMed @Abby1010 All right, settle down. Comment on the subject of the thread or not at all.

LionelTheLion said:

Every Last Minute

This isn't even a debate for me. She was SHOT. Are we seriously debating whether her life is better off because she was shot? Seriously?

My pain is from an injury too, but it was an accident. I had to work hard to forgive the other driver even though she had no intention whatsoever of causing a collision. If she'd intended to? If she'd calculated and committed a crime with the intention of hurting me? You better bet I'd want her to take it back given the chance.

LillyLove said:

Ehhhh, this isn't about her pain or her injury for me. If it was a cut-and-dry choice between "life with injury" or "life without injury," that would be one thing, but it's about the appropriate conviction for this criminal. Have you guys read up on Jason Mann (the shooter whose crime they're resentencing)? He is the epitome of young, white, male, rich privilege. His lawyer has pulled out all the stops to keep Jason from having to take any responsibility for his crime. I don't personally object to timeline rectification on principle, but it sure as heck bothers me when I see people using it as another way to scam the system.

> **RamaDamaDingDong** replied:
>
> @LillyLove So what, Mara just has to live in pain forever because you aren't sure Jason has learned his lesson? Entitled brats are everywhere. I don't care if Jason Mann is an entitled brat in jail or in public as long as he's not shooting anyone.

Chapter Twenty-One

....

MARA

April 13, 2011

7:31 a.m.

Robyn: Hey, time wrecker! How are you holding up?

Mara: Heh

Mara: Hiding in the family room. Trying to stay away from the windows.

Robyn: That . . . sounds bad

7:35 a.m.

Robyn: Because of the time wreck? Are there people outside your building?

Mara: Dozens of them, and more keep pulling up.

Robyn: ☹

7:40 a.m.

Robyn: Text me when you have a minute, ok?

7:48 a.m.

Robyn: Mara?

♦ ♦ ♦ ♦ ♦

Mara stood to the side of the kitchen window, trying to peer through the spaces in the blinds. How long before one of the neighbors pointed out which apartment she and Will lived in? How long before someone counted the floors and rooms and zeroed in their cameras on their window?

The first news van had pulled up less than an hour after Will left for work. How was he going to get back home? Would he be able to sneak through the crowd undetected? Not likely. His height set him apart from any crowd, even when he wasn't at the center of a scandal.

Mara's throat tightened.

Well, now the judge has to approve our case.

Mara tried to remind herself of what she and Will had talked about last night. It was never too late. Even if they didn't get the time wreck, they'd be able to put their lives back together. She could find a new job. Hopefully. Eventually. His family would be glad they'd turned away from sin and maybe even keep talking to them. Her parents would sweep it all back under the rug, like they always did. Everything would go back to normal.

But I can't go back to normal.

Living through the shooting, the injury, the unemployment—it had all been easier to deal with when there hadn't been a choice. But now there was. Could she really sit across the Thanksgiving table from Bonnie and

Chris, knowing that they wanted her—lobbied for her—to suffer? Could she ever accept her parents' praise for being strong when she knew how weak she really was?

And what about Will?

Their love story felt tainted now. Will had been the first person to see her broken down and to love her anyway. What if he didn't love the unbroken Mara?

Stupid. There was plenty wrong with her, with or without the help of Jason's bullets. It might take her longer to let her guard down, but there was no perfect Mara in any life map.

Mara tiptoed from the kitchen to the living room. It was foolish to act as if anyone could see her in there, safe inside the apartment. The news vans were out in the parking lot. The journalists couldn't get past the front steps, unless someone from the building let them inside.

Mara flopped down in her recliner and instantly regretted it. Her shoulder was seizing and her pain pills were about to wear off. She could take more of the pills, but the dose was so high. She didn't want to deal with any more of this nausea and tiredness when she could be taking the lower dose instead. Curse that pharmacist for refusing to fill the prescription yesterday. Curse all the pharmacists. Curse Chris for putting photos of her and Will on that stupid FundItUp campaign.

It still didn't give them the right to horse around with her medication, but what was she going to do? Complain? Sue?

They were up for a time wreck, anyway.

Will was going to swing by the pharmacy alone and try to get the prescription filled on his way home from work. "Maybe I should go," she'd told Will this morning. "It's not like I have a job anymore."

"You need to get some sleep. If you can hang in there until I get home, I'll do it," Will had responded. It was true she hadn't slept well the night before, but then, neither had he.

Now that the news media was stalking their building, Mara definitely wasn't planning to go back out.

Mara got out of the recliner and peered through the edge of the living room window. The slats on these blinds were longer and wider. She could get a better view of the outside. Maybe that meant someone outside could get a better view of her.

Mara backed up a few steps. The man was still out there. It looked like he was talking to Mrs. Hiddleston.

Mara gently turned the rod, pulling the slats of the blinds a little closer together. The room grew darker, but some of the sunlight still streamed in around the edges of the window. The sudden shadows made the living room look eerie and the quiet of the apartment only made it worse. Mara huddled back in the recliner and turned on the TV.

Golf . . . cooking shows . . . home decorating . . . sappy movies . . . Mara clicked through the stations until she landed on the last moments of an *Engaged or Enraged* episode. They were down to three couples now. It looked like they'd just done a makeover episode where each partner had to create an outfit for the other. Mara looked at the woman who was wearing bike shorts and a bikini top, and winced. "Hope your fiancé doesn't go into fashion design," she muttered at the screen.

The episode ended. Up next was a repeat episode of *Déjà Deirdre.*

That's timely.

Mara pushed up the foot of the recliner and propped a pillow under her shoulder. She'd stay right here until Will came home. With any luck, she'd manage to doze off a bit too.

◆◆◆◆◆

Mara was watching the third episode in a row of *Déjà Deirdre* when Will came in the door, with her prescription in hand.

"You're home early," Mara said. "Like, really early. What's wrong? Why aren't you at school?"

"Take these first, and then I'll tell you why." Will opened the paper bag and passed her the orange pill bottle.

"How did you . . . ?"

"Dr. Ricci called in and confirmed the prescription to the

pharmacist while I was standing right there," Will said. "It was ridiculous. The pharmacist still tried to argue they didn't have it in stock, but then the supervisor 'miraculously' found the exact amount you need." He rolled his eyes.

"Everything else okay?" Mara asked. *Please say you just took the day off. Please say you haven't been fired too. Please . . .*

"First things first." Will shook out three of the pills into her palm and walked to the kitchen. "Ginger ale or water?" he asked over his shoulder.

"Neither, thanks," Mara took all three pills dry.

Will brought her a packet of crackers and a glass of water anyway. "To answer your question: I'm on paid leave for the rest of the school year." Mara's stomach clenched and she let out a gasp. Will held up a hand to stop her from saying anything. "I know. I know. But look at it this way: I'm getting a paycheck, and we're keeping our insurance. If we're still in this life map when the next school year rolls around, I can call the union then. And for now—geez, I don't know how I'd be able to get in and out of this building every day." Will ran a hand through his flyaway hair, making it stand up even more. "I barely managed to get through the entrance without anyone following me into the building. I called the social worker as soon as I got inside," Will said. "Remember her? Traci Bryant? She said to sit tight and she and Nayana would think of something."

Mara took a deep breath, trying to force her knees and

elbows to stop shaking. It didn't work. "Do you think they're going to be able to move up the trial? How long are we going to have to live like this?"

That was the wrong thing to say. Mara felt the wrongness of it, hanging in the air between them.

"As long as we have to," Will said grimly.

Mara reached for her smartphone. The screen was lit up with text messages and missed calls, but she navigated away to the web browser. What she saw made her stomach churn.

"Will?"

"You aren't looking online, are you? Don't, Mara. Seriously. People can say what they want, but we don't have to read it."

Mara held out the phone to him. It shook a little in her outstretched hand. "You might want to read this."

IS MARA STERLING PREGNANT?

April 13, 2011

Anti-timeline rectification advocacy group One Life, One Time has taken up the cause of one Chris Sterling, whose FundItUp campaign to prevent his brother and sister-in-law's time wreck has gone viral this week. Now, OLOT has raised new concerns about the time wreck case at the center of the media firestorm. Those closest to the couple have raised their own suspicions that Mara Sterling may be pregnant.

Neighbor Sarah Hiddleston told the Associated Press, "It just makes sense. Last week, I had to help her up the stairs because she was so nauseated. We can hear her throwing up all the time too. These walls are terribly thin, just terrible."

If Mara Sterling is pregnant, One Life, One Time is even more justified in taking up the cause against this time wreck. Altering the course of the Sterlings' life map would almost certainly eradicate the possibility of this pregnancy. Particularly when a child is at stake, a time wreck is far too great a risk.

"This can't be happening," Will said, passing the phone back to her. He moved the blinds slightly to the side with one finger and peered through.

"Are there more people out there?" Mara asked.

"You don't want to know."

Will's cell phone buzzed, and Mara's stomach clenched in response.

"It's Traci," Will said, relief flooding his voice. He flicked the phone on to speaker.

"How are you two holding up?" Traci asked. She sounded breathless.

"Like goldfish trying to hide in a fishbowl," Mara said.

"I don't know how we're going to leave the apartment again," Will said. "There are people camped out front." That was enough to make Mara jolt out of her chair, rubbing her throbbing arm as she did. She walked over to the window, ignoring Will's whispered plea. *Don't look.*

Dozens of people were crowded onto the sidewalk in

front of their building. She could see one of the neighbors—Mr. Sylvan, the sweet old widower who lived two floors up—elbowing his way through. At every turn, someone was shoving a microphone at him or trying to take his picture. Out in the parking lot, a van was just pulling up. *Another reporter,* Mara thought, until a group of young girls with poster board signs piled out.

It was a strange thing, seeing her face and Will's plastered next to handwritten slogans. "One Life, One Time," several of them said. One had writing too small for Mara to read. Another had a picture of Jason's mug shot and read, "Keep criminals in jail."

"We know," Traci said. "Nayana and I have been monitoring the situation. The level of interest in your particular case is certainly unusual."

The protestors with their poster board signs approached the sidewalk. Several of the reporters turned their cameras toward them. Mara closed her eyes and barely listened to Traci until she heard her say, "The judge has approved an immediate trial date."

Mara opened her eyes and looked at Will. He looked surprised and—could it be? —a little disappointed too. "They can do that?" Mara asked. During all of Jason's appeals, trials were always months in the future, and inevitably ended up being postponed.

"Rarely, but yes. The judge agreed that since all the pieces were in place, it would be best to move along the process." Traci cleared her throat. "You two will meet us at the courthouse at nine tomorrow morning. Nayana will send you an email with the details. Protocol would be a written letter, of course, but in this case . . ." Her voice trailed off. "We've encountered a great deal of anti-rectification sentiment before, but nothing on this scale. I'm sorry you all seem to be bearing the brunt of it."

"People only care about ethical dilemmas if they can attach a face to it," Mara said.

"That's very insightful. I'd never thought of that," Traci said.

Mara had thought of that phrase many times. It was one of her father's favorites.

"Well, that's good, anyway," Will said, once Traci had hung up. He stepped away from the window and motioned for Mara to do the same. "We only have to deal with this until tomorrow morning."

Mara sank back down into the recliner. So he was looking forward to the trial. Too late to back out now. She tried to force a smile, but something stopped her.

"How does Traci know that there hasn't been another case that's faced this much attention before?" Mara asked. "People aren't supposed to be able to remember the original life maps. For all we know, everyone who's been through this has had protestors parked outside their apartment building."

"That's true," Will said.

Mara tried to piece together her thoughts through the ever-present fog in her brain. "Do you think they keep records somehow?"

"Who's they?"

"Nayana and the other people at the Justice Department. They have to have a way of keeping track of who's had a time wreck and who hasn't, right?"

Will shrugged. "It's the government. They probably have records of everything."

"But how?" Mara asked. "How could they keep records even if everyone's life map changes? It's impossible."

"Would the government really do something they couldn't regulate? I'm sure they have some super-fancy software or something to keep track of it." Will didn't seem too bothered. "Come on. Let's think about something else."

On TV, Deirdre Collins was back onscreen. "Today, I'm wondering who I might have been in my first life map," she said. "I've always loved animals, but I've never even had a pet—as far as I remember." Deirdre gave the camera an exaggerated wink. "I'm off to work on a farm today to see if it might hold clues to my past life. Maybe it'll feel familiar!"

Will rolled his eyes. "Yeah. Let's think about anything else," he said, and clicked the TV off.

In the suddenly silent apartment, the echoes of the protestors sounded louder and closer.

To: William Sterling; Mara Sterling
From: Nayana Patel
CC: Aaron Hendrix; Traci Bryant
Subject: Tomorrow

Message:

Hello Will and Mara,

I hope this email finds you well. As I'm sure you've heard from Traci, your trial date has been moved up to tomorrow. An electronic copy of the letter is attached. Please call with any questions.

---BEGIN ATTACHED MESSAGE---

Dear William B. Sterling,

This letter is to notify you that a trial date is set for the Timeline Rectification Case regarding the incident at Adams Morgan University Student Union on October 18, 2002. The trial date is

April 14, 2011
9:00 a.m.

District of Columbia Court of Appeals
Historic Courthouse
430 E. Street, NW
Washington, DC, 20001

If you have any questions regarding this case, please visit the Applicants for Timeline Rectification portal on the Department of Justice website. You may register for this portal even if you did not personally apply for this event modification. Please have the Case Number on this letter and your Social Security number ready for login.

Chapter Twenty-Two

....

WILL

Mara was asleep again. Will tucked a blanket over her and pushed the recliner back so she could stretch out. The recliner let out a long, slow whine, but Mara didn't even stir. It was good he'd been able to get her pain meds refilled, after all.

If the pharmacies they visited had been cold and unhelpful yesterday, today's visit had been downright hostile. The pharmacist glared at him through the entire phone call with Dr. Ricci, and the other staff behind the counter were completely quiet. He paid for the prescription and left as quickly as possible. He couldn't afford to let his anger get the best of him. Not now, when it felt like the whole world was watching.

Will could have sworn he saw Chris outside the pharmacy as he hurried out, but it turned out to be just another tall, blond customer. Then he thought he saw Chris waiting to cross at a street corner as he drove past, but that hadn't been him, either. He would have scanned the gathering crowd outside his apartment building, but there were flashbulbs going off and people yelling questions after him.

"Have you agreed to the time wreck, or could you still change your mind?"

"Who's really behind the time wreck—you or your wife?"

"Have you heard from your brother yet? Do you know Chris is coming up from North Carolina to see you?"

Will had practically run past them, not stopping until he was safely inside the building. The words *time wrecker* rang in his ears until he reached the apartment door.

Remembering Mara's face when she'd read the latest news—darn that busybody Mrs. Hiddleston—made Will even angrier. Of all the rumors to start, why did it have to be about pregnancy? Reflexively, he smoothed the hair on Mara's forehead, wishing he could erase the creased frown line while he was at it. Maybe in the next life map, pregnancy wouldn't be just a rumor.

Will peeked out the blinds again. It was dark now, and most of the protestors had gone home. He still saw a few people camped out on the sidewalk outside the building.

No one's altering time tonight. Go home. He let the blinds snap back in place, not caring if the tiny movement attracted attention or not.

There was a knock at the apartment door.

Will stood frozen by the window. Chris. It had to be

Chris. He'd had enough money to make the drive since yesterday, and it was only a ten-hour trip. Even factoring in stops for food and bathroom breaks, it was surprising Chris hadn't turned up on their doorstep yet.

And now here he was.

Will had been so busy dreading his brother's inevitable arrival that he hadn't thought through what he would say.

He can't do anything to you. Chris is your younger brother, for crying out loud. What's he going to do? He just wants to talk. You don't have to agree.

Will still couldn't force himself to move.

Another knock. More insistent, this time. Mara shifted in the recliner and opened one eye. "What is it? What's going on?" she asked.

"Nothing. Don't worry about it," Will said, finding his voice. Her eyes shut again, and Will strode over to the door. He would just tell Chris to leave. They had a chain lock on the door. Will could open it just enough to tell him to go away, that now wasn't the time—it was night time, for heaven's sake.

No, he couldn't. He'd broken the chain lock by accident last weekend. *The maintenance in this building really is terrible.*

Will bent down just enough to look through the peephole.

Tristan.

Will unlocked the knob and threw open the door. "Okay

if I come in?" Tristan asked, but Will had already dragged him inside and shut the door behind him.

"I hope I'm not bothering you too late," Tristan said, eyeing Mara asleep in the recliner. "Do you want me to come back tomorrow?"

"Honestly, I'm just glad you aren't Chris," Will said. "Did you have any trouble getting into the building?"

"Nobody seemed too interested in me," Tristan said. "One of your neighbors actually let me in. Got some awesome security in this place. I didn't even say who I was or who I was visiting."

"Great." Will rolled his eyes. "There's a mob outside the building today and our neighbors are still holding the door open for anyone who wanders in."

"Good thing you have a lock. Or two." Tristan nodded at the door, then turned and scanned the room. "So, can we talk?"

"Sure," Will said.

Wait. What did Tristan want to talk about?

"Will? Who is that?" Mara asked. Both eyes were fully open now and she was lifting the recliner back into a sitting position. "What time is it? What's going on?" The recliner let out another creak.

"It's a little after nine. Tristan's here," Will said. He turned back to Tristan and echoed Mara's question. "What's going on?"

"What do you mean?" Tristan asked. "Your names are all over the news, you have reporters staked out around your building, and you're asking *me* what's going on?"

"I mean," Will said, "why'd you come by?"

He hadn't meant to sound accusatory, but maybe he was. Even when Will had played piano for Tristan's church for the extra money, Tristan had never pressured him about religion. But now, he and Mara were all over the news as the biggest time-wrecking sinners in the country, so maybe Tristan was finally going to dip in his oar. Everyone else was.

"I wanted to make sure you were okay," Tristan said. "I've been calling all afternoon and neither of you were picking up." He looked uncertainly from Will to Mara and back again. "I guess I shouldn't have come?"

The question hung in the air longer than it should have. Mara frowned and sleepily rubbed her eyes with one hand. Will wondered if she even realized what was going on, or if she was still hanging on to the last layers of sleep.

Tristan was watching him. He didn't look confrontational, just sad. And a little hurt.

"I'm sorry," Will said. "Sorry. Chris is on his way up to DC and he's got it in his mind to confront us and help us turn away from sin, so I'm a little . . ."

"Oh," Tristan said, understanding dawning on his face. "You thought I was here to talk you out of the time wreck."

"Oh, God," Mara said, suddenly covering her face with

331

one hand. She groaned and unsteadily got to her feet. "Are there still people outside?"

"Just a few," Tristan said.

"Don't worry about it," Will said. "Sit back down. Try to rest."

Slowly, Mara made her way back across the room. She walked like a little old woman when she was just waking up. *It'd be nice if she didn't have to do that.*

"Feels like morning," Mara remarked, sliding in next to him on the couch. Tristan sat on his other side, still looking uncertain. He sat as stiff as a paper doll, barely touching the seat at all.

"I can go," Tristan offered again.

"No, stay," Will said. "Thanks for checking in on us. I'm sorry I was rude."

Tristan shook his head. "I don't even know how you guys are handling all this. I can hardly stand watching it on the news. You don't deserve this. Have you heard from your family at all?"

Will guessed that was directed at him. Everyone knew Mara's family wouldn't be showing up any time soon. "Not yet. Chris is probably on his way."

"I read the FundItUp page," Tristan said. "I'm sorry they're being like that."

Will shrugged. As angry as he was at his brother, he felt a little defensive too. "They aren't trying to hurt us. Mom and

Chris honestly think we're going to hell. They're trying to keep us from that."

"Funny way of showing they care," Mara snorted. "This is why I'm glad I don't believe in heaven or hell or any of that." She glanced over at Tristan. "Sorry."

"Don't," said Tristan. "I'm here as your friend, not as a pastor."

"Here's what I don't get," Mara said. "So, the protestors and everyone are trying to convince us to stay in this life map by . . . making us miserable? They're just making me even more glad I have the chance to get out. Why don't they try convincing us that this life map isn't so bad and see if that makes us stay? I mean, I don't need people to give me chocolates or throw me a parade or anything—"

"I do," Will interrupted.

"*But* a little sucking up would go over a lot better than all this protests-and-hellfire crap."

"They aren't really targeting you, if that helps," Tristan said. "I bet you anything most of the people kicking up a fit have a problem with time wrecks in general, and you all just happen to be the most famous case right now."

Mara sighed. "It must be nice to be that committed to something," she said. "Most people don't even vote because they can't pick a side before an election."

"You're committed to me," Will said. "And I'm committed to you." Mara smiled and squeezed his hand.

How had she answered Dr. Hendrix's question? The sudden thought took Will's breath away. *Why did Mara decide to go forward with a time wreck? Was she sure that they would meet again in the new life map? Or was she willing to risk a life without him?*

If Tristan wasn't here, Will would have asked. He would have asked, and then he would have pulled Mara up on his lap and they could have proved how committed to each other they were.

But Tristan was here, sitting right on their couch, and apparently oblivious to what Will was thinking. Tristan was looking off into the distance somewhere, lost in his own thoughts. "Everyone wishes they could be that certain about something," Tristan said.

Something in his voice made Will look up. He got the sense Tristan wasn't talking about them anymore. With a sigh, Will pushed his own questions to the side and focused on Tristan. "What's up?"

"I didn't want to bring this up since you all are going through so much."

"Well, now you pretty much have to," Mara said.

"The kid who had the gun at your school a week ago Monday? Did you know him?"

"No," Will admitted. "He wasn't in band."

"He was in the youth group at my church," Tristan said. "I saw him every week for two years. We had counseling sessions, even. And I still had no idea how much was going on with him."

"Oh, Tristan," Mara said. "Wow. I'm sorry."

"You couldn't have known," Will said.

"Yes, I could have," Tristan said. "It was my job to know. I tried to know. Ever since it happened, I keep thinking about any signs I might have missed, any conversations I could have misinterpreted."

"But you can never really know everything that's going on in someone else's head," Will said. He laid a hand on his wife's knee. *If only we could.*

Mara put her hand on top of his. "Don't we know it," she said softly.

✦✦✦✦✦

So much of their lives revolved around sleep, Will realized. Mara was always tired, especially after she took her medicine. For Will, tiredness was a catch-22. Closing his eyes felt like tempting fate—would he wake up with a nightmare or sleep through the night this time? On the nights he did have nightmares, falling back asleep was impossible.

After Tristan left to catch the last Metro train back home, neither Will nor Mara moved toward the bedroom. Mara stood in the middle of the family room, turning slowly on one heel as if she were trying to memorize every inch. "It all happened so fast," she said. "We read the first letter about meeting with Nayana just a month ago. Not even that."

"Well, if we checked our mail more often, we would have read it sooner."

The joke seemed to fly over Mara's head. "I don't know if I ever would have been ready to say goodbye to this," she said. "But I feel like we haven't had time to prepare. The trial is tomorrow."

"What happens with that?" Will had a sudden thought. "Were we supposed to get a lawyer to represent us or something?"

"Who would we call? My mom? Someone who doesn't want to cross my mom?" Mara said. "I think we're better off going it alone."

"Yeah." *We won't really be going it alone, though. We'll go into the courtroom together.*

"I guess we should pack," Mara said, hesitating over each word.

"Do we really have to? If they approve the time wreck tomorrow, won't they let us come back and get our stuff then?"

"I doubt it," said Mara. "Did you see how much Tristan had to go through just to leave the building? It's going to be a lot worse for us leaving tomorrow morning in broad daylight. The time wreck people aren't going to want us to keep doing that."

"The reporters and protestors aren't hurting anybody. They're being vultures, sure, but it's not like they're attacking people."

"The surest way to stop a time wreck would be to get rid of the participants," Mara said. "The court moved up the trial date. They want us as safe as possible."

"And if they don't approve the time wreck? What happens then?"

"We might want to disappear for a few days, anyway. Just to let things settle down."

Disappearing for a few days with Mara sounded good to Will. "What do we really need?" he asked. "Besides our toothbrushes, I mean."

"I'll get my meds, for sure," Mara said. "Plus some clothes. How many days do you think we have?"

It was a logical question, but it still stung. "I'm just going to grab enough underwear for a week," he said. "If it takes longer than that before our time wreck, they'll have to let us use a washing machine, right? Or else I guess we'll all suffer the consequences."

"Grab some T-shirts too," Mara said. "And your razor and shaving cream."

This was his Mara-in-charge. In the next life map, she could be a military strategist. Or an event planner.

She could be anything she wanted to be.

I hope she'll still want to be with me.

Will threw the contents of a dresser drawer into an old duffel bag. That should be enough clothes for both of them. When he returned to the family room, Mara had a gallon-size plastic bag of pill bottles in her good hand. She was staring intently at a framed picture by the TV.

It was their wedding picture. Mara looked like a china doll, dressed in white with lacy sleeves covering both arms. She'd tossed her veil over Will's head, too, and they were kissing under it.

That had been a good kiss. Will reached forward to recreate it, but when he lifted her chin, he saw that Mara's face had crumpled.

"I can't," she said. "This is so wrong, Will. The time wreck—it's almost worse than the shooting. We're letting Jason take away everything we've built."

"But we'll get it back," Will said. "Even better next time. Same us. Same you and me. No shooting."

Mara didn't say anything.

"Right?" He was hedging now, trying to push her to say the words.

"I'm not like you, Will," Mara said. "I can't just believe in something, no matter how much I want to."

It was now or never. "So what did you tell Dr. Hendrix that day?"

"I lied. I said I was willing to go through with a time

wreck no matter what."

Will's heart stopped.

"But only because I thought you were."

"What?"

"You came back from your appointment so quickly. I thought that maybe the PTSD was so bad you would do anything to get rid of it. And I wouldn't ask you to—"

"No."

"I wouldn't ask you to live through the shooting and the nightmares and everything else just for me. I would never ask that."

"But I would do it," Will said. "In a heartbeat. I would never give you up."

"But what if you're wrong?" Mara asked. "What if we don't meet in the next life map? It's a possibility, Will. We have to deal with it."

Okay, Will wanted to say. *Let's call it off. We can run away if we have to. Start over again far away from everyone and everything. We'll give ourselves new names and new lives. It won't matter where we are or what we do next as long as we're together.*

Yes. It would matter. Once the shock of it all wore off, when the media storm was a thing of the past and they were a long way away from their fishbowl life in DC, Mara would resent him for letting her give it all up. She'd think back to the time when they could have had a choice not to be in pain and chose to be together instead.

He couldn't let her do that. And she wouldn't let him do that, either.

"Okay, one step at a time," Will said. "We'll start somewhere else. What about our engagement picture?"

"What about it?" Mara laid the plastic bag on the top of the piano and unzipped the top with one hand. She retrieved the large bottle of chalky antacids, popped the top, and shook out two tablets.

Will took the silver-framed portrait off the top of the piano. Their smiling faces were covered with a fine layer of dust.

"This is going to happen again," Will said. "Exactly the same way. Right?"

"I want it to," Mara said softly. "I really, really do. I hate that we're risking this at all."

Will pointed to the picture again. "Look, we're sitting on the lawn at Adams Morgan U. See?"

Mara nodded.

"Jason didn't change that. Even after we do the time wreck, we'll still be going to the same school. Do you really think you'll be able to resist this face for four whole years?" He held the frame under his chin and batted his eyes.

"If I see you, I'll fall in love with you," Mara said. "That's pretty much what happened in this life map."

"So I'll make sure you see me," Will said. He waited for her to contradict him and say, "You can't promise that or how can you be so sure?"

But she didn't. "Perfect," Mara said, and she leaned up on her tiptoes to kiss him.

Will pulled back. "Hold up. Since when do you believe in fate?"

"I don't," Mara said. "But I believe in you."

A kiss could say a lot of things. *I love you* and *I miss you* and *goodbye*, usually. Sometimes it could say *you're the best thing that ever happened to me* or *I want to spend every last minute of this life with you.*

Will tried to make this kiss say all of that, plus one more thing:

I wish I could give you what you really need. God help me, I'm going to try.

I Was Almost Mara Sterling: How Would Her Time Wreck Change My Life?

By Katie El Doran

On October 18, 2002, I was a junior at Adams Morgan University. For the first time, I had elected to stay on campus during fall break instead of going home. I had an internship that semester and I needed the time to catch up on my schoolwork.

Sounds exciting, right?

On October 18, 2002, I watched as my roommate and all my friends left for long weekends at home, road trips, and concerts. Then, as the dorm became eerily silent, I sat at my desk to study.

I didn't emerge from my room until late that night, when I realized that I desperately needed something to eat. Sure, I could have walked to a nearby pizza place or hit up a local store, but I didn't want to walk around DC at night. I decided to stay on campus, where I felt safe. There was only one place that was still running over fall break: the Student Union.

I've gone over the events that happened next so often over the last eight years that I can no longer distinguish which memories are mine and which are scenarios I have imagined. I wasn't expecting anything noteworthy to happen that night, and therefore, I took no mental notes. I was probably still thinking about the work I had left to do, but who knows? Who remembers now? Maybe I was thinking of calling my family to say hi, or wondering what my friends were up to on their various adventures.

Here's what I do know: on October 18, 2002, I walked by the mail room. I checked my mailbox. I think I remember stopping and looking at the bulletin board by the Career Center. It's possible that I stopped by the student art gallery, as I often did. I know that I went to the café and picked up a small salad, a soda, and a pint of ice cream. I know that I checked out at 9:02, because I still have the receipt. And I know I decided at the last minute to walk out the back door instead of going back around, through the mail room, to the front exit. I knew I was going to be hitting the books as soon as I got back to the dorm room and I thought a quick walk would help keep me energized.

What I remember next is impossible to forget. I remember seeing a security guard running back to the Student Union. Then I saw another. And another. The friendly faces that so often checked my student ID or waved at me on my way to class were now stern. Serious. Maybe (in retrospect) even scared.

I stood still for a long time, trying to think of what to do. I didn't know what was going on. I heard sirens in the distance.

I was still rooted to my place when the police and paramedics arrived on the scene. That was when someone saw me, a lone girl standing awkwardly in the middle of a sidewalk. A police officer sat me down and asked me question after question, all while I tried to explain that I hadn't seen anything, didn't know anything. I understand now that he was trying to discern if I had been involved in planning the shooting. At the time, I was simply shocked and confused.

After the officer was satisfied that I was as confused as I said I was, he told me that the campus was on lockdown and I needed to go inside. A security guard escorted me to my dormitory and walked me all the way up to my room. Once I was alone, I remember turning on the TV, and that was when I found out what had happened.

As I watched the horror unfold on the local news, five little words have haunted my every waking moment:

That could have been me.

Every Last Minute

Did I see Will Sterling when I walked through the mail room? Sometimes I think I did and other times I'm sure I was alone. I didn't know Will then and I still don't. Perhaps we passed each other without noticing. Perhaps I was there just before he arrived.

Did I see Mara Sterling (then Gaines) in the café? I know I saw another girl there, but I'm not sure if it was her. I don't know Mara, either. I believe I saw Mara simply because no other girl has said that she was in the café that night. But then, who wants to relive October 18, 2002?

Jason Mann does. And apparently, Will and Mara Sterling do too.

I can't say I blame them. On paper, timeline rectification looks like a dream come true. I don't begrudge Will and Mara wanting to live their lives without this shooting. I admire Jason for being willing to work to change what he did.

My concern is in whether the timeline rectification will truly have the results that they desire. What if Jason hasn't truly rehabilitated? What if he decides to shoot again? What if this time, I don't make that split-second decision to take the long way back to the dormitory? What if this time, it's me, not Mara, who sees Jason first?

These are fair questions. I'm disappointed that the Justice Department hasn't been more forthcoming in assuring the public that the rehabilitation process is effective or that all the variables of the crime have been considered. We are all affected by the ripples of these tragic events. Jason, Will, and Mara are the principal players—but they aren't the only players.

On October 18, 2002, I could have been the victim of Jason Mann's shooting.

On October 18, 2002, I could still be the victim of Jason Mann's shooting.

Categories: #YSOLO, Perspectives, Politics, Millennials

Chapter Twenty-Three

....

MARA

Trial day. Mara remembered before she even opened her eyes. She kept them closed a little longer, trying to soak in the feel of her body against the mattress, the sun from the window hitting her face, and the sound of Will's long, slow breathing.

Chris hadn't come after all. Mara didn't know whether to feel relieved or scared. If he hadn't come to the apartment, had he somehow found out that the trial had been moved up? Was he planning to confront them there? Mara pictured the dramatic standoff on the steps of the courthouse, in front of the people and the cameras. Mara felt the heat rising in her chest.

No, he was probably just en route. Maybe he'd gotten to the District late last night and decided to wait until the morning.

Except this morning was already too late.

Mara started to roll over before the pillow she'd wedged

under her right side stopped her. Good thing too. The deep ache was already burning in her injured shoulder. She should get up. Take her meds. Take a shower. She should eat some breakfast to keep the nausea at bay. She should get dressed for court.

Should, should, should.

Mara lay still on her side of the bed, watching Will sleep, trying to memorize the spread of his hair on the pillow and the pattern of light, golden stubble dotting his jaw. Where they were going today, there were no guarantees they'd end up together—however much Will seemed to believe there was.

But they had right now. No matter what happened at the trial today, she had Will right now. She was going to soak up every last minute.

♦♦♦♦♦

Over the years, Mara had come to think of it as "their" courthouse. It was the first place she had remembered seeing Jason Mann in person after the shooting. She was grateful that she couldn't remember the night in the Student Union, but the pictures of Jason she'd seen in newspaper clippings and online articles had painted a vivid picture. She'd expected a teen with bloodshot eyes and his bleached hair sticking out in all directions, like his mug shot.

In that first trial, though, he hadn't looked anything like she expected. Someone had made Jason get a haircut. It had been smoothed down and gelled into a classic good-boy hairstyle. He wore a navy-blue double-breasted suit and khakis that fit him more naturally than the dirty T-shirt he'd been wearing in the mug shot. He'd looked like the kind of boy she might have run into at her parents' country club, the kind of boyfriend her family had probably envisioned for her. If things had been different.

After that first trial, she'd mostly heard of Jason from the endless series of updates from her lawyer. Jason—or more specifically, his lawyer—had appealed the length of the sentence. Asked for him to be tried as a minor, since he had only just turned eighteen. Asked for house arrest instead of jail time. There seemed to be no end to the special exceptions Jason felt entitled to.

Well, he's getting a special exception this time. If we get this time wreck—if he gets this time wreck—he'll never even know that he was once a school shooter. And neither will we. Mara gritted her teeth as she walked hand-in-hand with Will into the courtroom. Courtroom C, the placard said, but it hardly looked like the courtroom they had been in before, for Jason's first trial. It had gray walls and Formica tables instead of rich wood paneling. It was smaller, too, with just enough room at the table for her and Will with Nayana, Traci, and Dr. Hendrix.

A shuffling sound at the door behind them made Will

tense. Mara tried rubbing his hand with her thumb, but he appeared to be focusing just on his breathing.

It was Jason. Mara turned and watched him walk in, accompanied on one side by a guard and on another with someone Mara assumed was his rehabilitation officer. They sat at the other table. None of them so much as looked their way.

Probably for the best. Mara swore she could see the blood draining from Will's face.

"Hey," she whispered, giving him a nudge. "We're okay."

Will seemed to snap to attention. He gave her a wide, warm smile and squeezed her hand back. "There's nothing to worry about," he whispered back. "I've got you."

I'm not the one who was worried.

Mara looked left and right again, waiting for someone—anyone—to say something. The loudest sound in the room was the rehabilitation officer pouring a glass of water. Traci caught her eye and gave her a big smile, as if they were friends meeting for lunch instead of waiting for a judge.

When the judge entered the room, even that was anticlimactic. His robe flapped unflatteringly behind him, making him look like a short, squat boy playing dress-up in his father's clothes. The judge didn't seem impressed at all by the idea of timeline rectification. He didn't blink when Jason's charges were read aloud. His eyes didn't linger over Mara's shoulder.

Jason's lawyer began talking at length about his progress and rehabilitation. It was the same lawyer Mara remembered from all the other trials. *What a windbag.*

Nayana looked as if she were paying close attention to every word, but Mara could see her foot slowly tapping under the table. Traci was less discreet. She sighed loudly and then tried to cover it up by faking a coughing fit. Mara nudged Will to see if he noticed, but he was staring down at his hands as if the hangnail on his thumb was the most interesting thing in the world.

Mara felt that someone was staring at them for five long minutes before she was brave enough to turn and check. Sure enough, Jason was looking right at them. Normally, people looked away quickly when they were caught staring, but Jason simply met her gaze. She wished she could read his face. She wished she could read his *mind.* Was he staring at them because he was seeing, for the first time, how much hurt he'd caused them? Was he hoping he'd get a chance to make it right? Or was he just staring them down, hoping they wouldn't mess up this last chance for him to have his freedom?

Maybe neither. Maybe both.

Mara couldn't tell.

"Before hearing remarks from the timeline rectification specialist assigned to this case," the lawyer said, "is there anything you would like to tell the court, Mr. Mann?"

It sounded to Mara like he was chastising a young child. *Say you're sorry and go take turns on the slide.* Jason stood up, buttoning the top button of his suit coat as if he were the lawyer.

"Your Honor, I would just like to express my personal regret for my actions on October 18, 2002. While it's true that I was young and experiencing difficulties of my own at the time, I did know better than to discharge a firearm in a public area. I also deeply regret the impact of my actions on Mr. and Mrs. Sterling, who I did not even know at the time. I hope that I will be allowed a chance to take back what I did." The lawyer moved forward as if to shush him, but the judge nodded for Jason to continue. "But regardless of Your Honor's ruling today, I am deeply sorry for my actions and for the hurt that I have caused."

The whole room seemed to shift at once when Jason sat back down. Traci and Nayana both cleared their throats, but only Nayana stood up. Dr. Hendrix started jotting notes on his yellow legal pad, but when Mara peeked at the page, she saw he was just doodling. She gripped Will's hand tighter. *This is it.*

Now Nayana was speaking. Her voice sounded clear and sure as she said all the little phrases Mara had come to hate:

"Disastrous, life-changing consequences."

"Incurable chronic pain."

"Suffers from post-traumatic stress disorder."

"Both parties would clearly benefit from a timeline rectification."

Mara waited for the judge to say something, like, "Really? They look fine to me." Or else, "Well, it doesn't seem like anything they can't handle. They've done a great job so far. I'm impressed."

But the judge just nodded, looking back over some of the papers. Her victim impact statement was probably in there. Hers and Will's. Mara realized she was holding her breath.

"The court has considered the nature and circumstances of the offense. I have also heard and considered the aggravating and mitigating factors of the original offense for Mr. Mann. The defendant has no prior criminal history, did not attempt to conceal his involvement when he was discovered, and has successfully completed a rehabilitation program. The permanent impact of Mrs. Sterling's physical injury and Mr. Sterling's psychological distress have also been considered in determining the propriety of resentencing Mr. Mann to complete a timeline rectification.

"It is ordered that the defendant, Jason Mann, shall proceed with a timeline rectification to the offense as soon as such rectification can be arranged. Until that time, defendant is to remain in custody and transported to the simulations with security."

The bang of the gavel thundered through Mara's body, from the burning sensation behind her ears down to the deep, sinking pit of her stomach.

So this is how our lives unravel.

5 Fast Facts You Need to Know about the Timeline Rectification HOAX

April 14, 2011

1. Nobody Remembers Having Had a Timeline Rectification

This is the most glaring proof of all, so we put it first. Seriously, thousands of people have had timeline rectifications and not one person remembers it? Not one of these timeline rectifications was botched?

*Update: Some commenters have noted that Deirdre Collins claims to have evidence of having a timeline rectification. For more on why we know her claims are bogus, click here.

2. Yet Somehow, the Government Has Data "Proving" That Timeline Rectification Works

Huh. So there's a massive crime problem in the United States that is actively being solved by an equally massive rehabilitation-and-rectification movement, thoughtfully provided by the government. And it totally works. And nobody even has to be bothered by memories of the original crimes. We'll just have to go ahead and take their word for it that all kinds of crimes have been miraculously undone.

Sure.

3. Total Arrests and Incarcerations Have INCREASED Since 2000 . . . the Year That Timeline Rectification Was Supposedly Approved

Time wreckers would love to have you believe otherwise, but go ahead and do a little digging. A simple Internet search will tell you that's completely false.

4. The "Rehabilitation Program" Is Bogus

What is this magical rehabilitation program that turns convicted criminals doing hard time into poor, misunderstood souls who just need another chance to go back and make a better choice? Were they not aware that they were doing something illegal before? Was being charged and jailed not enough of a hint? Were they not aware of the difference between right and wrong?

5. Amazingly, Crimes Are Still Occurring

These claims about timeline rectification would be somewhat plausible if we could see some shred of evidence that it was working. Read your local paper. Watch your local news. Heck, look out your window. Crime is still happening. It's an everyday part of our existence.

Now let's stop talking about the fairytale that the government is going to solve all our problems by undoing our crimes and start looking for what it is they're trying to cover up.

Chapter Twenty-Four

....

WILL

"How long do we have?" Mara asked. Will noticed that she winced every time the van went over a speed bump, but her voice stayed steady. Traci and the security guard—Ken, a large man whose chest seemed to strain against the shoulder strap of the seat belt—sat across from them.

Since they'd been hurried out of the courthouse and into the large, dark van, Will had half-wondered if they were being protected or if they were being kidnapped. Traci talked nonstop about moving them to a secure location, whatever that meant.

"I can't give you an exact ETA," Traci said carefully, "but it's going to be quite a while before we arrive. Do either of you need snacks? Drinks?" She moved toward her large, cracked leather briefcase, as if it held a vending machine.

Maybe it does. It is a pretty big briefcase.

Will shook his head. So did Mara. The van was moving fast, zipping in and out of traffic like they were on a high-speed chase to nowhere. They were heading outside of the District now onto a highway. I-66, Will guessed, although he wasn't at the right angle to see the signs.

Will took the time to get his bearings. It had all happened so fast. After the trial, he and Mara had been whisked away to another room. A room without Jason, Will had noted. A wave of relief swept over him. They'd have to be around him again at some point. But at least it didn't have to be right now.

In the inner room, Will and Mara had had to surrender their phones. Then, they'd had to be searched—again, even after going through the metal detectors before the trial—and the security guards had needed to look through the duffel bag they'd packed too.

"Any laptops? Watches? Anything at all with a tracking device or signal?" Traci had asked, before she handed over the duffel to the gloved security guards. Mara cringed when the guards took everything out of the carefully organized bag for inspection and then haphazardly threw it all back in.

That was when they had met Ken. Traci had introduced them as if they were meeting at a cocktail party. "Ken, this is Will and Mara Sterling."

"I'll be your security detail," Ken said. His face gave no trace of a smile and his arms seemed permanently crossed over his sizeable chest. Ken's bald head gleamed shiny and brown under the fluorescent lights.

"Nice to meet you," Will had said weakly, while Mara mustered a "Hello." Ken nodded in response and retreated to a back wall.

"Congratulations," Mara whispered to Will, as soon as Ken seemed out of earshot. "You finally met another guy as tall as you."

"I'm pretty sure I weigh less than one of his biceps," Will said, keeping a wary eye on the back wall. Ken was watching them. Maybe they hadn't been out of earshot after all.

Now that they were in the van, speeding off to who-knows-where, Ken's demeanor hadn't changed. Traci still seemed to be determined to turn this time wreck into a social event by being bubbly and friendly. She was talking Ken's ear off about the best place in the District to get crabs that were "as good as the crab shacks in Annapolis." Ken barely nodded and grunted in response.

They had taken an exit off the highway. Will lost count of the turns and side streets the driver took them down. Wherever they were going, they were far outside the District. Will watched out the windows as the highways gave way to smaller roads. Less busy. Better.

They were in Virginia now, he guessed. Gradually, the smaller roads disappeared, too, and there was only a highway with large, vacant fields on either side. Occasionally, a church or farm would appear in the distance. Mara was looking warily out the van's window, either trying to guess where they were or trying to forget what they'd left.

"How're you holding up?" Will asked, leaning closer to Mara. Traci was too busy talking and Ken was too busy tuning her out for either of them to listen in.

"I feel like I have whiplash. Not physically. Like, emotional whiplash," Mara said.

"Tell me about it. It feels so weird to be without my phone. I have no idea what's going on in the world now."

"Gotta keep up with those web comics and cat memes?"

"I meant the news," Will said, bumping her knee with his. Mara grinned before suddenly turning serious.

"I feel like I've left without saying goodbye," she said. "I didn't text Robyn this morning, and we didn't even check on Tristan to make sure he got home okay. Your brother could be anywhere right now."

"What do you think is going to happen if he gets to our place and figures out we aren't there?" Will asked. At least when he'd had his phone on him, he'd felt like he could keep track of Chris's updates on his FundItUp campaign. Now, he only had his own guesses to occupy his mind.

"Your mom is going to lose her mind if Chris doesn't report back to her that we're safe, sound, and turned away from sin," Mara said. "And my parents are going to figure out that we're definitely having a time wreck if we're missing from our apartment."

"I guess it's good not to have our phones after all," Will

said. "Some things are probably better not to know."

"I don't need to read the news to know how my parents will react," Mara said. "It's always the same. I'll never be good enough for my parents' legacy. This time, I'm just being a more public disappointment than usual."

Will wasn't sure what to say to that. *Not our problem? Maybe it's not that bad?* "You're not a disappointment," he finally said.

Based on how Mara leaned in on his shoulder, that was the right answer.

Finally, the van turned in at the parking lot of a motel. Traci gestured to them to wait while she checked in. She returned with two key cards and motioned for Will and Mara to follow her.

Their room was going to be on the third floor of the motel. The stairs creaked warily underneath their feet as they climbed. Ken swept room 312 before he allowed Mara and Will inside. Will didn't know whether all the precautions made him feel safe or not. Sure, there were a lot of people who would want to stop a time wreck—but would anyone actually kill them to do it?

Given Ken's terse expression as he stepped out to guard the door, it seemed like a possibility. Will tucked an arm around Mara's waist and surveyed their new home. For the rest of this life map, anyway.

It wasn't much of a room, but then, it wasn't much of an

occasion. There were two double beds with blue-and-gold striped comforters. They were separated by a nightstand that held a lamp and a clock radio. The peeling beige wallpaper was punctuated by gold-framed abstract artwork. Will could tell at first glance that the two pieces over the bed were hung crookedly, while the one across from the bathroom was about five inches too low. That was going to bother him.

"Ken will be staying in a room down the hall," Traci said. "If anyone else contacts you—anyone at all—dial three-one-four on your room phone immediately. That'll connect you straight to Ken's room. He'll bring you your meals, too, and the van will come and pick you up in the morning. We'll begin our first simulation then." Traci paced a bit before putting her hand on the doorknob. "Can you think of anything else you might need?"

"I think we'll be okay," Mara said. "Thanks."

"Oh! Also, I know you both know better, but I have to say it. Please don't make any outside calls or attempt to contact anyone. Your safety is the top priority here."

"We know," Will said. *Actually, preventing anything that could put a stop to the time wreck is your top priority.*

Traci hesitated a bit. "For whatever it's worth, I'm sorry this has been so tough for you two. You really deserve all the best."

Chapter Twenty-Five

....

MARA

Spending the whole night offline had been strange. Without the steady stream of updates, Mara drove herself half-crazy wondering what people were thinking.

"It doesn't matter what anyone thinks," Will had said, as usual. But Mara noticed that he kept checking the peephole at the door and picking the phone up to be sure there was a dial tone. As if anyone could find them here, in this middle-of-nowhere motel.

For the first time in a long time, Mara spent most of the day reading. Every now and again, she would look up, surprised to find herself stretched out on the lumpy comforter of a no-tell motel instead of ducking in and out of the front lines in a Revolutionary War battle. Will was reading too—one of his thrillers. No wonder he kept checking the peephole and the phone line.

The van arrived the next morning at 7:00 a.m. sharp. They had a long ride ahead of them, Ken told them, and Mara wished she'd had the foresight to bring her book with her. Instead, she and Will looked out on the passing fields and occasional barns as they sped down the highway. They weren't going back to DC—they were heading even farther south. Or west. Mara wasn't sure.

They came to a stop at a complex of large, gray buildings with metal roofs. If they had passed by it on the highway, Mara would have assumed it was just some type of farm equipment, maybe a place to store grain or something. The buildings were unmarked and the complex was ultimately forgettable—something a traveler would see and forget in the blink of an eye.

Which made it the perfect place for an outpost of the Department of Timeline Rectification.

Ken led them into the first building, which had cracked linoleum floors, plain walls, and glaring fluorescent lights. Everyone else was already there. Nayana Patel and Dr. Hendrix were talking quietly by the computer. Traci Bryant was comfortably situated in a chair, chatting with a tall man. Mara recognized him from the trial as Jason's rehabilitation officer.

To the side, sprawled across another chair, was Jason.

Mara stepped a little closer to Will. Jason was in his gray prison uniform today. Without his sport coat and tie, he looked vulnerable again. Like someone who could feel. Someone who could hurt.

Someone who could snap.

Nayana turned and waved Will and Mara over to her. "I see everyone's here. We'll begin now," she said.

Someone had arranged two rows of the maroon waiting room chairs to face a large projector screen. Will and Mara took a seat on one side of the front row.

"You okay?" Mara whispered to Will when she saw him sneaking glances behind them.

"He's sitting on the other end of the back row," Will whispered back. "Nowhere near us." He put an arm around the back of Mara's chair, which was sweet until his hand brushed against her throbbing shoulder. She flinched.

"Sorry! Sorry," Will whispered. He moved his arm down and held her good hand instead. Mara wished he could put his arm around her. It made her feel safer.

"In this initial phase, we're going to watch a simulation on screen. We've used your witness statements, forensics, and the footage from the security camera to compile a detailed timeline of the event," Nayana said. "Take notes and record your initial impressions as you watch. If anything feels confusing or inauthentic, please speak up." Traci passed down memo pads and ballpoint pens. Reluctantly, Will let go of her hand and they both got ready to write.

Dr. Hendrix spoke next. "It's important that we're all here, doing each part of the simulation process together. Each of you will benefit from the rectification, so you all have a vested interest in ensuring that the simulations are accurate and that the eventual rectification will be successful. After our work today, we're going to use the data to create a more realistic simulation for our next session. You may find that these initial simulations of the event are triggering. If you do, I encourage you to signal Traci or myself with a raised hand to indicate that we need to take a break."

Mara cast a look toward Will. Was he ready for this? He'd seemed to sleep well last night, but watching the event unfold in front of him couldn't be good for his PTSD. Mara awkwardly tried to pat his thigh but succeeded only in leaving a long, dark pen mark on his jeans. Will raised an eyebrow at her.

"Sorry," she whispered.

Dr. Hendrix flicked off the lights, plunging them all into darkness. Nayana must have turned on the computer screen then, illuminating the room with a spinning color wheel.

"It should load in a few more seconds," she said.

Mara felt Will shuffle closer, so that their hips and knees rested against each other. The closeness helped. She hoped it helped him too.

Finally, an animated sketch of the Student Union appeared on the screen. There was the entrance to the college bookstore on the right, and the long, empty hallway to the left. Straight ahead was a bank of student mailboxes. Cartoon Will was standing at one of the mailboxes. He looked like a paper doll, with a swirl of blond hair and large silver glasses.

"I look like a character from the Sims," Will said, under his breath.

"I think you look like a hipster," Mara muttered back. "All you need is a beanie."

Will stifled a laugh. "Yeah. I liked time wrecking before it was cool."

Nayana shushed them.

The screen panned slightly to the right toward the bookstore. Cartoon Jason was wearing a white T-shirt and jeans. He was pacing back and forth in front of the bookstore, kneeling by the water fountain, then jerking up and pacing again. Even though the character's face was flat, the movements alone made him look anxious. Mara felt almost as though she should avert her eyes. It felt private, watching Jason have a breakdown, even if it was just a simulation. One minute of his jerky, puppet-like movements stretched into two, then three. Mara could hear the other people in the room shifting in their chairs.

"All this footage was taken straight from the security camera," Nayana said, as if another explanation could make the silence less awkward. It didn't work.

Finally, the screen pulled back, showing Jason on the right, Will at the mailbox embankment in the middle, and the long hallway to the left. Mara's heart started to hammer.

I'm going to come down that hall.

Cartoon Jason ran both hands through his hair and reached down to his side. To the left, Mara saw another figure emerge. Cartoon Mara had long, dark hair and a pleated gray skirt. She was holding a white box. It had been a Styrofoam takeaway box, Mara remembered. She'd gone to the Student Union for mozzarella sticks from the café.

Cartoon Jason pulled a gun and aimed it up at the ceiling. He fired a shot.

Beside her, Will jumped. "I'm okay," he whispered immediately. "I'm okay."

Onscreen Will looked frozen. He stood flat against the mailboxes, looking to his right and left again. Onscreen Mara froze too. The simulator played a yell—could that really be her voice? No, it had to be a sound effect they'd pulled for the simulation—and Cartoon Mara turned and ran. Jason jumped back and then lowered the gun toward the hallway. He pulled the trigger. Another shot. And again.

More screams. Cartoon Will ran out of the mailroom and toward the screaming. Mara watched him picking up her limp figure. Jason dropped the gun and ran offscreen.

When the simulation stopped, Dr. Hendrix flicked on the lights. The silence in the room was profound.

"That is some crappy-ass animation," said a voice from the back. "My little sister designed a better video game when she was five."

It was Jason. His voice was so unfamiliar that it took Mara a full minute to place it. When she did, she turned around slowly, moving her entire body so she wouldn't have to swivel her neck and set off her shoulder.

Jason was sitting back in his chair with his hands laced behind his head. Like he was critiquing a movie, not watching footage of his own crime. Something inside Mara snapped.

"Seriously?" Mara said. "Seriously? You put us through all this and you're going to make smart remarks about the video quality?"

"What?" Jason said. His eyes looked like they were laughing at her. "What am I putting you through? Sorry, I'm getting ready to go back in time and make everything better for you. I'm such a jerk."

"Asshole," Mara hissed.

"Okay, okay," Dr. Hendrix interjected. "Let's go ahead and take a recess to regroup. We'll meet back in ten minutes and move on to Phase Two. Get a drink of water, use the restroom. The next phase is going to be a bit intense." He looked back and forth from Jason to Mara. "We're all here to make a difference in each other's lives. I expect everyone to come back ready to work together."

BREAKING: Will and Mara Sterling Reported Missing
Sterling Family Pleas for Public's Help

April 15, 2011

WASHINGTON, DC—Christopher Sterling, who gained notoriety in recent days with his popular FundItUp campaign, has reached his brother and sister-in-law's home in Washington, DC and reported that they are missing.

According to the FundItUp campaign, Sterling had requested funds to cover time off work and gas money so he could drive the nearly ten hours from the family home in Deer Hill, North Carolina, to Washington, DC, where William and Mara Sterling live. Christopher believes that his brother and sister-in-law were offered a timeline rectification, or "time wreck," for the 2002 Adams Morgan University shooting, which wounded Mara (née Gaines) Sterling. Christopher made the journey to try to talk them out of it. The cause has been taken up by One Life, One Time, an anti-timeline rectification lobbying group.

"When I arrived, the windows were dark and there was no response to my knock on the door," said Christopher in an impromptu press conference on the apartment building's front steps. Due to the notoriety of the FundItUp campaign and William and Mara Sterling's suspected involvement in a timeline rectification, reporters and protesters have been camped outside the building for days. "I was worried for their safety and then I saw the door had been forced open."

Witnesses report that the chain lock on the inside of the front door was broken and there was some splintering around the door frame. William and Mara Sterling were not present in the apartment.

"We've reported Will and Mara missing to the authorities, but no one seems to be concerned," said Christopher. "My mother and sister are on their way up to join me in the city so we can search for our missing loved ones. We ask for the public's help but especially for your prayers."

Comments:
KingDiva said:
Saw the door had been forced open, huh? And none of those reporters happened to see who did it? Yeah, right. Bloodthirsty vultures broke and entered the home, straight up.

> **MsSimoneSays** replied:
> I think the brother was the one who broke in and all the cameras just conveniently turned away.

LoveLaughLive said:
My thoughts and prayers are with this poor family! I am out in Oklahoma and cannot travel to Washington, DC to help with the search due to a recent knee replacement but just know that I am holding you in my prayers! Good for you for trying to stop this time wreck!

Ilikecake said:
OMG those poor people. They probably ran away to get away from the cameras. Can you imagine being at the center of this story? I don't know if they were really offered a time wreck, but I

sure hope so and I hope they take it.

MsSimoneSays said:
Bonus: if they DO have a time wreck, then this whole stupid FundItUp campaign and "human interest story" will disappear into the ether or whatever. If the shooting never happens, then they'll never be offered a time wreck and then there won't be this dumbass controversy taking over our news feeds.

> **PhilosophicalAtheist** replied:
> Amen to THAT.

> **MrBrightSide** replied:
> Small quibble: The shooting will have happened, time wreck would be offered, and news story will have gone down . . . just not in the life map we're aware of. Timeline rectifications are a shifting of consciousness to a different life map more so than a literal changing of time.

>> **llamallamallama** replied:
>> Duuuuuuuuude. *mind blown*

Chapter Twenty-Six

....

WILL

Mara was shaking when she and Will filled up their paper cups with water. They walked the halls until they found a small conference room. It was private enough, even with Ken trailing behind them.

The second the door closed, Mara exploded. "I knew it. I knew it! He's not sorry at all. He's an entitled, egotistical brat who finally found a loophole to get him out of jail."

"Take a drink. Calm down," Will said, passing her a cup of water.

"Calm down? We just upended our whole lives for this asshole while he sits there smirking and you want me to calm down?"

"We upended our lives for *us*," Will said. Something about comforting her made him feel stronger too. "And even if he is a jackass, it's still going to work out for us. I promise."

"How can you promise that?" Mara cried. "Will. You

cannot control him. I cannot control him. The Department of Justice cannot control him. This all depends on whether Jason chooses differently. Otherwise, we're just signing up to get shot again."

"He's not going to do that," Will said.

"How do you know?"

Will started to explain until he realized that he really couldn't.

Because Jason wouldn't make the same mistake twice. Why not? Most people don't even make that mistake once.

Because he's sorry. Jason definitely wasn't as sorry as he could be. Will agreed with Mara there.

Because it doesn't make sense for him to do all the work for another opportunity and then waste it.

What about Jason Mann had ever made sense?

Will opened and closed his mouth before he realized that he probably looked like a fish. Mara was waiting, a fresh I-told-you-so barely contained in her expression.

"I guess I don't know," Will said. "But I hope so. I really hope he'll do right this time."

"Hope isn't a strategy," Mara said.

"So what do you want to do?" asked Will. "Are we going to walk out of here and say we're not doing this anymore? We can, can't we? They can't force us to go through with it. We're the victims."

"The judge already ruled," said Mara. "And besides, what

would we be going back to?"

Will found himself looking at the door, as if Cliff and Chris and his in-laws and the media were literally standing on the other side. They weren't, of course. Just Ken and his all-hearing ears.

"We'd have each other," Will said.

Stupid. Stupid. Stupid. If having just him were enough, they wouldn't be here right now.

But when he looked at Mara, she didn't seem to think it was stupid. "There's always a choice," she said.

"Now you sound like me."

Mara one-shoulder shrugged. "I always knew you'd make a rule-breaker out of me someday."

Was it wrong of him to feel hopeful? Will knew they had no right to back out now. They couldn't keep running away from their problems.

Or could they? What if they just . . . disappeared? Will pictured grabbing Mara's hand and running away with her, out of this strange building complex and across the long, plain fields and highways that separated them from DC. They could run and keep running. No time wreck. No Jason Mann. Just him and Mara, going whatever direction they wanted to go.

A knock on the door startled them both. "Two minutes, please, and then we'd like everyone back in the conference room," Nayana said through the door. "Are you two all right?"

"Fine," Mara called back. She drank the rest of the water and crumpled the wilting paper cup in one hand. Will felt his heart disintegrating with it.

♦♦♦♦♦

Traci gave them both a wide, warm smile when Will and Mara walked back into the room. She was the only one who did. Jason, his corrections officer, and Nayana all looked at Mara a bit warily. *What, you afraid of someone telling you the truth?* Will was privately glad he got to see Mara tell Jason off a little bit. Even if they wouldn't remember it in the next life map.

Thinking like that made Will's head hurt.

Dr. Hendrix sat at the computer now. He watched Will more than Mara, with the type of squinty-eyed consideration that made Will feel like a textbook case study instead of a person. Will looked down and took his seat next to Mara.

"Good, we're all here," Dr. Hendrix said briskly. "Now, for the next portion, I've created a simulation of the *rectified* life map. It begins at the same point in time as the incident we just saw—three minutes before the first shot was fired. This is my understanding of the most likely trajectory of events if Jason chooses not to shoot in the next life map. What I need each participant to do, particularly, is to think about how realistic this course of events is for you personally. I know it's difficult, but try to think of any factors at all that would cause you to take any different actions. Ms. Patel, Ms. Bryant, obviously your input is appreciated as well." Will noticed he had left out the name of Jason's corrections officer. Whether on purpose or by accident, Will couldn't tell.

Dr. Hendrix turned off the light, and the projected image of the animated Student Union shone brightly on the wall. It felt strange, seeing himself onscreen, even if he was just a computer-generated cartoon. Animated Will was standing at the mailboxes, just like he had been before.

The screen panned out and revealed Jason pacing in the hall. He still looked upset, but not with the same panicked motions as before. He walked slowly toward the mailboxes, stooped low, and turned the combination dial. It was empty. Cartoon Jason stood up, stretched, and leaned his forehead against the wall.

Onscreen, the animated Will seemed to notice Jason's distress. "You okay?" he asked, walking over and putting a hand on Jason's shoulder.

The animated Mara walked past the mailroom, balancing her Styrofoam containers and remaining completely oblivious to them both.

The simulation ended and Dr. Hendrix turned the lights back on. Will felt as though he'd been slapped. *I have to talk to*

Jason? And comfort him too? He glanced quickly at Mara, who was frowning slightly at the screen.

"Any remarks? Suggestions? Questions?" Dr. Hendrix asked.

"Nope," said Jason quickly. "Looks right to me."

"Not to me," Will said. "Seriously, I don't feel like I would walk over and talk to him. Not in this life map or any other."

Nayana raised an eyebrow at him, but Dr. Hendrix nodded for him to keep talking. "Why not? You present as a very empathetic person. All the information from your childhood seems to indicate the same. If you didn't know him—which, in this life map, you don't—it's predictable that you would reach out to someone in distress."

Will tried to think of something to say to that. If Jason were just anybody, sure, he probably would have. But Jason *wasn't* just anybody.

Was he ready for Jason Mann to disappear back into the crowd of people he didn't know?

"Maybe I would have, but maybe I wouldn't," Will said. "I can't remember exactly what I was thinking about before it happened. Maybe I was distracted, like Mara."

"When Mara passes by, you and Jason are completely outside her field of vision," Dr. Hendrix said. "You will be in the same vicinity as Jason, and he will obviously be upset—not volatile, but given his life circumstances at the time, he will be under some stress."

Will shrugged. "So what? If I don't talk to someone I don't know in the new life map, is time going to unravel?"

He heard Traci laugh, which somehow annoyed him more than Dr. Hendrix's condescending smile.

"We're simply trying to imagine the most likely course of events for this point in time. If Jason doesn't shoot, how would he act instead? How would those around him react to those actions?" Nayana asked the questions smoothly. But Will wasn't in any mood to be soothed.

"*If* Jason doesn't shoot?" he asked.

"*When* I don't shoot," Jason corrected. Something in his voice made Will turn around. If Jason didn't look exactly humble, at least he wasn't smirking anymore. "I don't really want to think about this part of my life either, you know. I'm not proud of what I did. I'm not proud of a lot of what led up to it, either. I screwed up. I know that. I didn't go to class and I didn't study because I didn't think I had to. There's a whole building on campus named after my dad, for God's sake. Who's going to expel the kid whose family practically funds the engineering department?"

Will didn't move. He could barely breathe. Everyone in the room was watching Jason now.

"And then when I got suspended, it was just like—I was a nobody. I went to the dean and he didn't even make time to speak with me. I asked, 'How do I get an academic suspension when I've only been here half a semester? Can't I just go to class the next half and make it up somehow?' And he looked at me like I was the biggest idiot he'd ever seen and said, 'There are no classes to go to. You were dropped from all of them for lack of attendance. Don't come back to this school until you're serious.'"

Will did not want to feel sorry for Jason Mann. He and Mara had spent the last eight years cleaning up the mess Jason's terrible decisions had made. He did not want to feel sorry for him. He did not want to pity him.

But he kept listening anyway.

"That should have been my wake-up call. Hell, a lot of things before that should have been my wake-up call. I should have left, gotten a real job, and spent years clawing my way back into my father's good graces. I thought I was going to. But—" Jason slid his eyes downward. For the first time, Will saw Jason look ashamed. "I wanted to be notorious."

♦♦♦♦♦

"Dr. Hendrix is right, you know," Mara said. "You probably would have reached out to Jason."

Will locked the door of their motel room and double-checked the chain. "Maybe."

"It's not a bad thing," Mara said. "It's one of the things I love about you."

"That I comfort attempted murderers?"

"That you're kind to people."

"Aw," Will said. "Thanks."

People don't turn their heads and notice the kind guy by the mailboxes.

Mara was already settled in on one of the two double beds, remote in hand. "Should we risk watching the news? See if we're still headliners?" she asked.

Will shrugged. "Why not?"

Mara flipped through the cable channels, skipping over a home-decorating show and a Lifetime movie before she got to the news. The reporter was talking about a traffic jam in southeast DC. The images felt so familiar to Will—definitely the rows of taillights stretched out along the highway—but here in the motel, it all felt so far away.

Will was about to say, "See? For once people aren't talking about us," when the news anchor said, "And after the break: has this young man's search to reunite his family hit a dead end? Find out what's next in the case time wreckers are calling hashtag YSOLO: You *Should* Only Live Once."

To Will's horror, there was a clip of his brother, surrounded by microphones. "I haven't been able to find my brother and sister-in-law. I'm just asking everyone to help, however they can." The news station's logo and theme played, and then it cut to commercial.

"Fantastic," Will said flatly, at the same time that Mara

said, "Jackass." Will raised an eyebrow at her.

"Sorry," Mara said. "I'm sorry. He is your brother. I should probably get a swear jar or something. Put in a quarter every time I cuss."

"Why? It would only have fifty cents in it. You never had a problem with it before today." Will waited a beat before adding, "Besides, it wasn't cussing when you called Jason an asshole this morning. That was just telling the truth."

Mara shrugged. "Maybe he's not as bad as I thought." Will's expression must have revealed the sinking feeling in his stomach, because Mara hurried to add: "I'm not saying it's right or even understandable what he did. I feel like he's sorry, though. I feel like he really does want to go back and fix things."

"Let's hope so," Will said.

"Well, obviously we want him to be sorry, or else this whole thing is for nothing."

"Yeah," Will said. "I guess . . . I want to forgive him. I really do want to move on." He left the rest unspoken. *But I'm still struggling.*

"I know how you feel." Mara said. "Believe me, I know."

Statement of Congressman Gaines Regarding the Safety of His Daughter and Son-in-Law

Press Release April 16, 2011

Congressman Gaines Responds to Concerns That Daughter, Son-in-Law Are Reported Missing

On behalf of my wife and myself, I want to thank the many concerned constituents, friends, and citizens across the country who have reached out to share their support when my daughter and her husband were reported missing yesterday. We want to assure you that Will and Mara are indeed safe and sound. They are staying with relatives for the time being, as their home was unfortunately no longer safe due to the intense public scrutiny surrounding their rumored timeline rectification.

I apologize for not immediately addressing the situation. As you can imagine, the first priority for my wife and I yesterday was helping our daughter and son-in-law reach a safe location and settle in. Now that we have returned, we want to assure the public that they are, again, safe and sound and ask that you respect their privacy as they regroup and heal from this difficult time.

Additionally, I hope this serves as a reminder that, particularly in these times when information is easily accessible on the Internet, it's important to stop and critically evaluate your sources before acting. In the coming weeks, I will be introducing legislation that will better protect victims of libel, cyber-bullying, and other forms of privacy invasion.

Chapter Twenty-Seven

....

MARA

When the van brought them back to the building complex the next morning, the large conference room looked completely different. The projector screen was dark and all the chairs had been moved to the side, making the room seem even bigger than it had the day before. Nayana was on her hands and knees, marking off sections of the linoleum floor with masking tape.

Mara nudged Will. "If we're about to do a dorky trust-building exercise, I'm out," she whispered.

Will snickered. It was good to see him laugh again.

Dr. Hendrix knelt on the floor with a tape measure and a diagram, measuring and remeasuring the lines Nayana had already taped. He was going to ruin the crease in his chinos. For some reason, that made Mara smile.

Will leaned in toward Mara. "What do you think? Are we going to play precision hopscotch?"

Mara started to respond when she heard two more people

shuffle in behind them. It was Jason and his rehabilitation officer. Jason kept his eyes down and walked to the other side of the room. The rehabilitation officer—Mara thought his name might be John—gave them a quick, tight smile and nodded before following him.

Mara glanced back at her husband. Will had left again. Fallen away inside himself, back to a place only he could remember. A place he couldn't help remembering.

Mara squeezed his hand. Will didn't seem to notice.

"We're ready," Nayana announced, rising to her feet. She wore her roll of masking tape on her arm like a bracelet. "Since we've already gone over the simulation, today we're going to reenact the event with the desired outcome. I know Jason has been preparing for this through his rehabilitation, and I'm sure all of us are ready to relive this moment the way we wish it had gone."

Dr. Hendrix directed Will first. "If you'd just stand behind this tape line, please. Right, just there. This represents where the mailboxes will be. Jason, you can wait over by the window. This tape here marks the door to the Student Union. Mara? Your turn, dear. These lines mark where the hallway is. Perfect."

Mara bristled a little at being called "dear," but she turned her attention to Will instead. Even from her new position, ten feet away, she could see he was barely breathing.

Mara tried to think of a question that would distract them

from starting the reenactment. Will needed more time. "So this tape is supposed to be the blueprint of the Student Union, basically. And I'm supposed to be standing in the hallway?"

"Yes, exactly," Nayana said. Her soft-soled flats squeaked a little on the floor as she circled around them, pointing out each of the markings. "This is where Jason began in the simulation—right by the building entrance. This tape marks the mail room, where Will is standing. And as you mentioned, Mara, this is the hallway here."

That meant in the actual building, there would have been a long wall between her and Will, and another blocking her view of Jason—at least until he came around the corner. But no matter how hard she tried, Mara couldn't pretend that these were really walls instead of tape markings. She had a perfect view of both Jason and Will. There was nothing separating them.

Will was staring straight ahead still. This couldn't be good for him. Mara had to say something.

"Is this completely necessary?" she asked. "Do you think we could watch the simulation again instead?"

Dr. Hendrix answered that. "We've found it's most effective to have the participants actually go through the motions, if you'll pardon the pun. In the next stage, we'll have a virtual reality setup to help you reexperience the modified event. At the moment of the actual timeline rectification, your consciousness will be returning to this point in time. In order to really counteract any of the elements that might have encouraged Jason's original actions, we want the modified actions to feel habitual. We're going to reenact this event until it feels natural, and at the moment of timeline rectification, you'll feel that it couldn't possibly have gone any other way."

So it was going to get even more realistic than this. Mara twisted the hem of her shirt. *Will can't take this. He looks like he's about to pass out.*

"The first time will be the hardest," Traci said, walking toward them with a tissue and a bottle of water. Will shook his head and stared off in the distance. Focused. Breathing. Mara cringed in sympathy.

"Whenever we're all ready, we'll begin," Nayana said.

Minutes ticked by, when everyone tried to look as if they weren't watching Will. Mara gave the evil eye whenever anyone so much as glanced his way. *Let him be. Give him time.*

"While we're waiting, please try to picture yourself back at that moment, just as you were in the Student Union. The more realistically we can execute the reenactment, the easier it will become with practice," Nayana said softly.

Not you, Will. Mara wished she had telepathy. *You do whatever it takes to get through this.*

Maybe she did have a little ESP. Will finally breathed deeply and looked squarely over at Nayana. "I'm ready," he said.

Nayana nodded and pushed a button on the computer. A countdown clock appeared on the screen.

"When the clock reaches twenty seconds, Mara, you're going to walk in this direction, just as if you were walking down the hallway away from the café. Jason, you'll proceed in this direction, as if you're going to check your mailbox. See the taped X on the floor? That's the location of your box. Stop when you reach it," Dr. Hendrix said. "Will, remember what we discussed yesterday. When Jason approaches, do whatever feels most natural."

Eighteen. Nineteen. Twenty. Mara couldn't help sneaking glances over at Jason as she slowly began to walk. In the real Student Union, she wouldn't be able to see Jason from here. Will, either. She tried to imagine the tall cinderblock walls instead. They'd probably be lined with photographs or paintings from the art students, or have flyers for upcoming student events.

Jason was walking toward her. Mara felt a wave of nausea as he came closer. He was near enough that she could detect the peach fuzz on his chin, hear him clearing his throat. Jason looked anxious. Was he just playing the part, or was something wrong? Mara hesitated. Somehow, she couldn't quite take another step closer. Footsteps—long, fast, strident ones. Mara turned in time to see Will half-running toward her, stepping straight over the taped lines until he was close enough to grab her arm. Will jerked her back, sending a ball of fire singing through her right side. Mara gasped.

"Are you . . . ?" Jason said, half a second before Will pulled Mara back again. She cried out, but Will didn't seem to notice. Her husband loomed over Jason and pulled his arm back, like he was winding up to hit him.

"Stop right there! Stop!" Traci said, rushing in. Nayana flicked the countdown clock off, and Dr. Hendrix pulled Will away from Jason.

"Totally normal," Dr. Hendrix said. "Totally, totally normal. Let's take a break, shall we? A quick break?"

Traci and the rehabilitation officer had escorted Jason to the other side of the room. "Nayana, I think it's best if we end the session for the day. This isn't productive."

"What do you think, Mara?" Nayana said. "Are you okay?"

It was too late. Mara knew everyone could see the hot tears rolling down her cheeks. She gently squeezed her right arm, wishing she could wring the pain out.

So much for being strong.

"Are you okay?" Will sounded horrified.

"No, I'm not okay," Mara snapped. Now her nose was running too. Her voice sounded thick and whiny. "Why'd you have to pull on me like that? What's wrong with you?"

"Oh, God," Will said, realization dawning on his face. "Mara, I'm so sorry. I just . . . I saw him and I felt . . ."

"I was fine," Mara said. The tears rolled faster now. She

didn't even object when Traci pressed a tissue into her hand. "He wasn't even going to do anything" Her shoulder throbbed in time with her anger.

"Okay, okay," Traci said. "Okay. Come with me."

"I'd like to set up another session with you," Dr. Hendrix said to Will, so low only he and Mara seemed to hear. "It can be very triggering for a victim to be confronted with the assailant, even years later. That was my fault. This was a critical moment, and I didn't prepare you enough for the experience."

Traci led Mara to a chair while Dr. Hendrix walked with Will out into the hall. Mara blinked back tears enough to see Will flinch when Jason and his rehabilitation officer passed by. Mara, Traci, and Nayana were left alone in the room.

"You're in a lot of pain, aren't you?" Traci asked, trying to soothe her.

Mara didn't bother to respond.

"Has Will ever reacted that way before? Ever hurt your shoulder?"

She must be crazy, Mara thought, but Traci's brown eyes were wide and sincere. The picture of a non-threatening social worker.

"He didn't mean to," Mara said. "He was pulling me back because he was triggered. He wasn't here. He thought it was happening again."

"It was an extremely trying situation for him," Nayana

said. "Extremely trying. I should have rescheduled as soon as I saw Will was having trouble with the reenactment."

"He said he was fine," Mara said, blowing her nose. "But then, he always says that."

Nayana nodded grimly. She knelt and began peeling up the tape with her hands. Traci patted Mara's knee.

Mara looked over at Will, standing by the door with Dr. Hendrix. *He looks so small*, she thought. Usually, Will's height made him seem to tower over everybody. Today, he seemed like he'd sunk within himself. Dr. Hendrix was talking to him earnestly.

"We'll take the rest of today off, but unless you hear otherwise from me, assume we'll be back here tomorrow," Nayana said. "I'll be checking in with Jason and coordinating with Dr. Hendrix to make sure we're all on track."

"And I'll be in touch with you both later today," Traci said. She gave Mara's good arm a friendly squeeze. "Go back to the motel and relax. Put some heat on your arm and just regroup for a bit."

"Thank you," Mara managed to say. Ken reappeared out of nowhere—it was so creepy how he did that—and led her out into the hallway. She felt like a child leaving the principal's office. Not that Mara ever had been sent to the office or gone to detention in school. Will never had, either. *What had happened to him?*

Jason did. Jason happened to us.

Chapter Twenty-Eight

WILL

Every bump the van hit on the way back to the motel gave Will with a fresh jolt of guilt. Mara wasn't outwardly complaining about how he'd hurt her. She was comforting him, which made it a thousand times worse.

"You were triggered. You have PTSD. You were trying to protect me," Mara said.

"I panicked," Will said. "I shouldn't have panicked."

"Give it time," Mara soothed. The van went over another bump, and a little more color drained out of her face.

Will looked over at Ken. In three days of following them around, Will couldn't believe that their security guard was as impassive as he looked. Surely Ken was listening in. Judging them.

Why shouldn't he be? Everyone else was.

"When we get back to the room, I'll warm up one of your heating pads," Will said, before he remembered that they didn't have a microwave in the room. Or her heating pad.

"That's okay," Mara said. "I'll be fine. I'm just going to take a nap."

"Right." Will felt like an idiot.

The van pulled up behind the motel and Ken did his customary sweep before taking them inside. "Thanks," Will said, just before the door swung closed. Ken surprised him by responding with a gruff, "You're welcome."

Will checked the lock and chain lock on the door after Ken left, all the same. He picked the phone up out of his cradle to be sure there was a dial tone. He half-expected Mara to tease him for being paranoid, but when he turned around, she was already arranging the pillows in one of the beds and gingerly lying down.

It's just to keep the pressure off her shoulder. That's why her back is toward me. All the same, Will felt her reproach long after her breathing slowed and she let out soft, low snores.

This is not who I am. Not really. Dr. Hendrix had said as much to him out in the hall after the simulation. "Right now, Jason is a trigger to you. Your brain is hard-wired to feel threatened when you see him or when he approaches you. I should have worked with you to resolve that before asking you to work with him this closely."

It felt like excuses. Will's dad always had excuses too. He was stressed at work. He was worried about money. He'd had a rough day. Even as a little boy, Will could recognize his father's heavy-lidded "I'm sorry" expression. He'd come to hate the way his dad would press his hands together and earnestly explain that he had lost control, yes, but really, it wasn't his fault.

When his dad had finally left, Will had secretly felt relieved. Over time, it turned to guilt. Maybe if Will hadn't been such a difficult child. Maybe if he'd been better at sports, his dad would have been proud of him and wanted to stay. Maybe if Will had taken more responsibility for Chris and Becca, his parents would have had more time together. Maybe then they would have still been in love.

Excuses, all of them. Will's dad had made his choices, and now Will was making his.

No more. He might only have a few weeks left in this life map—days, even—but he was putting a stop to this now. If he got another chance at a simulation, he was going to do it and he was going to do it right. No excuses. No guilt.

Will looked over at his sleeping wife, and for once, everything felt right. He could go through with the simulations. He could go through with the time wreck. He could go through with anything, just to make things right for her.

♦♦♦♦♦

Will made it a point to be true to his word. For the next week, he and Mara and Jason went through the motions like line workers in a factory. Fair enough, Will supposed. They were assembling something. Assembling a new life map.

Will walked through Nayana's carefully taped lines on the floor three times before Mara visibly relaxed. Five times before Jason didn't seem tense, either. Ten times before Will himself felt his breathing was normal, heard himself talk through the script out of habit.

"Good," Nayana said softly, after the fifteenth run-through. Dr. Hendrix smiled and nodded his approval. Even Traci, who had regarded Will suspiciously every day since he came through the door, seemed pleased.

"Let's take a quick break," Dr. Hendrix said. "The next segment of the simulation takes us a step farther: we'll be using virtual reality to create a more realistic experience. I'd like to start by working with each participant individually before we attempt the experience as a group."

The tips of Will's ears burned. *That's because of me.* Next to him, Mara squeezed his hand.

"Will," Dr. Hendrix said. "You'll be first."

The rest of the group dispersed, just like Will's students had at the sound of the bell. Thinking about his old life made Will feel briefly disconnected. Was he really here, simulating a time wreck with his wife and the man who'd shot them? Shouldn't he be back at school, teaching sixth-graders how to play their instruments and seventh-graders how to create a harmony? Will shook his head and focused on matching his strides to Dr. Hendrix's as they walked out of the room and down the hall.

"How are you feeling, Will?" Dr. Hendrix asked. He led Will into a small conference room and shut the door behind them.

"I'm feeling pretty good," Will said. He did a quick gut-check to be sure. No knots. No anger. No fear. "That went a lot better than I was expecting."

"I'm not surprised," Dr. Hendrix said. "You've been working very hard. This next step, though, makes things a bit more intense. We've taken the computer simulation we ran the first time and made it more realistic. Not terribly realistic, you understand. It looks like a Grade-B video game." Dr. Hendrix smiled at him, as if they were connecting over something they had in common. Will hadn't played video games since college.

"I'd like to talk you through your first experience with the virtual reality headset," Dr. Hendrix said. He handed Will a large black-and-gray headset with dangling elastic straps. It smelled faintly of rubbing alcohol. Will wondered how many other people must have worn this headset before. What their life maps looked like now.

"This is going to fit over my glasses, right?" Will said. He strapped the headset on, relieved that it didn't pinch the earpieces of his glasses after all. He held his breath and waited.

Nothing. Will saw only black.

"You're tense," Dr. Hendrix said. "Tell me what you're thinking."

"I thought I was going to see the Student Union," Will said. "I thought I'd be back. I thought I'd see Mara . . ." The first Mara he'd ever seen. The Mara that was bleeding and dipping out of consciousness, collapsed on the floor. His heart raced.

"How would you describe your anxiety level right now?"

"Bad," Will said. "I feel . . . I don't want to see this."

"Okay. Good. That's honest. Now, let's talk about what it is that you're going to see. You're going to the Student Union. You're checking your mailbox. Maybe there'll be a letter from home, right? Maybe some flyers or a postcard from a friend? Then a boy you don't know walks up behind you, and he checks his mailbox. He's upset, and maybe you reach out to him—or maybe you don't," Dr. Hendrix said quickly. "Then you go your separate ways, and you go on with your evening. How does that sound? Is that something you can do?"

"That sounds fine." Will swallowed. He couldn't stand to meet Dr. Hendrix's eyes. Sweat gathered on his neck, threatening to drip down his shirt.

"That's all you're going to see. A normal day for a freshman in college."

The sound of Dr. Hendrix's voice was ringing in his ears,

and Will felt warm all over. Too late. Will pulled off the goggles and sat forward, leaning his head against his knees until the dizziness passed.

"Sorry about that," Will said when he was able to sit back up.

"Nothing to be sorry about," Dr. Hendrix said. "You're doing just fine."

Will wiped more sweat off his forehead. "Really? I don't feel fine." He reached for a tissue, which Dr. Hendrix passed to him without comment. "What if I can't do this?"

"Nonsense," Dr. Hendrix said.

"No, but really." Will swallowed. "What if it gets to the day of the time wreck and I just . . . can't? What if I panic?"

"You won't," Dr. Hendrix said. "I won't allow the timeline rectification to take place until I'm confident that each participant is ready. If you're not ready, we'll keep practicing."

Will swallowed hard. The idea of practicing this scenario over and over again wasn't terribly comforting.

"What I perceive as your primary issue," Dr. Hendrix continued, "is a lack of trust. You don't fully trust Jason to rectify his actions and you don't fully trust yourself to control your reactions. At some point, you need to look at what happened in the past, with the shooting and recently with your reaction, and accept it for what it was. Then you need to ask yourself, do you trust that that won't happen this time?"

Trust. There was a word Will was starting to hate. He had to trust Dr. Hendrix. Trust Nayana and Traci. Trust the justice system. Trust Jason.

Trust himself.

"Will?" Dr. Hendrix repeated the question. "Do you trust that that won't happen this time?"

"Yes." *No.*

Will put the virtual reality glasses back on anyway.

Chapter Twenty-Nine

....

MARA

Mara rubbed her temples at the end of the day. "I don't think I'll ever get used to that," she said, putting her virtual reality glasses back in the tray. Nayana quickly picked them up and wiped them down with an alcohol wipe.

The others were already filing out. Was it her imagination, or was Jason walking a little faster now? More purposefully, as if he were going somewhere important instead of being transported back to his cell for the night. He finally saw hope for his future, Mara thought ironically.

"Every time we do that, I feel a little surprised when I take the glasses off and find myself back here. I mean, I know while I'm doing it that it's a simulation, but it's so realistic that I kind of get wrapped up in it," Will said.

Something he'd said made Dr. Hendrix nod to himself, looking pleased. Well, why shouldn't he be? Mara had her own doubts about whether Will could handle the simulations after the first disastrous attempt. She wasn't sure what kind of psychiatrist voodoo Dr. Hendrix had been doing in his private sessions with Will, but it was working.

It wasn't just in the simulations, either. Will had slept through the night every night since they'd started working with the virtual reality glasses. He'd stopped glancing behind him and freezing up whenever he heard footsteps coming. It was so nice to finally see Will so relaxed.

I never knew him like this before. She and Will held hands on the way out to the van. *He's had PTSD as long as I've known him.* Sometimes it had been better, sometimes worse, but it had always been there.

Ken slid the van door closed and nodded to the driver to start. Mara looked out at the long stretches of countryside rolling past their windows. They were taking a different route back to the motel, she noticed. Not obviously different—every farm looked about the same, at least to Mara. But they were going the other direction on the highway, then down a gravel road.

"Does the government not pay for shock absorbers?" Will asked as the van bumped and jostled down the gravel road. Mara swore she could hear rocks spinning off the wheels.

"The usual route is blocked," Ken said. "Sorry. Try to enjoy the scenery."

"I'd enjoy it more if my teeth weren't rattling," Will said, but he was grinning. Everything about him seemed buoyant lately. *This must be what he was like before college.* Everyone in

Will's hometown had always called him easygoing. Relaxed. Chill.

No wonder his old friends—and even his brother and sister, to an extent—had always complained that Will had changed after college. It wasn't college that had changed him. Not really.

"Penny for your thoughts?" Will said. "You've been so quiet."

"I'm not thinking anything, really." Mara forced a smile. *And thinking how much better your life would have been if you'd never met me.*

Lucky Will.

◆◆◆◆◆

Watching *Déjà Deirdre* had become a regular ritual for Mara and Will. Since they'd been moved to the motel, it had been hard to keep track of what day it was. Mara had to stop and count to realize it had been twelve days since the trial, including weekends. Without their phones or computers, they were blissfully distant from every part of their old lives. No Facebook updates. No text blasts. Just her and her husband, alone for as much time as they had left together.

The cable on the motel TV was consistent, though. At eight o'clock, the reality TV channel played either *Engaged or Enraged* or *Déjà Deirdre* depending on the day. Today was a long string of Deirdre Collins episodes back-to-back, starting from the beginning of the season and going straight through to the newest.

"I think the finale is tomorrow," Mara said.

"Think she'll come to terms with her identity by then?" Will asked.

"Depends on if she got signed for another season."

"Ouch," Will said. The theme song started and he hummed along.

Mara vaguely remembered the episode from last night, when Deirdre went to a speed-dating dinner. "I didn't realize people still did those," Mara said.

"That's what you said last night too."

"Ah. Painkillers."

"I'm impressed you remember last night's show at all. I wasn't sure you were awake while it was playing."

"Off and on. I remember Deirdre kissing some guy with a full tattoo sleeve. Didn't seem like her type."

"That's what she was trying to find out." Will raised his eyebrows and spoke in a falsetto. It was a frighteningly good imitation of Deirdre Collins. "'If I've been through this life before, I might have already met my soul mate. Tonight I'm gonna find him!'"

I don't want that to be me.

"Mara? You got all quiet again."

With her good arm, she pulled Will to her and kissed

him, hard. He seemed surprised for a minute before enthusiastically kissing back.

If they could change their next life map by rehearsing their should've-been moments, then surely their love would carry over too. Even if she and Will didn't see each other that night, they would have to lay eyes on each other at some point. Four years. Same university. They would cross paths eventually.

Mara pulled him down on the bed, ignoring the stinging pain that shot through her arm. Some things were worth the pain. And some people were worth everything.

Will ran his hands over her body, slowly, as if he were trying to memorize everything about her.

He did know everything about her. Everything.

How could she stand to let this man go?

She didn't have to let him go. Not yet. And she was going to love him right up until the end.

◆◆◆◆◆

The knocking on the door was sharp, commanding. Mara jolted awake at the same moment that Will flew out of the bed. She could hear him pulling on his jeans and a shirt, stopping to fasten his belt buckle before he tiptoed, almost silently, to the door.

It was late. Mara squinted at the radio clock on the

nightstand. Almost midnight.

Who could be knocking on the door at this hour?

Maybe this was how the time wreck happened. Nayana had made it sound so orderly. "It will be just like the virtual reality simulations, actually. You'll take the van here in the morning and we'll proceed as usual. True, you'll have an injection before putting the virtual reality glasses on, but otherwise you may not even realize it's happening." As if they could just pretend so hard that their rehearsed life became reality.

"Who is it?" Mara asked, sitting up in bed. Her shoulder was throbbing and she shivered as the air conditioning hit her bare skin. Will was at the door, hunched over so he could squint through the peephole.

He straightened up and came back to the bed before he answered. "Get dressed," he said. "It's your dad."

"My dad?" Mara pulled on her T-shirt and shorts, cringing as she eased her right arm through the sleeve. She tripped in the dark and barely caught herself on the end of the bed. Her shoulder seized again.

"You okay?"

"Can you get the light?" she asked. "Wait. Don't. We should call Ken and have him talk to Dad." Mara found the duffel bag that sat open on the room's other bed and found her bathrobe. She wrapped it around her and cinched the belt tight.

"Are you sure?" Will asked.

Mara stumbled over to the nightstand and picked the phone up out of the cradle. There was the dial tone. Good. *Now what number were we supposed to call for Ken?*

There was another knock on the door. "Mara," came her father's voice. "I know you're there. Open the door, please."

It was the *please* that made Mara hang up the phone. Did he sound . . . worried? And he was here, in the middle of nowhere, looking for her. When was the last time her father had been concerned enough to do that?

She looked at Will, trying to read the contours of his face in the dark. He shrugged.

"Maybe something's happened," Will whispered. "Maybe we should talk to him."

"Please, Mara," her father said through the door. "Open the door."

Why hadn't Ken heard him out in the hall? Unless Ken wasn't there after all. Mara nodded once at Will, and he turned on the light.

She checked the peephole too, just to be sure. The concave lens made her father look shorter than usual. His bald spot looked shiny in the reflected light of the hallway.

Mara slid open the chain, then the latch, then the lock on the doorknob. "Dad?" she asked, suddenly conscious of how childish she sounded.

"Mara. Thank goodness you're safe." He stepped into the

room and closed the door behind him. Hugging him felt awkward. His cologne was still overpowering, the arc of his arms more formidable than comforting. The congressman stepped back and nodded at Will, as if he was acknowledging a constituent.

"Don't worry," Congressman Gaines said. "I've come to take you somewhere safe."

"Back home?" Mara asked, trying to force her foggy brain to focus on what he was saying. Why wasn't the motel safe? And where was Ken?

"No, not home," her father said. "Not for a long time. We found a place for you with some of my mother's family. You might have met them back when you were a teenager. Do you remember Ida and Eileen?"

Mara searched her memory for their names and came up blank. "Who are they?"

"Your second cousins. They'll be able to house you away from the public eye until things die down a bit." He patted Mara's good shoulder. "I know how easy it is to get swept up in these things. You're just lucky I could track you down. Don't worry. Your mother and I have everything under control. We've made the arrangements and handled the press already."

"What's going on? Why do we need to leave here?" Will asked.

Congressman Gaines answered his questions as if Mara

had asked them. "Obviously with the media attention surrounding your time wreck, there's been a big outcry from the public. I trust the people in charge of this . . . rectification"—he said the word as if it faintly disgusted him—"have sheltered you from most of it?"

"We've seen the news," Will said.

"What's on TV doesn't cover half of it. Do you have your phones or computers? No, of course you don't." The congressman answered his own question. "Will, when your brother came forward and said he hadn't been able to locate you, it put a lot of things into motion. The combination of the general distaste for rectifications and your family's religious objections in addition to my position in the government—well, a lot of people have been trying to find you two. These things are much safer when the participants are anonymous. Once people can attach a face or a name to an issue, it makes things personal to them. This storm has been brewing for a long time and once you went public about your involvement . . ." Congressman Gaines waved an arm, apparently to indicate that riots were inevitable.

"What do you mean, they've been trying to find us?" Mara asked.

"You're just lucky I was able to find you in time," Congressman Gaines repeated.

Mara searched her father's face for some shred of comfort. Some hint that he had come here to protect her, to rescue her, to save her and Will from handling all this alone.

She couldn't read his face. She never could.

"What exactly are people saying?" Mara heard herself ask. "What's really going on?"

"I have it handled. You just need to come with me."

"No," Mara said. "I need to know what's happening."

Her father huffed out a low sigh and reached for his phone. Mara reached for it, but he tugged it away, pinching and scrolling at the screen until he came to the page he was looking for.

"Here's one example," Congressman Gaines said. "I can help you. You're in a mess right now, sure, but you're not so far over your head that I can't bail you out."

Finally, he offered Mara the phone. She held it closer to Will so they could both read at the same time.

Online Event: Join the Search for Will and Mara Sterling

Date: May 12, 2011

Time: 10:00 a.m.

Location: Meet at Eastern Market metro station. After 10:00, we will begin dividing into teams and canvassing DC.

Message from the organizers: Earlier, Congressman Gaines (Mara's father) made a statement that Will and Mara are safe with relatives. Congressman Gaines claims that Will and Mara are not missing, nor are they considering a timeline rectification. We know from the Sterling family (Will's parents) that THIS IS NOT TRUE. Will and Mara ARE pursuing a time wreck, and if they aren't in their home, then it is VERY LIKELY that they are already training to "rectify" the 2002 shooting.

Will and Mara were seen leaving their apartment on April 14, 2011 and some sources say they were seen entering a courthouse, although reports from eyewitnesses are conflicting. We do know that Will and Mara have NOT been seen since then!

Chris Sterling reported his brother and sister-in-law missing on April 15, 2011. Despite this, NO ONE IS LOOKING FOR THEM! Since Congressman Gaines's statement, Will and Mara are no longer reported on any Lost and Missing websites!

HELP US FIND WILL AND MARA STERLING!

125,067 people are planning to attend this event. Click here to register—free!

Chapter Thirty

....

WILL

"That's tomorrow," Will said. "I mean today." It was after midnight, wasn't it? In fewer than ten hours, over a hundred thousand people were planning to search for them.

"They probably won't find us," Mara said. Her voice rose as if she were asking a question. "They're searching in DC. We're way out in the boonies somewhere."

"I was able to find you with a little effort," Congressman Gaines said. "How much effort do you think thousands of people are willing to put forth to locate you? This is dangerous. You need to get out now. Gather your things and come with me."

Mara wanted to go. Will could see it in her face as she looked up at her father. She didn't believe that Congressman Gaines was telling the truth, not quite. Her father had obviously lied to the press when he said they were already with relatives. Was the congressman really trying to protect them? Did he really believe that timeline rectifications were wrong, or that they were in danger? Or was he still just trying to manage his family's public image?

Either way, escaping from DC and the timeline rectification was tempting. Will put one arm around his wife. Hadn't he daydreamed about this exact thing? They could run away from the time wreck, their old lives, everything. They could start all over again. He and Mara could face everything together, exactly the way it was meant to be.

Congressman Gaines cleared his throat. "I'll give you two a moment," he said. "But just a moment. We need to get moving. Gather your things, and I'll take you. The car is on standby."

The door clicked shut softly behind him, leaving Will and Mara alone. "What do you think?" Mara whispered, angling herself toward Will. "Do you want to go?"

"Yes," Will said. "I want to run away with you. I don't want to face a life without you. Any life, no matter how good the rest of it is. We can do this. We can start fresh, just the two of us. We never have to come back here." He held on to her as he said the rest, grounding himself. Grounding her. "But we won't."

"What?" Mara asked.

"It's not right," Will said. "We can't give this up. The shooting never should have happened and I'm not going to let it happen to you."

"I don't need this time wreck," Mara whispered. "I was

doing this for you. And now you're doing so much better—you haven't had nightmares since we started the simulations, and you're more relaxed now, and I know things aren't perfect but maybe with some more treatment, it'll be even better. Let's just go. Let's just go and live our lives."

"But what about you?" Will asked. "You have a chance to finally feel better, and I don't just mean your shoulder." He swallowed, forcing out the words he knew he had to say. "It's one thing for you to be the victim of a crime when there was nothing we could have done to stop it. It just . . . happened, and you survived it. But now that we have a choice—"

"Stop," Mara said. "Don't say it."

"If you choose living with this crime so you can be with me—I can never live up to that. You would resent me and . . . and honestly, I would resent me. I would hate myself for letting you live through that for me."

"But we can't guarantee what happens after the time wreck," Mara said. "What if we don't find each other again? What if I live out my whole life without ever knowing you?"

"You won't," Will said. "I'll find you."

Mara started to laugh, even as she buried her face in his chest. "You can't promise that."

"Why not?" Will asked. "We've felt what it's like to meet our soul mate. How could we ever be satisfied with anything less?"

Mara wrapped her good arm around him so tight Will

could feel her fingers curling through his shirt. "Don't let me go," she said. "Please."

"I have to," Will said. "So I can find you again."

♦♦♦♦♦

The van bumped and jerked down the gravel road toward the highway. The sun was barely peeking up from the horizon. Will knew that he probably ought to be tired—how many hours had he and Mara managed to sleep last night after her father left? One? Two maybe? Instead, Will was oddly alert. He wondered if Congressman Gaines was still out there somewhere, waiting nearby in case they changed their minds. Maybe. His father-in-law clearly wasn't used to being told no.

And now here they were, being shuttled off to the building complex before it was even fully dawn. They would probably be there before he knew it. Will wished they could slow down instead. Give themselves just a few more minutes together in this life map.

Ken had been the one who rushed them to get ready and out of the motel this morning. Now he was sitting on Will's left, silent and surly, knees spread far apart and arms crossed so that he took up as much room as possible. Every time Will looked over at him, Ken glowered.

On his other side, Mara was staring out the van window

as if she were trying to soak in the view. Her hand was securely tucked in his and they sat hip to hip, knee to knee, foot to foot, hanging on to every inch of each other as long as possible.

Will felt as if dread would swallow him up as they turned onto the highway. The rectification had to be today. Had to be. They'd rehearsed so many times already and if people were really searching for them, surely Nayana and Dr. Hendrix would want to move things along. Every minute they waited before the rectification was another opportunity for someone to find them and put a stop to it.

It felt like they were speeding down the highway, even though they were only going fifty-five miles per hour. Will saw the odometer from the backseat—one of the benefits of being tall. Fifty-five miles per hour wasn't too fast to jump out of a moving van, was it? They could jump and roll, just like they saw in the movies, and run off to . . . somewhere. Maybe Mara's dad was still waiting nearby, even after Ken had kicked him out of the motel.

Will gave Ken another sidelong glance. Instead of returning it with a scowl, Ken stayed fixated on a point down the highway. Will strained to see what he was staring at.

It was the building complex and there—Will's stomach sank—was a throng of people surrounding it. The driver slowed.

"Oh, no," Mara groaned. "How did they find out where it

was?"

"People have a way of finding things out," Ken said grimly. "Especially if the ones being guarded don't communicate with their security team."

That sounded a lot like the twenty-minute lecture Ken had given them last night, when they'd finally dialed the phone and told him that Mara's father was there. Originally, Will had thought they could ask Congressman Gaines to leave quietly—"Can we not end this life map by calling a security guard on my dad?" Mara had asked—but Congressman Gaines hadn't expected to be turned down. By the time Ken got involved, it took the motel manager and three policemen to wrestle Mara's father down the hall.

Maybe it was Congressman Gaines who had told the crowds where to find them. Will weighed the thought and dismissed it. After last night, Congressman Gaines probably wanted to forget all about this life map too.

The driver had slowed all the way down to forty miles per hour now. The closer they came, the more people Will could see crammed in the parking lot around the buildings. There had to be hundreds, at least. Ken unclipped a walkie-talkie from his belt and flicked it on. "ETA two minutes. What's the plan?"

Dr. Hendrix's voice crackled through the other end. "Get as close to the door as you can. Make sure they get inside."

Every muscle in Mara's body tensed. They were close

enough to see that plenty of people in the crowd were holding signs—Will thought he could see his and Mara's faces on some of them. The van slowed down further and pulled into the office park. Even though Will knew the windows were tinted, he pulled closer to Mara, trying to shield them both from the hawk-like eyes watching the van.

There were police holding the crowd back. "This is government property," one policeman said into the megaphone. "Be advised that you are trespassing and you can and will be removed."

"Circle once around," Ken told the driver. "See if we can get to the back entrance."

The van moved slowly through the crowd, which only reluctantly moved back. Something large hit the window inches from Mara's head. A shoe. Will's pulse quickened even as he tried to reassure himself. It was only a shoe.

"So how do you think we'll meet in our next life map?" Mara asked suddenly, squeezing his hand.

Will tried to think. His heart was hammering along with the chants of "One life, one time," that pulsated through the crowd.

"Maybe we'll meet each other in the library," Mara said. She was looking intently into his eyes. "We both like to read. That's kind of how we bonded that day in the hospital, isn't it?"

"Um," Will said. "I guess."

"Will," Mara said, reaching up and pulling his face closer to hers. "Look at me."

Once he started looking in her eyes, he couldn't stop. She knew that. How long before these deep-brown wells would be unfamiliar to him? How many minutes did they have left together?

"Stay with me," Mara said. "I think we're going to be at that little café across from campus that had the gritty coffee and the weekly poetry slams."

"And you're going to be reading some dark poetry about finding your one true love."

"I hate poetry. That's never going to change. No, I'm going to be in the little corner by the window, trying to read my book while I eat their imitation biscotti and chew on chocolate-covered espresso beans."

Looking into Mara's eyes, Will could almost completely tune out the chant from the crowd outside. "And then I'm going to come up to you and ask if anyone is sitting in the chair across from yours."

"Which Robyn totally was, but she'll be a good friend and find a seat at the little coffee bar so I can talk to the cute guy who's flirting with me."

"Right. And then I'll say, 'So what are you reading?'"

"Because that's such a great pickup line . . ."

"It worked in this life map."

Mara was still looking intensely into his eyes, pulling him

along with her into the first meeting she imagined. "And I'll say, '*Hitchhiker's Guide to the Galaxy*,' because I'll still be eighteen and I'll only have read it half a dozen times by that point."

"How many times are you going to re-read that book?"

"Forty-two. And you'll say that you don't read science fiction, which I won't immediately hold against you because you do have a pretty cute smile."

"And I'll say I like reading thrillers and true crime because we won't have lived through one yet. Or ever, hopefully." Thinking that made Will start to panic a little. The crowds were only separated from them by inches, really. How secure was this van? Was it bulletproof?

Sweat dripped down Will's neck.

Mara squeezed his hand with her good left one. "And by the end of the afternoon, I'll give you my email because I hate giving out my phone number."

"And I'll write and rewrite the perfect email to ask you out and then as soon as I hit SEND, I'll be positive that it's the dorkiest, most idiotic email written to a beautiful girl in the history of time."

"But I'll answer it and we'll meet up again and we'll talk even longer this time."

Yes. That was what was going to happen. They only had to make it out of the van, out of this life map, and into the next. "And we'll fall in love and get married and have children," Will said.

"And we'll live happily ever after."

The van pulled to a stop. Will watched the police officers pushing the crowds farther back, making a narrow aisle between the van and the door of the building.

"Here we go, kids," said Ken. Was it Will's imagination, or did he seem gentler now? Ken wasn't scowling at them anymore, that was for sure. He looked almost kind. "Wait for my signal, okay?"

Ken opened the van door and the crowd erupted in screams and camera flashes. Ken swept left, then right, and nodded for them to follow him.

Will and Mara laced their fingers together and ran, hand in hand, matching strides, holding each other up against the angry chants that thundered all around them.

"One life, one time. One life, one time."

"Do the crime, do the time."

"Time wreckers!"

No, Will thought. *Rectifiers.*

ABOUT THE AUTHOR

Ellen Smith is a freelance education writer and speculative fiction author. When she isn't busy writing, Ellen can usually be found reading, crafting, or playing piano. No matter what she is doing, Ellen is always wondering, "What if?" Ellen lives with her family near Washington, DC.

REVIEW EVERY LAST MINUTE

Did you enjoy *Every Last Minute*? Please take a moment to leave a review!

Mara and Will's story continues in Book 2 of the Time Wrecker Trilogy: *Any Second Chance*. Keep in touch to stay updated on the next book in the series!

Facebook: https://www.facebook.com/ESWrites/
Instagram: https://www.instagram.com/ellensmithwrites/
Twitter: https://twitter.com/EllenSmithWrite
Website: www.ellensmithwrites.com

www.ingramcontent.com/pod-product-compliance
Lightning Source LLC
Chambersburg PA
CBHW030646120726
47905CB00001B/86